THE GIRL WHO'LL RULE THE WORLD

by

Jolie Booth

THE KING'S ENGLAND PRESS
2016

ISBN 978 1 909548 68 8
THE GIRL WHO'LL RULE THE WORLD
is typeset in Book Antiqua,
Castellar, and Franklin Gothic
and published by
The King's England Press
111 Meltham Road
Lockwood
HUDDERSFIELD
West Riding of Yorkshire

Printed and bound in Great Britain by

4Edge Ltd
Hockley, Essex

In loving memory
of Terry Chapel,
Nanny & Granddad

Until one is committed, there is hesitancy, the chance to draw back, always ineffectiveness.

Concerning all acts of initiative (and creation), there is one elementary truth, the ignorance of which kills countless ideas and splendid plans: that the moment one definitely commits oneself, then Providence moves too.

All sorts of things occur to help one that would never otherwise have occurred. A whole stream of events issues from the decision, raising in one's favour all manner of unforeseen incidents and meetings and material assistance, which no man could have dreamed would have come his way.

Whatever you can do
Or dream you can,
Begin it.

Boldness has genius, power, and magic in it.

BEGIN IT NOW!

Mistranslation by John Anster, attributed to Goethe.

LAMMAS

Esmeralda woke to the alarm on her mobile phone. It was 9.30am. She had been in the thick of a particularly vivid and prophetic dream, but the memory of it now slipped out of her mind like a well-spent member. She lay for a moment gathering her thoughts, watching the small black flies continually circling her lampshade, and tried to recall the reason for setting her alarm. Her room was dark. It always was. Only a pathetic trickle of light ever made it through the window from the lofty heights of the courtyard that her room backed onto. Every surface in the courtyard was dripping in pigeon shit, and the pigeons themselves squatted ominously in their own faeces, winking at Esmeralda through the window panes with their yellow beady eyes.

She wondered if it was her name that had led her to a penchant for ugly but intriguing men?

She always found amusement in people's inability to perceive parallel universes. "They're everywhere you look," she commented idly, watching a bird and a butterfly partaking in a dogfight, "and are as clear as the end of your nose."

"But the end of your nose is a blur," he replied.

7

"I was just telling everyone how you are the light of my life," he told her as he answered the phone.

"Why, thank you," she replied.

"I've decided that I'm going to write a book."

"I remember asking my tutor when I was at secondary school if he could tell me where I was supposed to use a comma. He told me to use it wherever it felt right..." She looked introspective for a moment before concluding, "I didn't go to a very good school."

"I don't like non-committal punctuation marks. Especially the semi-colon. " She snuggled down into his armpit.

"Don't worry, I've got you."

She woke up in his arms. She had been in a very lucid sleep, always aware that she was lying next to him. It took her a long time to get used to sharing a bed with a new lover, as she found it impossible to fall into a really deep sleep whilst she still fancied the pants off someone and was too sexually excited to be able to relax properly. Which was exactly how she was feeling right now, counting down the seconds until he showed signs of life, so that they could commence with the mating ritual that is the morning wriggle. That figure of eight frottaging on each other's legs, this way and that, until one of you could resist it no longer and finally raised your sleepy body against the mighty force of morning gravity and plonked yourself on top of the other.

"That girl's got custardy tendencies," noted Esmeralda.

As much as we try we can't escape from Mother Nature. We box ourselves in and try to make it feel safe, but she is always there, cooing at the window, and doing figures of eight around the lampshade at the centre of our world.

She was impressed that the computer's spell and grammar check insisted Mother Nature was spelt with capitals in the same way that God is. iPod sounds a bit like the name of a god.

Language is so patriarchal… the linear formulation of thoughts and feelings. Box it off, segregate it, and understand it. Fuck that for a laugh.

Esmeralda dragged herself out of bed, wrapped herself up in her blue towelling dressing gown and grabbed her Faith in Nature lavender and geranium shampoo and conditioner. Being the only girl in a house full of boys meant that she was the only one who ever bought toiletries, so she had to keep them squirrelled away in her room. And besides, if the boys did ever buy toiletries, they were always the big brand types or the dirt-cheap variety, both of which were full of harmful chemicals that Esmeralda had decided she wanted to avoid. Her shampoo was free of SLES. Esmeralda didn't know what SLES was, but she was certain that she didn't want it in her shampoo. She was happy to ply her body with harmful chemicals all weekend, but not in the safety of her own shower on a weekday, thank you very much.

She marched into the bathroom, took off her dressing gown, and began running the hot water tap. She pulled off her pyjama bottoms, went to the loo, and then set about the highly skilled art of balancing the taps. She was the only one in the house who had perfected the technique of nurturing the water flow to the exact temperature between freezing cold and scalding hot. The boys in the house had to either have baths or cold showers.

Once it was running to her satisfaction, Esmeralda stripped off her pyjama top and climbed into the shower. She washed her hair with the shampoo, and then

9

conditioned it with the conditioner. Then she used the shampoo to wash her body. No one had bought soap in an age. She lathered up under her armpits and shaved them. Then she lathered up her between her legs and shaved her bikini line. She could never decide one way or the other about her bikini line. Half of the men she shagged were the kind of men who expected shaved bikini lines and the other half were the kind who advocated the natural look. But Esmeralda had an obsession with preening and she could never resist the urge to neaten up her pubes, even though she never bothered shaving her legs. Plus, she hated hairy bum holes. She couldn't stand the thought of someone doing her from behind and being distracted by what looked like a spider trying to escape from her arsehole. After shaving, she rinsed herself down, turned off the taps, dried, and returned to her room. The whole procedure had taken less then fifteen minutes.

Bridget Jones can kiss my spotty arse.

"I love my daughter," said her mother, "because I'm always left feeling inspired after I've spent time with her."

"My daughter is everything I ever wanted to be!" said her father to her friends, much to her embarrassment.

"I did the whole 'Fury at the Father' thing when I was studying feminism," she explained to her friend, who was pouring vast quantities of sugar into her coffee. "You know… renounced my faith, stopped talking to my dad, dumped my boyfriend, that kind of thing. But then I realised that all that anger was giving them far more energy than any of them actually deserved."

"My mum," replied her friend, "once said that her world was created purely out of her relationships with other women. Any men who might enter her realm from time to time could only do so with her permission."

"Wow!" replied Esmeralda "Your mum sounds cool."

"The relationship between a mother and her daughter is the most important relationship in the whole wide world. Remember that, girls. Love your mothers!"

"I'm keeping your memory alive," she told the photo. "Now I don't know if you were a nice person, and quite frankly, you give me the heebie-jeebies, but I love your house and appreciate the artistic efforts that you went to in keeping your memory alive. I have your diaries and holiday snaps. I'm happy to be a vessel for your memory."

"Thank you," replied the woman in the photo.

They drove the Land Rover through the Broads, rather than along the motorways. It added two hours to the journey, but it provided much better views. It was nice to put a face to all the places she usually passed through on the train. She had spent time stuck at most of them in the past and had cursed their names. But now she discovered they were all quaint little villages, full of personality, and she felt a tinge of guilt.

After an hour or so, they pulled off onto a dirt track and christened his new vehicle. She liked the relationship she had with him. There was no question as to their intentions. It was purely sex when they were having sex, and the rest of the time they thought of each other as an awesome person and a good friend. She had lots of lovely men and women in her life who were like that. It would be tough breaking the news to them all the next time she went exclusive with someone.

"I'd never done it in a car before this summer," confessed Esmeralda.

Corrupting young people had become her favourite new pastime. She had even, for the first time in her life, been toying with the idea of breeding. But then she caught a train during the school summer holidays and quickly thought better of it.

"I always give my lovers labels rather than using their names. At the moment I'm shagging the eighteen-year-old, the twenty-one-year-old, the rock star, the composer, and the porn star," she confessed, "I suppose it's a distancing technique."

Like the *Verfremdungseffekt*.

"Love is when their shit don't matter," he murmured.

"My slug heart feels like it has been rained on by salt," she wailed. "It burns, master!"

Tapping her fingers over the keyboard of the new laptop felt amazing, like slipping in between satin sheets after a lifetime sleeping in Hessian. She wondered why the computer was insisting that she spelt Hessian with a capital H. Had Hessian been a person with an appetite for coarse fibres or was she spelling it wrong?

The pigeons were mating again. She had woken to their strangled warble. *I'm in love and it's wonderful!*

"Hello, my lover!" he waxed lyrical down the phone.

"Hey, gorgeous, how are you?"

"I'm great. And you?"

"Wicked. Are you at work?"

"Yep."

"I'll be quick, then. I've got good news and great news. What do you want first?"

"Erm… the good news."

"He was wrong about the festival dates. It's not this Saturday."

"Excellent. And the great news?"

"I'm free all weekend, so I will come to yours whenever you want me to."

"Well then, come as soon as you can!"

"Of course. Can't wait to see you."

"You're like a crystal on a string that's spinning around my head," said her mother, making Esmeralda's heart wrench with joy.

"Well, I hope I'm not making you too dizzy." Esmeralda replied.

Every time she thought about the conversation it made her squirm and grin so inanely that people looked at her in the streets as if she were mad.

"I don't have to be sexy!" she shouted at the group of fat, red-faced men as she threw up outside the sex club in the centre of Amsterdam's red-light district. The mushrooms had worn off now and she realised she'd smoked far too much weed. Her puke was a luminous pink though which was rather exciting.

"You can take the girl out of Essex but you can't take the Essex out of the girl... cause she's had so much of Essex in her."

"I'm rubbish at remembering details. All I can go on is what I think and feel," Esmeralda mused.

"But it's all about the details," she snapped.

For yet another moment that evening, Esmeralda really hated her.

"If anyone feels like hitting themselves over the head with a coal scuttle... don't. It's not a good idea," he said.

She woke up thin. She loved it when that happened. Esmeralda set about choosing her clothes for the day. Without consciously meaning to, her clothes always reflected the seasons. In the summer she wore bright colours and in the winter she normally always wore black. Each season would be set around a different theme. This summer it had been polka dots in red and white or blue and white.

Last winter she had worn Goth Victoriana. Winter was starting to creep in again now, and it was all about black outfits with pink accessories. She had dyed pink chunks in her bleached blonde hair and was currently donning a pair of black pin-striped trousers, a black and white striped long-sleeved top, a black trilby, and a pair of pink sneakers. She looked like something out of a Tim Burton film.

"Who is your hero?" he asked her.

"My heroes are Sally Bowles from *Cabaret* and Holly Golightly from *Breakfast at Tiffany's*. To be honest, I've basically stolen their personalities... I don't know," she said, pushing back her cuticles with her thumbnail, "but I've always known that I'm better than them."

The train was delayed. She tried to remain patient whilst the stupid train squatted silent as the grave at East Croydon station. She began to think about all the times she had travelled towards the arms of a man that she was in love with. Once she had travelled forty-five hours from Sydney to Nottingham so that she could be with the man she loved. Upon arrival he had been playing his music so loud he couldn't hear her at the door. She had been stuck on his doorstep for nearly an hour, before one of his housemates showed up and let her in. In her earlier days she would have been beside herself with anticipation mixed with a little *soupçon* of blind fear. Nowadays she just felt pain-free excitement. *This last year of being single is the best thing I have ever done*, she thought to herself.

"Drinking coffee gives me arthritis but it helps me shit. It's a real conundrum."

"There is no I in eye."

"The oranges of words and phrases, the lemons of past tenses."

"The world is my harem," he proclaimed.

The commune was cold and draughty, full of cat hair and screaming children, but it induced the feeling one gets from camping – that there is less need for washing, that you will never get a hangover, and that you have suddenly become a thousand times more resourceful.

Esmeralda spent the morning picking plums from the wilting tree dripping heavily in fruit. It was an absolute treat. She had not had a garden to work in since she had left home ten years ago. September had sneaked in an extra week of summer and Esmeralda bopped around amongst the stinging nettles to the tunes on her iPod, plucking the plums from the branches that she was able to reach. Her hands were feeling arthritic. She had drunk too much coffee the day before, but the pleasure she was feeling from the sun on her face took precedence over any ailments. Her father had told her on the phone earlier that it had been a bumper year for crops and would be a vintage year for wine. There were certainly plenty of plums. She had managed to harvest three carrier bags full.

I hate people who copy me. I'm obsessed with individualism. If I had twins I'd send one to a boarding school and one to borstal.

"I'm a mean, not very lean, on the hammers machine," she explained. "My body is not a temple. It's a skip," she announced.

When she woke up she was still as drunk as a skunk. After an hour or so of writhing and staring into space she thought that it might be time to get up and brave the world. Picking the sleepy dust from her eyes she raised herself weakly, climbed out of bed, stumbled dramatically into the corner with her arms flailing, had a little giggle, and then went for a cold shower.

They kept shagging harder and deeper. All she wanted was for him to crawl up inside her and snuggle up around her heart.

A life without passion is a fate worse than death.

Esmeralda looked at the young man that she had fallen in love with. He was tall, thin, and incredibly good-looking. His dark hair flopped over his dazzling blue eyes, full of stars. There was so much fire burning in his belly it was part of the very fibre of his being. Like hell was missing an escaped fire pixie.

"This is the most comfortable my bed has ever felt."

"My bed isn't comfortable any more. I need to find something the same size and shape as you," he said down the phone.

She wondered how many women he had been with.

A pigeon dive-bombed her head as she sat minding her own business in the park. Pigeons were always dive-bombing her head. She wondered if that ever happened to anyone else.

"Hi… Yes, I want to make a complaint… Right. I've just been dumped in the middle of fucking nowhere because I had been given the wrong information by one of your lot and went and got on the wrong train going in the wrong direction. So the ticket guy told me I needed to swap trains and told me I needed to buy a ticket to make up the difference on my ticket, because I was now two stops away from where mine was valid. But the fucking rail service doesn't accept the cash cards I've got, which means I couldn't pay for the ticket. So he tells me to get off on the next stop and that I'll have to try my luck going the other way. I wait for half an hour to get on the train going the other way, but when it arrives the ticket guy won't let me on because the bastard on the last train had radioed through to him to say that I wasn't able to pay for my ticket and to not let me on the fucking train!"

No one likes a jobsworth.

The guy sitting opposite her on the train was really cute. She moved her leg a little bit closer to him.

"What do you want from me?" he asked her.

"I want you to be interested in my past but not to buy into any of my baggage. I want you to believe that I will be everything that I believe I will be and yet also excited to discover how things actually pan out. But most of all... I want you to be fearless and brave about love. Will you do all of that for me?"

"I promise you I'll try."

That conversation never really took place. In reality they had never once discussed their liaison. He made her go all tongue-tied.

Playing it safe dulls the heart and blunts the senses.

"I don't like saying I love you," she explained to her friend, "because I believe that my feelings are going to be growing deeper and deeper. Which means that if I tell someone that I love them now then I'll have nothing left to say to capture the strength of my feelings in the future. It means I'll just have to keep saying 'I love you" and 'I love you' all the time until it becomes like a punctuation mark and loses all of its meaning."

"You think too much," said her friend.

Esmeralda suddenly had the idea of moving out of her house-share with the cast of *Planet of the Apes* and into a flat on her own. As soon as the thought crossed her mind she became flooded with fear. The thought of living on her own terrified her. *That's interesting,* she noted. *I guess that means I should do it?* Esmeralda got quite a kick out of facing her fears.

I'm going to move out and write a book, Esmeralda decided. *It's probably not going to be a very good book, but it will be my book and that's all that matters.*

Destiny: "You know in your heart it will be an amazing book."

Experience: "You're so full of shit."

The insufferable disgust of the optimist...

Esmeralda found herself stuck at Wymondham train station. It had taken her two hours to travel less than ten miles and even that was in the wrong direction. To say she hated the train services was an understatement. It was a shame, she felt, because she was actually rather fond of trains and train stations. Wymondham was wonderfully quaint, with its overflowing hanging baskets and hand-painted signs. It oozed all that was yummy about the country. But the service she had just received from the ticket guards and the rail enquiries phone line had oozed with all that was malignant about England. Privatising the rail service, handing it over to businessmen who were completely void of integrity and had no interest whatsoever in the common man or the effects their crummy services had on people's lives, was a mistake from beginning to end. *Just think*, thought Esmeralda, *how many opportunities have been missed, relationships left in tatters and uncomfortable nights spent in dangerous empty train stations, all because of the incompetence of the privatised rail service. That Margaret Thatcher has a lot to answer for.* Esmeralda breathed in the fragrant evening air of Wymondham station and imagined all of the tears that had been spent on behalf of that wretched woman. *This country has cried more than a river over you*, she thought to herself.

"The saying 'It's not cricket' has become obsolete because it doesn't mean anything anymore. Nothing is 'cricket' these days. It's all gone down the pan. Damn willynillyness. It pisses me off," she moaned.

"I hate willynillyness. That's why my love for you will never die," he replied.

After all that no one even came to check her flaming ticket. Although she had technically got the journey for free, it had cost her two hours of her life.

She chomped down on the stumpy piece of liquorice root, her substitute for the never-ending stream of tobacco she had always smoked.

Hastings was like a time-warp, with empty throbbing arcades and grease-ridden fish and chip shops. But she liked the feeling of dilapidation. The town was full of possibility. Brighton had won city status for the Millennium, but since then it had lost its charm as a washed-up seaside community and had become a badly-managed culture shock.

The train pulled into an empty station in the middle of nowhere. Looking out of the window she noticed that the standard long thin signs that normally announced the name of the station was just a blank white rectangle. *This looks like my kind of a stop*, she decided, and alighted from the train. She had never been to Orpington, but one of her true loves had gone to college there.

She lay next to him, with the cold autumn light blaring in through the open window bringing with it cool air that delicately lapped at her exposed skin. She realised that for the first time in her life, she felt completely free. The past no longer created her present. She was exactly where she wanted to be and with whom she wanted to be with. She was falling in love and although it was still terrifying, she was feeling fearless. Everything that had led her to where she was now had been an adventure, a journey, a rallying of experience and insight. The time was now, the place was here and nothing was anything other than it should be. She turned and looked over at his tanned lithe back and inhaled his sexy pungent smell. Mixed with the morning air, it tasted of complete contentment. Everything was perfect and she felt as free as a bird.

"I hate falling in love. It makes me think of a farmer sticking his hand up a cows arse and pulling out a gushing, bewildered, mucus-covered calf," she told her friend.

She wondered what star sign he was. Her birth chart was all fire and earth, hence the important people in her life were either water or air signs. It also meant that she had a penchant for water, always living by the sea. *He must be a water sign,* she decided. *Hence our mutual attraction and his penchant for fire.*

"The duvet is covered in love juice."

"It's covered in sex juice?"

"No… I said love juice."

The greatest thing you'll ever learn is just to love, and be loved in return - Moulin Rouge.

Breakfast was divine. For years she had thought that breakfast was spelt breakfeast, because it was a feast at the break of day. It made sense, she guessed, that it was when you broke your fast, but she didn't like the idea that a fast was being imposed upon her by a word. Surely fasting was a choice one made for religious or health reasons, or to raise money for charity? *And I'm sure that sometimes I eat in my dreams,* she thought to herself.

Noting the books on his bookshelf, Neil Gaiman, Brian Froud, *Where the Wild Things Are. I could be happy here,* she thought.

"She's a gorgeous ball of sexiness," he said.

"I'm in love and it's glorious!" she wailed.

20

Esmeralda woke to the sound of the tarpaulin crashing with the wind against the sides of the cart they slept beneath in a makeshift shelter. It was the middle of summer and they were all working at a Tudor re-enactment that was held annually at an old house in Suffolk. She snuggled up closer to the young man she was sleeping next to, one of those friends whom she considered her brethren, having spent every summer with him at the re-enactment since they had been young children. She desperately tried to go back to sleep. The visitors would be arriving soon and she wasn't feeling anywhere near capable of conversing with the public.

Unfortunately the damage she had done to herself the night before began to creep into her consciousness and all she could think about was drinking cool fresh water. Still, she managed to ignore her thirst for about an hour, before finally caving in. Eventually she untangled herself from her friend's gangly limbs and located an old tonic bottle they had filled with water. Gulping down half a litre, she looked around at the dishevelled mess under the cart where they were sleeping. Bodies and cans were strewn everywhere, along with bits of Tudor costume, and it stank of wood smoke and stale beer. She looked down at her sleeping friend and recalled how he'd rather unexpectedly tried to kiss her last night after they had left the campfire. Esmeralda was glad they hadn't gone and messed that one up. It would have been a tragedy.

It was the same with breakfast. In the summer she always wanted to eat muesli with soya milk, drizzled in honey. In the winter, without any conscious thought, she suddenly only fancied porridge made with soya milk, drizzled in honey and sprinkled with raisins.

21

She decided to get off and wait for the next fast train. It was a huge risk but she was feeling rather reckless.

They went to the pub for a pint and she told him all about songlines.

"Knob end," she slurred.

"We could just sneak off to bed?" he suggested.

"We could actually do that, couldn't we?"

"Damn straight. I mean, I know we are the party, but we are also entitled to an early night once in a while."

"Gosh. I've never even considered that as an option..."

"Come on, let's do it."

"I feel so naughty!"

They had cuddled up next to each other, in their sleeping bags, under the cart. Then he had rather unexpectedly tried to kiss her.

She thought about the man she had last been in love with. He was tall, ginger and filling out a bit at the sides, but she had always loved the way that he managed to pull it off. He was somehow still very sexy and the girls all went mad for him. She'd loved his artwork and his passionate drive. Even though he had cheated on her three times before she'd finally come to her senses and dumped the arsehole, he had taught her to call herself an artist, and this fact alone meant that she would always consider him a dear friend.

Everyone comes into your life for a reason.

"The baker's hand's smelt... because he kneaded a poo," she laughed.

"When was the last time you washed? You smell of cat piss," he asked her.

The risk had been a success. The train slid in between the platforms like a silk tie between two smooth thighs.

Esmeralda crawled out from under the cart and stumbled to her feet. *Fucking hell, I'm still pissed,* she thought to herself.

The bright morning light burnt her eyes as she staggered a few feet away from the cart, undid her trousers and flopped down onto the grass for a piss. She had never understood why women squatted down to piss. It meant that it went all over your shoes, legs and dribbled down your bum. If you sat straight on the grass and pissed slowly then it just seeped down into the ground and you'd only get a bit of a damp bottom. Plus it meant you could do it anywhere, as you only needed to drop your trousers a little way and no one ever suspected you were pissing, especially if you looked them straight in the eye as they walked past. Esmeralda sat on the thick grass enjoying the sensation of relieving her extremely full bladder whilst comfortably partaking in her favourite view in the world - a tree that looked like a witch, whose large hooked nose and pointy chin waved in the wind, looking as if she were cackling at Esmeralda's toilet exploits.

This technique is called "sneaky weeing" and Esmeralda had been taught it by an amazing old witch who had been the mother of one of her friends when she was just a teenager. Unfortunately the woman had succumbed to alcoholism and came to a rather untimely end, but her legacy lived on in Esmeralda's sneaky wees. It even worked on Brighton beach, where afterwards she only needed to roll over a few stones to cover the damp patch and everyone was left none the wiser. It was better than having a dick even. Men still needed to go somewhere to piss. She need only move a few feet away.

"Men treat you completely differently when you have blonde hair. I'm embarrassed for them. It's like watching a moth butting a window pane," Esmeralda told her friend.

"I think conflict makes you evolve. Wars boost the economy and every time I get dumped I get a new haircut, do a bit of exercise and make darn sure I'm a lot sexier than I was when the bastard was fucking me," she told them.

The gaggle of women cackled in unison.

"There's no plot or story."

"The Aborigines," she explained to him, "believe that the ancestors, who were animal-like spirits, rose up out of the earth and travelled across the land singing all of the landmarks, elements and living things into being. When a pregnant woman first feels her baby kick, she remembers the land features of where she is standing and then goes to tell the elders. They believe that the song of the ancestor jumps up through the legs of the mother and kick-starts the baby into life, which means that the baby's spirit belongs to that songline, rather than to the tribe or its family. The elders know all of the songs of the ancestors and the paths that they took, so when the child is born, they teach the child the songline that it belongs to, then when the child has grown up, it will go on walkabout across the barren landscape of the outback, using the song as a map. They will meet others on the same songline as themselves along the way. They are their brethren and they will help each other out with information about food and watering-holes, but they'll also spend some time hanging out together and enjoying each other's company."

"I think it's important to keep one's love as far away from one's self as possible. Both age-wise and geographically," Esmeralda told her friend.

"You say 'one' a lot, don't you?" he said.

"I know," she replied. "That's because I'm a bit of a cunt."

It was one of those moments when a person chooses to cross over from one universe and into another. She had met up with one of the guys from her course. He was a lovely chap, very talented and, from time to time, she took him as one of her lovers. He was looking very dapper and she had made an effort too, in her pin-striped suit and trilby. The show they went to see was thoroughly enjoyable and afterwards they sauntered down the stairs of the theatre and into the bar, content with an evening well spent. But when they got into the bar, they discovered a loud gang of crusties, all of whom turned out to be her friends. One of the crusties, a little androgynous skinhead girl by the name of Little Teddy, had also, from time to time, been one of her lovers, and had been living up a mountain in Spain for the last three years, so they were very pleased to see each other.

The next thing she knew, he had gone home on the last train, kissing her on the cheek goodnight, reassuring her that he expected nothing less. Esmeralda suddenly found herself drinking cheap red wine from a shiny silver sack, in a big top tent, surrounded by circus types, dogs and small children. In the morning she peeled herself out of the soft arms of Little Ted, located her clothes and caught the train home.

"Where have you been?" asked her housemate as she walked in through the door.

"I ran away with the circus," she replied.

"Oh... That was quick."

The shower was freezing cold, but it was exactly what she needed after a night at the circus.

"Wow. That's amazing!" he said, visibly impressed with the idea. "So they believe that the world is created out of songs?"

"Yep."

"That's wicked."

"And I really believe it's true. If you think about it, we are born on the same wavelength as some people and not others. And the reason why the world seems like it's such a small place is because when we go on walkabout around the globe, we visit the places that call to our particular songline and we meet like-minded people along the way, who exchange information with us about other places we'd enjoy and hang out with us for a bit. You'll inevitably know all the same people too, all of us being of the same songline."

"Cool," he said, "I've never thought of it like that before."

She decided to stop off in Cambridge and visit an old friend. "I'll meet you at the station and we'll go straight to the pub."

"Great plan."

"Can we ride on the roof?"

"Go on, then. But don't stand on the bonnet, and hold on tight."

"Excellent."

"And it can only take eight of you."

"OK."

She wondered if it was the mother who sat down to teach the songline to her baby or if it was the elders?

They had recorded her snoring. She had passed out at some point and couldn't remember the later part of the evening. She woke up on the seating area in the trailer. His brother and sister had slept in the bed and he was asleep on the seating opposite her. She was sure that he had arranged for them to have their own caravan. Either everyone woke up in unison or the noise of their movements had woken her up, but they were all awake now, sitting up and already tucking into the booze left over from their pilfering expedition at the party the night before. She remembered being at the party, but didn't remember getting back to the trailer.

"You passed out," his sister told her, "and were snoring like a bastard... I recorded you." But luckily she couldn't find the recording on her phone.

She had found the entrance to fairyland. It wasn't quite what she had expected, but it would have to do. The next day, she left him, safe in the knowledge that something special was flourishing.

A cloud of sparrows swooped down and caught onto the telegraph wire.

"Do you remember when sparrows used to be the most common bird in the country?" she asked him.

"No. It's always been pigeons in my lifetime..." he replied.

"I guess you're too young," she mused. "It used to be sparrows, hands down."

He called her his summer girl, which had made her heart skip several beats. Donning a trilby, she entered the balmy evening.

She realised that she hadn't listened to music for ages. When they finally reached the entrance to the new poncey "place to be" club in London, they found that they weren't all on the guest list. Whilst she ended up having to pay £20 to get in, several of the lithe, blonde, success stories she was with had already sauntered their way through. Inside, the club was wall-to-wall with tossers. Everyone was so busy trying to look good, they had completely forgotten about enjoying themselves. She pushed her way through the stench of perfume and cigarettes to the bar and ordered two vodka and Red Bulls. Three women stood on her feet in stilettos on the way and not one of them apologised. When the barman had finished pouring the drinks, she handed him a £20 note. He stood and stared at her with contempt.

Embarrassed, she produced another tenner and waited for her change. He gave her two pounds back.

They ran away from that soulless hole and made their way to a proper club - one that was open all night, sold cheap drinks and was wall-to-wall with hot South American guys laden with pills. She and her mate scored a couple and then danced their arses off. They soon gathered quite a following of suitors and picked their way amongst them, snogging some, getting drinks off others and giving the odd lucky one their number.

Her head was full of cotton wool. *I'm too tired to sleep,* she thought to herself. *I'm too stoned and too broken. I'm going to have to watch porn and frig myself to sleep.* She wished he were there with her. A warm pair of arms would be lovely right now, along with a slow cosy screw. That's the only trouble with being single - the lonely nights when you just want a bloody cuddle. She would have really fancied her mate's boyfriend if he hadn't have been her mate's boyfriend.

Esmeralda woke up. The pigeons were mating again. She had woken to their strangled warble a million times. *I need to move to the countryside,* she thought to herself.

"I've got another car that needs christening."

"Great."

She donned her bright pink pants and her low-slung jeans, which allowed her pants to peep slyly out of the top of them. She liked the fact that her pants matched her hair. They were exactly the same shade of pink.

It had turned out that the man she loved was an Aries. He was all fire. She was suddenly aware that there was a chance she might get burnt. Being fearless in love isn't the same as being reckless.

"Sweet dreams, fire child."

28

It's time to write a book, she thought, *but if I'm going to write a book, then I will need a room of one's own. If those twats can write a book, then so can I. I'm going to write a book about writing a book.*

"We were just talking about shooting things, then about tinnitus and then about blowjobs. I just love the conversations I have with my family..." he snorted.

"I don't want the summer to end," she mused.

"You can't fight time."

"I know, but why does it insist on going so fast?"

Esmeralda had felt an old enemy creep up on her over the course of the weekend. A twinge of jealousy had leapt up whenever he had mentioned a woman he had been with. He wasn't being an arsehole mentioning them, he was just being normal, but it had made her uncomfortable. She hated the feeling of jealousy. It was her least favourite emotion in the world and she hadn't felt it once in the whole time she had been single. She hated it so much that it was almost a good enough reason never to allow herself to fall in love with anyone ever again. But she knew that was stupid. The whole point of falling in love is so that you allow someone else into you innermost bubble, which of course is going to make you feel vulnerable. Besides, Esmeralda had an addiction to facing her fears that far outweighed everything else. The whole time she had been single she had been having trouble remembering the word "compromise".

Esmeralda sat around the table with the female trinity. The Crone – a midwife and a mother of three who had just gone through her menopause; The Mother – a musician, songwriter and a single mother of four; then there was Esmeralda – residing somewhere in the undefined realm between Virgin and Mother, which she liked to call Slut. They talked, over many cups of tea, about their lives. They shared stories, supporting each other's points of view and congratulating one another on their voyage of discoveries. Calmly they shared out their nuggets of gold around the table.

People can only intimidate you with your permission - Eleanor Roosevelt.

Esmeralda felt like she had been lost in a bubble of hedonism all summer. She was looking forward to settling back into her routine bubble again. Well… sort of.

She was on her way to see one of her oldest friends. It was always weird seeing her because their paths had taken such different directions over the years, but at the same time it was good because they both could see the whole distance of where the other had travelled from over the other one's shoulder.

Whilst chatting to her oldest friend, she smiled as she realised that she was talking in metaphors again and her friend had always laughed at her for doing this. She knew that her friend would be thinking this too, but there was no need for either of them to physically acknowledge the situation in any way. They both knew what the other one was thinking.

There was a fairy caught on her jumper.

Esmeralda listened to one of her best friends rutting with her housemate in the next room. *How sweet*, she thought to herself. It was obvious that they still liked each other.

"I love dancing. When I dance I feel like the sexiest person on the planet," she told him.

"You are the sexiest person on the planet," he reminded her.

"Oh yes… You're right," she agreed.

She missed the sea, but she was loving the countryside.

The smell of woodsmoke engulfed her and permeated every pore in her skin and every fibre of her clothing, in the way that only woodsmoke can.

Her world was made up of bubbles, each with its own location, group of friends and season. Not to mention the bubbles of her past that she still possessed a membership to, even if just in memory. Each bubble was formed of a thin film separating each of them, one that she passed through as easily as a ghost through a wall. *No wonder it's all so confusing,* she thought to herself. *I'm like a glob of cuckoo-spit hanging on the bush of life.*

The landscape of his bubble passed out of view. The nourishing feminist rants, the parties with his youthful vivacious friends, the crystal healing and the organic home-grown food, all disappeared into the darkness. Now she was heading towards the landscape of her routine bubble, with its squirrelled-away toiletries, her cynical housemates, her Nathan Barley studio and a long list of unanswered emails.

She was looking forward to partaking in a bowl of frozen Acai with muesli and a drizzle of honey.

She loved honey.

And the word drizzle.

Her longest relationship had been with an extremely attractive man who had been her brethren for many years. There had always been a strong chemistry between them and they had loved each other very deeply. But they had been with each other during the chrysalis stage of development and as they had turned into beautiful butterflies, they had found that their love for each other had been caught up in the empty chrysalis shell they were leaving behind. She was aware that the man that she loved

31

now was still a chrysalis and she didn't want to go through all that again. *I'll meet you on the other side*, she decided.

"Hi Mum!"

"Hello gorgeous, how are you?"

"I'm great, thanks. I'm stuck at a station, so I thought I'd give you a call."

"Where are you?"

"Deepest, darkest Norfolk."

"How's the last few days been?"

"Er… it was good, but it's put it all into perspective a bit more."

"In what way?"

"Well… I can see that for it to work, we need to spread what would normally happen in six months, over a few years."

"Right?"

"Because there are limitations at the moment on how well we can communicate with each other. We get on really well when we are around other people and the connection between us is incredibly strong. But when we are on our own, we don't really have much to talk about."

"Why do you think that is?"

"Well, there's the age gap, obviously. And then, because he didn't finish school, he can feel a bit threatened by stuff that seems too academic. And then also, he hasn't flown the nest yet and experienced what's out there in the world. All we really have to talk about is the few memories we have created thus far and whatever is happening at the present moment."

"Do you think that's going to be a problem?"

"Well, no. He is an amazing guy and as soon as he gets out there and has spent some time in the world then we will have loads to talk about. Our communication will grow the more we build a backlog of experiences together. And he knows that I totally adore him and I know that he adores me. We're on the same wavelength and all that, but this can't happen now. It's too big an age gap."

"It's good that you can see the limitations at the moment and that that doesn't mean anything's wrong."

"No, 'cause in some ways it's great, 'cause our communication is completely grounded in the present, which is extraordinary. It's something really special. It's not about stories and old baggage. And it's good not to be over-analysing the situation, or trying to define our feelings with words; we are going completely on our own instincts. And people don't listen to them enough. At the moment my instincts are telling me that this is something fun and light."

"And you will know when it's the right time for it to move into something more serious. Are you exclusive to each other then, or don't you know?"

"I don't know. I think that it might be a good idea for us to just carry on as we have been. I'll see him again loads next summer, but in the winter it's probably best if we just get on with our own thing. I like the idea of him being a fair weather friend."

"And that means you are taking your time with it."

"Yeah, that's it. Listen, the train is coming. I'll call you back in a bit."

"OK, darling."

"Thanks for that, Mum. It's weird 'cause I don't have anyone else I can talk to about this. I can't talk about it to any of his friends and none of my friends know him. It's like a dream I keep entering in and out of."

"Well, you know I'm always here."

"Sure do! Love you lots."

"Love you too, darling. Speak to you soon."

"Bye!"

"Bye."

It was nearly a full moon. *My period didn't really happen this month*, noted Esmeralda. It only lasted a day and the blood never even turned red. She wished her periods would go back to normal again. Damn contraceptive pill. She had liked it when her periods had coincided with the full moon. It made her feel in tune with things.

The train pulled into Brighton station. It was the only place she had ever lived that she loved coming back to. It always made her smile. A much-needed sea breeze cooled the sweat between her nose and her sunglasses.

The air was full of fairies. Not the winged variety with breasts, but the fluffy stars that float around the place, having begun their lives on thistles. Esmeralda wondered why we couldn't be satisfied by the magic and wonder of these fairies and had to go around making up fake ones.

She wasn't saying that she didn't believe in fairies, by the way.

There was a cute guy on the opposite platform and he kept checking her out. She smiled at him.

Esmeralda listed her plans for the next year in her notebook...

- Move into a room of one's own.

- Learn to drive and get a van.

- Get *uber* fit.

- Enjoy my last year at school to the max.

- Be a space for "Anything is Possible" in the next year.

Esmeralda felt old. She had just had the best summer of her life, but her body was bearing the brunt of it now. She certainly wasn't as young as she used to be, plus she had spent the whole summer with people who were five to ten years younger than her, which had been a constant reminder of her own mortality. But it had been good fun. They had fed Esmeralda the powerful optimism she had been in desperate need of. One thing was for sure, though, and that was that this summer she had noticed something settling inside of herself. She had settled into womanhood and who she was as a person. Her 28th birthday was looming and she knew that the next two years of her life were going to be the most exciting yet. Great changes were afoot as she was entering the next stage of life. Esmeralda smiled at the door to her future and her fingers twitched like antennae with anticipation. It had been one hell of an adventure so far and the next ride looked set to be even more exciting than the last.

ITALY

"I think I was about eleven years old. I owned a pair of bright pink fluorescent dungarees – I had a real thing for fluorescent colours and these dungarees had neon-yellow pockets and buttons all over them. They were quite a sight – and I lived in them.

"We went to Italy, where Dad had been working for the last year. Dad seemed to me to be very important and did very important things. He was a computer programmer and I didn't know what that meant. He worked in London, which was a big important place, *and* he worked for a year in Paris and a year in Milan, and I didn't even know where those places were! This made him a very important and special person. Far more impressive than Mum, who was training to be a teacher and everyone knows what a teacher is and all the teachers I'd ever met had not been very exciting people. I liked my Mum but she did normal things.

"I was dead excited about going to Milan and seeing all the exciting places where my Dad had been hanging out. We spent a few days in Milan. I can't remember where we stayed, but I can remember trying to visit the Duomo and not being allowed in because my Mum and me had bare legs and shoulders. This was my first brush with orthodox religion and I didn't like the way it made me feel. As if my skin was dirty or something. Instead of going in the Duomo therefore we went up on the roof and enjoyed the amazing views. There were lots of statues of little naked cupids that had lost their heads and Dad put his head on one of the empty necks so it looked like he had a little cupid body. Then he stuck his finger between the little cupid's legs so it looked like he had a little willy and I thought that was really funny. I liked it when Dad was naughty. I remember there being a statue of the Madonna on the roof. She was white and gold. I wondered why they had a statue of a pop star up there and was confused as I was sure the cathedral was older than her.

"In the square in front of the cathedral was a man selling fresh broken-up bits of coconut in a beautiful fountain of ice and running water. It was cold and refreshing and exotic. I got addicted to lemon sorbet and we had to stop every time we passed the multi-coloured ice cream stalls, piled with unusual exciting flavours.

"We also went and camped for a few days by a lake at the foot of Mont Blanc, which we thought was a funny name as it sounded like Mont Bonk. All the way there we listened to Madonna's new album and I learnt all the words to *Little Jessie* because I thought it was a brilliant song. I remember my arm got sunburnt from where I was leaning it out the window. We camped by a lake called Lake Maggiore, which was partly in Italy and partly in Switzerland. We went for a drive around Switzerland and I remember seeing someone cut their grass with a scythe, and all the houses looked like cuckoo clocks. The lake was beautiful. It was fresh water so my brother and I used to run down to the lake every morning to swim in it, instead of having a shower. It was full of little fish that would nibble your toes if you sat still for long enough. One time we met some Italian kids who jumped in and swam around with us. They were a girl and a boy. I really liked the boy. When I got back to England we found we had a photo of him and I lied and told everyone he was my boyfriend. We took our airbeds down there and used them as lilos. I think I remember Mum and Dad not getting on for some reason on that day. In these situations I would always think that Mum was being a spoilsport. I was a real daddy's girl.

"Dad hired a speedboat and we drove it around the lake. We went really fast, which was exciting. We all had a go at driving it. I love driving speedboats.

"We ate lots of great food. There was a waiter at the local bar at the campsite who kept flirting with me and who I kept going to for Coca-Cola, which I would ask for in Italian. We went to a restaurant next to the water and I wore my pink dungarees and a new headscarf I had bought in Milan that had lots of different acid men faces all over it. There were punk acid men, flamenco acid women, lots of acid faces in a row like acid traces, pirate acid men and baby acid men. They were each their own bright fluorescent colour. At the restaurant I had folded-over pizza for the first time. We bought some fishing rods and sat on the decking and tried to catch some fish. I can't remember if we actually caught anything.

"We had driven all the way to Italy in my Dad's Triumph Acclaim, which was much cooler than my Mum's clapped-out Opel, and at one point a huge lorry drove into the back of us and we all got whiplash. I think we also ran out of petrol another time and Dad had to walk for miles to go get some more."

"That was the first family holiday we ever had abroad and it was such an adventure. But the most exciting thing was how Dad was making money now, and there was a whiff of success hanging over the family. We had moved out of our council house, which Margaret Thatcher had allowed us to buy, and we had moved into a new house on a new housing estate. We had two cars and went camping abroad instead of camping in Robin Hood's Bay. It felt great. Although I wasn't really old enough to understand debt, I knew we were in a lot of debt, and Dad would sometimes shout at the computer, head-butt the walls or the steering wheel in his car, setting off the hooter for all the neighbours to hear.

"Not long after that, the recession hit. I didn't really know what a recession was, but I knew it meant that my Dad's computer programming company folded and he had to sign on the dole. He was very ashamed and didn't like the fact that Mum had become the breadwinner. She was a fully fledged teacher by now.

"My Dad got a job at the local college, plugging in light bulbs and that kind of thing. Then he had an affair with my drama teacher and left us. It didn't matter financially; Mum could look after us on her wage and we soon got used to living on a small amount of money again. He had left her with all the debts though, which was mean.

"It took many years for me to go back to doing drama again."

MICHAELMAS

She woke up in her own bed. She hadn't slept that deeply in ages. Esmeralda lay there stretching her arms out, relishing the comfort of her own smell, her own surroundings and her own lovely bed.

The house was full of pigeon mites.

Get your own fucking shampoo, Shane! was scrawled in biro on the side of the empty Head and Shoulders bottle.

"It's so depressing and so incredibly right-wing. It's an example of the abused child becoming the abuser. They formed the 'Promised Land' to escape from the labelling and the ghettos, but they have created a world where they label people and put them in ghettos," her friend told her.

"Yeah, I'd recommend going there… for less than a week and if someone else is paying."

"Live in London once," exclaimed Esmeralda, "but leave before it turns you into a hard-headed knob-end. Live in Brighton once, but leave before it turns you into a soft-headed knob-end."

"Can you help me dye my hair?" her friend asked.

41

"I really want to lose a stone in weight," moaned Esmeralda.

"If I get jowls like my father and my sister… then I'll consider surgery," mused her friend.

"I'm dreading my tits turning into spaniel's ears if I breastfeed, which I'm sure they will. But I refuse to make my child suffer just so I don't have weird-looking tits."

"You have to allow yourself to ease into the pain," explained the older woman, who did not appreciate the term 'Crone'. "By the time I had my last child, I had learnt to connect with the baby and I was in tune with her every step of the way. I could feel exactly what was going on in my birthing canal and she came out with her eyes wide open and took straight to my breast. It was the most spiritual experience I had ever had."

Her friend who was a midwife taught a technique called "Orgasmic Birthing".

Esmeralda was quite a hippie, but she thought she might have found her line.

"There's this indefinable time after the menopause, when you're meant to be the Crone. I'm fifty years old but I may live for another fifty years. I'm only half way through my life. Am I really expected to be a Crone for half of my life?"

The thorn bushes were bulging with blackberries. Winter was on her way.

She loved the sound of his voice. He sounded like the chap from *The Good Life*, who was always doing voiceovers for commercials. He sounded like autumn and apple pies.

The yellow Lamborghini slid along the road like a slice of processed cheese.

"I'm full of cheese and tea," scoffed her friend, as soon as she answered the phone.

"That's weird," replied Esmeralda. "I just wrote the word cheese."

Esmeralda respected midwives. She had met two in the last year and they were both totally sorted women, working in the shadows of the towering pillars of modern medicine and stupid politicians who thought they knew best. These women worked hard towards making the most natural thing known to mankind seem as normal as possible, despite the attempts of medicine to turn it into a "medical event".

Facilitating what is happening, rather than lead to what you think ought to be happening. If you must take the lead, lead so that the mother is helped, yet still free and in charge - Tao-te Ching

They sat drinking tea in a bohemian eatery that was done out like you had died and gone to Harvest Festival heaven.

"How old are you?" asked the thirty-something with two kids.

"Twenty-seven"

"Ah, so you have to take that into consideration. You're coming up to your Saturn Returns."

Esmeralda looked at her confused.

"Have you heard of that?" she asked.

"No. What is it?"

"It's when Saturn returns to your chart, which happens after every 28 years in total, but some people are also affected by the seven year quarters of its movement as well. It's when people tend to go through really big changes. Most people can think of something significant that happened in their lives when they were 7, 14, 21, 28, etc. It's when a lot of big things tend to happen, like getting married or divorced or having kids. I was 28 when I had my first child."

Esmeralda had only realised she was a woman two years ago. Before that she had thought that she was a boy. Not only did she think she was a boy, but she thought she was the alpha of all alpha males, with the biggest balls in Christendom. She had been proud as punch the day that she received the highest marks in a masculinity test she had taken in her A-Level psychology class. She always hung out with guys. She was competitive with men, and was currently living in a house full of alpha males, trying to give as good as she got. Being a radical feminist and all, she used to think that men and women were basically the same creature - that everyone had a varying degree of masculinity and femininity in each of them and this had little to do with whether they actually possessed balls or tits. But in the last few years she had realised how different she was from the men in her life. They had grown up to be very different creatures indeed. Her male friends were patriarchs and she now felt every bit the matriarch.

"If you hate women you're called a misogynist, but what are you called if you hate men?" asked Esmeralda.

"Don't know. I've never heard of a word for that before," replied her friend.

"What about pasogynist?" offered up Esmeralda.

"Did you just make that up?" asked her friend.

"Yes..." admitted Esmeralda.

"That's quite good," her friend commended.

"I love porn. It makes me imagine how much damage I would do if I had a cock."

A rat scurried across their path.

"That's the second rat I've seen in as many days," she observed to her friend.

"Life is without meaning. But that isn't a bad thing. It's like having a blank slate... You can chose to put whatever you want on it. I believe in all gods, fairies, and that I've got bigger balls than any man I've ever met."

"Hanging out with eighteen-year-olds looks like it's done you the world of good."

"Are you taking the piss?"

"No. I mean it. You're glowing. Are you pregnant?"

"Don't fucking say that. That wouldn't be funny at all."

"It will be the third time I've got it right."

"Great."

She had a mosquito bite on her leg the size of a side-plate.

"I can't think of a single famous person alive today whom I could call a hero."

"Steve Irwin used to be my hero."

"My friend came up with the term spoorking," she explained. "A spoon and a fork are both useful instruments, but you put them together and they become utterly useless. Well that's just like a couple when they first get together. Separately, they are both fantastic people who are real laugh to have around, but you put them together and they become utterly useless. They have become a spoork. It's an absolute tragedy, but it's happened to the best of us.

"The ridiculous thing is that when I split up with my last boyfriend I said that I wanted to be single for at least two years. And it was like I cast a spell. Immediately things came into my life that were going to take two years to complete. My course, the projects I've taken on, my 'Saturn Returns'. They're all going to take the next two years to happen. The universe is supporting me with my wish. But I'm doing everything in my power to sabotage myself. I look for love in every man I meet. I'm acting like a naughty school girl, trying to pull one over on myself."

"But you get those disposable spoon-like forks", she contested. "Like baby forks. And they're well useful. You can spoon the maximum amount of food into your mouth and they're round with soft edges so they're safe for babies to use."

"I know. That occurred to me as a hole in the argument too..." she conceded. "Well, I guess then it boils down to a case of design. Normal forks and spoons are beautifully designed, individual and durable. Whereas those spoon-fork things are homogenised, tacky and disposable."

They looked at each other for a moment and then began to laugh.

"Before you have sex, tell him he's not allowed to make a sound, because it makes you feel sick. They respect you so much more."

"Relationships are like playing a game of Jenga. You keep giving up parts of yourself until it all crashes down around your ears."

She could feel herself becoming more powerful every single day. She could feel the discomfort and uncertainty of her twenties ebbing away - being replaced with resolution, boundaries and a sense of purpose.

"I realised it wasn't working when I read him a poem I'd written for him and he took it the wrong way. He thought I was saying that he is a slapper."

"But if you think about it, you didn't like it when your last boyfriend described you as having a potty mouth, did you? You said you didn't want the man you loved to see you in that way. Maybe he just didn't like the way you were describing him?"

"That's a good point."

"I wonder how he does want you to see him, then?"

"That's what is doing my head in." whined Esmeralda, "I have no fucking idea."

She was concerned that she had never had a secret. Every event, conversation, and thought she had ever had in her life had been shared with everyone that she had ever met. She suddenly felt very exposed.

She took her nose ring out and she didn't mention it to anyone. She knew that no one would notice, even her nearest and dearest. At last she had a secret.

"Rohypnol is wasted on men", she explained at the pub. I live with four boys. If I had some rohypnol I'd spike them all and dress them up in pretty frocks. Then I'd take photos of them sitting around having a tea party with fancy cakes and touching each other. They'd know nothing about it until I'd invited them all to the opening night of my exhibition."

Esmeralda had always been into science. Her favourite toy as a child had been a science kit, until one day her brother poured all of the chemicals down the toilet, to see what would happen. She had never quite forgiven him for that.

She had woken this morning with her science head on her shoulders. Esmeralda had been roused from a very, very deep sleep. She was loving her bed at the moment. For the last week builders had been working on the flat downstairs and had roused her from her dreams with drilling and hammering, every morning, right under her head. She didn't mind, though. It made a change from the pigeons, plus she was back at school and celebrating her freedom from the cycle of hedonism that had consumed her for the summer months. Already this morning she had got up and spent half an hour exercising, grounding herself in the moment, opening up her breathing and putting herself back into her body. Now she was in the bathroom inspecting herself in the mirror. Her roots were showing, which meant that her hair had grown about half a centimetre since she had last dyed it at her mother's house. Her nail varnish was all chipped off and had grown away from her cuticles, leaving little pink islands sprinkled in glitter, floating in a sea of nail. Her nails had only grown about two millimetres. She had painted them on the same day that she had dyed her hair. This meant that her hair had grown at twice the speed of her nails. She also cut her toenails on the same day and so she now inspected them. She found that they hadn't really grown at all. She wondered if that meant the sun stimulated hair and nail growth. She had once read in a girlie magazine that the expectation of sex stimulated hair and nail growth, but she didn't know if that was really true. Her hair did grow quickly and she was always expecting sex, but she thought that girlie magazines were the spawn of Satan, so it was probably safe to assume that it was a load of old bollocks.

Esmeralda brushed her teeth and put on her dressing gown, accidentally knocking a cross off the shelf above the mirror with her sleeve. She had made the cross six years ago for a photo shoot. It was covered in glitter and had a sentence from the Bible written across the top which read: *I will greatly multiply thy sorrow and thy conception; in sorrow thou shalt bring forth children; and thy desire shall be to thy husband, and he shall rule over thee. Genesis 3:16.* A Barbie doll was nailed to it in the place of Jesus. Esmeralda was also really into religion. Even though she had renounced her faith in the Christian God over a decade ago, she still believed in something greater than herself, but she didn't have the audacity to presume what in hell it could be. Smoothing the hair down on the Barbie doll, she replaced it on the shelf, unlocked the door and returned to her room.

Do not read beauty magazines, they will only make you feel ugly - Baz Luhrmann.

"When I was growing up," Esmeralda discussed with her chums, "we had a female Prime Minister and then of course the Queen. It couldn't help but instil an enormous sense of self worth in a young lady."

"Have you ever wondered if you could handle chopping up a body?" asked her friend, changing the subject.

"Yes."

"Do you think that you could?"

"I hope so," she replied, " because it's the kind of thing that you'll only ever know for certain when the situation arises, but will inevitably be the kind of situation where it's vitally important that you can handle it."

Thank God for that, thought Esmeralda, as she found the toilet roll down the side of the toilet. She had just relieved herself of a coffee-fuelled poo, before noticing the toilet roll holder was empty.

"The trouble is with matters of the heart, dear brother," – she was giving her brother advice again – "is that you can't for love nor money ever know what is going on in your heart of hearts. Knowing is a cognitive process and the heart does not work on this frequency. The heart is part of the body, so the only way to understand what your heart is actually after is by looking at your actions and weighing these up with your intellect. For example, physically, you know that at the moment you are not going to be meeting your intellectual, fun-loving, ambitious or worldly wise equal, so any relationship that forms, no matter how overwhelmed with love you may feel in the present moment, isn't really what you are looking for. Your soul mate is not in Essex. Now you're moving, at first you aren't going to be playing as big as you want to be, but in time you will be taking life by storm and will be meeting bright young things who really get your juices going. Until your actions fit with the kind of person you believe yourself to be, you can't be meeting the kind of partners that your heart truly desires. Until you feel like your actions match with your view of yourself, stay fucking single. Simple really."

"What other people think of you is none of your business," she told him.

His eyes lit up.

Her brother was her best friend now, though.

"Girls with brothers are useless," explained a mate of hers. "Their friends are all blokes and there is always that one guy hanging around that's her 'good mate' when really he wants to lay her. Girls with brothers are definitely easier to pull, though. Whereas girls who have sisters are much higher maintenance, but it's worth it 'cause they're always surrounded by a flock of knickers. She'll slag you off to them all the time, but they'll all fancy you anyway, so it doesn't matter."

She realised that it was always going to be hard for her to be in a relationship again, because she was an active member of so many different realities. Whoever she ended up with would have to see her in all of her different worlds for him to fully grasp the kind of person she was. Although she remained the same person whoever she was with, it was the fact that she got on with such a wide range of people, from different backgrounds and age groups. That was one of her greatest assets, one that could not be overlooked by someone who was in love with her. There was no way though for him, or her, to fully grasp this asset without spending time with her in all of her different worlds. And they wouldn't enjoy doing that unless they were that kind of a person too. She'd only met one other person who was like that and he lived a million miles away.

The soundtrack to *Eternal Sunshine of the Spotless Mind* began to play on her iPod and it transported her back to her last relationship. After watching that film together they had wept bitterly into each other's arms. They had both known the end was nigh.

"I am gay," announced her mobile phone as a text message came through. She realised that one of her new fifteen-year-old best mates had been tampering with her phone.

"I think there is something to be said for homosexuality being hereditary."

"Why's that?"

"Well, my dad is bisexual," she explained, "and so am I."

"Your dad is bisexual?" he queried.

"Yes. He realised just before he got married to my drama teacher, but decided that it didn't matter and went ahead with the wedding anyway. But it meant that he had spent the whole of his life denying his inner artist, in case anyone thought he was a soft sissy and suspected that he was gay. Now he doesn't care and is embracing himself as an artist."

"Poor bloke."

"Yeah, but he's happy now."

"Janis Joplin had the same problem. She struggled with her sexuality and her art."

"I think it's quite a common theme. I guess it's what happens when you feel society won't allow you to fully express yourself."

"I'm not sure if it's a case of nature or nurture though. I suspect its more nurture. I don't buy into this idea of a gay gene."

"The pink gene?"

"Yeah," she laughed, "apparently it's bent." They all chuckled.

"I don't see religion and science as polar opposites, I think they are two halves of a circle," explained Esmeralda as she folded up her sheets. Her friend sat on the edge of her bed smoking a roll up. "Science explains how the car works and religion tries to figure out who invented the car and why."

"The engine is science and Ford is God?" asked her friend, for clarity.

"Something like that."

"I love happy accidents," Esmeralda exclaimed.

"I'm pregnant... It was an accident," fretted her friend.

Esmeralda went with her to the clinic. Both of them had been down this road before. They both knew how unpleasant an experience it was. She was going to try the tablet this time, thinking that it might possibly be less fucked up than the operation. It turned out that this was not the case at all. She had a horrible old time. If ever you're going to get it done, let them knock you out cold.

"I love sex."

"Sex with him was amazing, but he always wanted to do it in the same position," she mused.

"Which one's that?" her friend asked.

"With me on top."

"Well... at least it wasn't with him on top the whole time..." she noted.

"Good point."

"My favourite position is doggy style, with my face rammed down into the pillow."

"That's Tracy Emin's favourite position too."

"How in the blue blazes do you know that?" she asked her.

"I read it," she replied.

Another of her friends had a shelf of cute yet screwed-up-looking kitsch dolls, one for each of her abortions. She had six dolls and had given birth to one child. She thought nothing of it and didn't find the experience in the least bit unpleasant. But she also assigned to the 80's mode of feminism that was all about the mastery and then denial of the female condition. Plus she went private.

The phone said "Private Number" on the display. *I'm not answering that,* thought Esmeralda. *It's probably my cult.*

Her family had a history of following cults, because they were the kind of people who liked to believe in the things that are greater than themselves. They weren't really cults, though, they were just groups of people taking some time out of life to reflect on things for a bit. However this always tended to attract a lot of lost souls whose behaviour would then freak other people out a bit. These days most people see religions as evil and distrust anyone who is deeply passionate about anything. Cynicism is the new world order.

"Why not just believe?"

She felt like a queen bee. All she wanted to do was dance her arse off or be filled to the brim with cocks. She sat squirming in her seat, doing secret circles.

An Irishman had once broken her heart. She didn't trust Irishmen anymore.

"The worse way to be dumped is when the bastard just stops ringing you or answering your calls. You're left deserted on the merry-go-round of romance, going dizzy with denial."

Good girls go to heaven, but bad girls go wherever they like! was scrawled on the toilet wall.

"Suicide is so selfish," he bitched as he strode towards her, "Imagine jumping in front of a train at rush hour. If you going to kill yourself, you could at least do it quietly."

Eat your taboos.

His eyes were glazed over as he walked along the street. He was plugged into his iPod and lost to the soundtrack of his own self-masturbatory movie, making love to his own ego.

"Can I fuck you up the arse?"

"No, I only do anal sex with people I'm in love with. I think it's crass otherwise. Can I fuck you up the arse?"

"What with?"

"I've got a strap-on."

"A strap-on? Let's have a look!"

"Say hello to my little friend! This is Bert Murphy."

"Your strap-on has got a name?"

"Yep. It's the same name as my teddy bear and it's what I'm going to call my first born child."

"Even if it's a girl?"

"Damn straight."

"Poor kid… It's huge."

"Are you up for it?"

"Go on then. If I'm going to let anyone shag me up the arse, it might as well be you."

"Loving your logic."

She couldn't stop herself from writing. The floodgates were open now and it was all pouring out. She had written all the way from Cambridge to Brighton yesterday and then had continued writing when she got home. It was now the next day and she was writing again. It was 3.23pm, she had been writing since 10am and she still hadn't even broken her fast.

"Never let a man fuck you in the arse unless he lets you fuck him in the arse first," she advised her friend. "That also goes for going down on him."

She used to hate Thai women because her ex-boyfriend had been obsessed with them. It was daft, though, because she had exactly the kind of features that most Thai women coveted. With a little cute round nose, huge eyes and perfect lips, she looked like a Manga character. She didn't have a problem with them any more though. She had got over her issues with them as quickly as she had got over the fella.

"I sometimes prefer bad works of art to good works of art, because… they're so full of possibility."

She hated women who drove Land Rovers.

Intelligent women scare the blue blazes out of men.

She thought it was tasteless the way that famous feminists behaved. Germaine Greer parading her love for young men like it deserved some kind of medal and Julie Burchill taking pride in her fascism. She thought that it made them worse than men, because they really ought to know better. She had become a simulacrum of herself. It was a tragedy. She is more hack than human now.

And I never… not once… put myself in a position where I'd be around young adolescent boys to any significant degree. I'm 50 years old now, and I still think about boys. But I've kept it under control for all these years and led a pretty dammed good life. I hope SADBOY can do the same. Been there, didn't do it – Anon.

Esmeralda got home from school and found the living room empty for a change, so she flung herself on the coach and switched on the TV. There was a film playing. She had found the end of a pure weed spliff in her pocket earlier in the day. She hadn't smoked a shred of tobacco all summer and had hardly touched weed in the last year. Being stoned didn't mix well with school and she was at school almost every day, plus she was trying to conquer her asthma, but the summer holidays had bought with it her usual pageant of bad habits and it would take Esmeralda a little while to shake them all off again. This was the last of her weed, though, so that sorted that one out. She sparked it up and sucked the stinging smoke down deep into her wheezing lungs.

She was reading *The Unbearable Lightness of Being* and was deliberating on the theory of eternal return.

She was a little bit like all of the characters.

Postmodernism rules, OK.

Postmodernism rules, OK?

"Are you looking at my tits?" she asked the Georgian.

"No," he replied in his sexy eastern European accent.

"Why not?" she sulked, "I love men who look like they could kill me with their bare hands."

One of the sexiest moments in her memory was when she pulled a guy in a hot tub at a festival and they went for a shag in the shower. She offered up her gorgeous rump for him to dishevel whilst she gripped tightly onto the shower pipes. There was a moment, as he grabbed hold of her hips, just before he plunged himself deep into her expectant vagina, where he brushed his left thumb over the tattoo at the base of her back. This moment of acknowledgment, through the haze of the drugs and booze, was a moment when she felt like he had truly seen her. He had noticed something unique and special about her, probably the only discerning feature he'd recognise on her if they ever met again, and it drove young Esmeralda wild. That moment became the inspiration for many a future wank.

We are caught in a perpetual groundhog of All Fools' Day. Imbeciles rule the world, dozy muppets parade themselves as celebrity gods, knuckleheads look down on bohemians with patronising scorn and willynillyness prevails.

"This decade was called the naughty noughts," Esmeralda pointed out to her mother, "Well, it's lived up to its name. We've all been very naughty indeed and there is naught left for us to believe in or value."

"I am the devil queen! I can do anything!" she screamed into the night.

She was fed up of having to keep quiet while she masturbated or when she was fucking. Back in the day she had been a right screamer. When had that stopped? She couldn't wait to have a room of one's own.

"Whey hey!"

"Yo, beast! Where are you?"

"I'm at home. Where are you?"

"We've just parked up outside your house."

"Excellent!"

The group of attractive young men had turned up to play with her for the weekend. How wonderful, she thought to herself!

She didn't like to over-use the exclamation mark.

"Do you want to fuck me in the arse whilst I'm looking like an eight-year-old?"

"I'm not a paedophile."

"That's all right, I'm not an eight-year-old."

"I was reading *Where the Wild Things Are* out loud to him whilst he has fucking me," she boasted later that weekend.

"Let the wild rumpus begin!"

"I think women should be allowed eight-year abortions," decided her friend. "Gives you the chance to get to know them first, see if it's going to work out or not."

"I don't think you have anything to worry about. You did have a period, even though it was really light, and they are regular. But I can give you a pregnancy test if you want, just to put your mind at rest..." The nurse began to search through the cupboards in the room.

"That would be good. It's just a friend said that they thought I looked like I was glowing and that they've guessed correctly that their friends have been pregnant twice before," said Esmeralda weakly. She hated mainstream health practitioners; they always made her feel stupid.

"Have you been suffering from morning sickness or anything?"

"No."

"And do you have any reason to think that you might be pregnant?"

"No..." said Esmeralda, although with her kind of sex life, it was always a bit of a grey area. It's not that she wasn't careful, it was just that the sheer volume and lack of routine made her forever uncertain.

"I can't actually find any tests. You could always buy one from the chemist, but they're expensive. Have you used one before?"

"Yes."

"Oh... I wouldn't worry about it till your next period is due, though. It's not going to change things, whatever the outcome is and whatever you decide to do...don't worry," she conceded, "I'm sure you're fine."

She was surprised at the state of the living room. It had seemed like a quiet night in yet the floor was covered in empty wine, gin and beer bottles, plus the annoyingly messy fiddly remnants of spliff-rolling.

She discovered the joy of wanking without fantasying, focusing on nothing but the sensation of her pleasing herself. Imagining the tentacles of her clitoris extending right up inside of her body, throbbing like an electrical pulse. It gave her the deepest orgasm she had ever experienced.

She was in a capital mood.

"How was your summer?" she asked her pal, back at drama school.

"Shit. I've been working the whole time. I feel like my soul has been sucked out of my body."

"You're kidding?"

"No. Sometimes I manage to find work that keeps me ticking over in my head, but this job is so brain-numbing."

"Why don't you sign on?"

"I've always tried to avoid that."

"Listen, signing on is nothing to be ashamed of. This country doesn't support artists, yet our art is one of its main exports. Fuck it! Let the country support you. As soon as you get the money to pay it back in taxes, then you can do it then. Or at least make sure you support another artist in getting their shit off the ground one day. Seriously, you deserve it. If we lived in France the government would be paying us a wage. In this country, we are treated like shit. Normally when I see you, you are so full of ideas and inspiration. It's a crime to see you like this."

"I fucking hate feeling like this."

"They're closing down the theatre museum."

"What will happen to the archive?'

"It's getting locked up in the Victoria and Albert."

"Why on earth?"

"The building is going to the Royal Opera House. I think they need a new dressing room."

"I fucking hate this country."

"I used to get a sadistic pleasure from signing on, because the people who work at the Job Centre did everything in their power to make your life hell, but at the end of the day they had to spend their lives talking to annoying shits like me, whilst I got to spend all day drinking cider in the sun."

"I used to take acid and sing *Phantom of the Opera* into my mirror, willing him to appear and rescue me from life."

The wind was in a particularly tricksy mood.

"Please mind the gap."

She thought about her first love. He had proposed to her outside school and had bought her a gorgeous engagement ring made of emeralds and diamonds in the shape of a little flower. They had thought their love would last forever. She hadn't seen him for years now. The last thing she had heard about him was that he'd gone mad and thought that she had put a voodoo curse on him, which was a little extreme, she thought, but was secretly rather flattered.

It had rather taken the wind out of her sails.

Her feedback session had thrown things into disarray. She had gone in with a sense of foreboding, but she certainly hadn't seen this one coming. Esmeralda was expecting a grilling for missing classes, but she actually received a painful mirror, revealing her greatest inadequacies as a human being. They told her that her work was too showy. That she always had to stick in a bit of pizzazz into everything she did and that this lacked delicacy, truth, beauty or intelligence. It was all too much of a performance. That wasn't really what they said, but that's how she took it. She then went that extra mile and translated this into a reflection of the rest of her life. She suddenly decided that her whole personality was cheap and over the top. That her bawdy and showy behaviour was a smokescreen, covering up her vulnerability, her true self, the gold within her. This revelation had left Esmeralda feeling very stupid and exposed. How could she possibly produce good work if she was incapable of being honest? She looked at her clothes, her pink hair and thought about her list of exploits over that summer. She suddenly felt very ridiculous.

The very best word in the whole world is goo.

"By the time I'm 40 I want to be living in a Gaudi apartment with a dwarf for a butler," proclaimed Esmeralda.

"Wouldn't life be great if it was like a musical? If on cue, everyone burst out into song and a well-choreographed dance routine?"

"That sounds like my idea of hell," he said.

"OK, so I'm being a little hard on myself."

"OK, so am I being a little hard on myself?"

Genius is mainly an affair of energy - Matthew Arnold.

"I'm concentrating on being calmer and quieter. Less over the top and silly."

"So... basically you're going to stop being Esmeralda?"

She realised that she hadn't looked at any porn for months.

"It's the thing that I keep coming back to. I've been told before: talk less, be serious. Every time I set off to try and be less over the top, I go off on an adventure, learning loads of amazing things along the way, but I always miss the point of being small and come back to this same point again. Maybe if I try to achieve something else I'll manage to learn to be small by accident?"

"I don't think you should think of it as being small," said her Mum. "Think of it as being still. There is a quote in the Bible that says: Be still and know that I am the Lord."

"I think that's it. It's where my gold is. I'll find it when I find the space to be silent. When I stop trying to survive and allow myself to just be."

"I don't mean to get all Christian on you, but there's another good quote in the Bible that says: Be still and you will hear a small voice."

"I don't mind, Mum. It's good advice."

A mentor had once told her that one day she would have to choose between one side of her personality or the other. At the time she hadn't understood what her friend had meant, but as she grew older, she realised exactly what she was saying. Half of Esmeralda's personality was a hippie who liked being drunk in a field and hanging out with beautiful people who were full of love and knew what was really important in life. The other half of her personality was an ambitious young woman who wanted to take over the world and surround herself with go-getting successful people who were having it all and knew what was really important in life. Over the summer she had immersed herself in the hippie world and had loved it. This was a nourishing world, free from stress and inferiority. But now she was back in the rat race world, she was driven once more to be world famous, better than her "friends" and proving that she was "worth it". This wasn't a nourishing world. This was a world that made her feel anxious and inferior, but a big chunk of her personality really did give a shit about playing this game and winning. She was torn. If she gave up the rat race she would be much happier. Yet winning the rat race had been the engine of her life and she had always believed that she could do anything she wanted.

If she quit the rat race, would it be because she was scared that she could not win it after all?

"I don't think that's true, though," said her best friend. They had been on the phone to each other for an hour. "You're a multi-faceted person and you're more than capable of encompassing both worlds. I think it was short-sighted of her to think you'd have to kill half of yourself off."

"I guess so. There's no real reason why I can't have it all."

"And imagine if you did jack it all in and move to the country. You'd go mad with boredom. You would be building a village of tree houses and winning jam-making competitions in no time. Actually… that sounds great. I want you to move to the country!"

"Here, take this…" said the woman to Esmeralda as she was leaving.

She placed a large piece of rose quartz into Esmeralda's hand.

"Are you still here? What do you want?"

Am really interested in the email you sent out – but it says it starts on the 16th Sept? This must be a typo?

"Ahhhhhhhhhhhhhhhhhhhhhhhhhhhhhhhhhhhhhhhhhhhhh hhhhhhhhhhhhhhhhhhhhhhh!" screamed Esmeralda, and she yanked desperately at her hair. "I'm dyslexic. I have to be dyslexic!"

Every time she sent out information on anything she would get one of the details wrong. Remedying these mistakes took up half of her life and it was exhausting. She was convinced she was number-dyslexic.

She finally got through to her best mate on the phone, who had been involved in the most monumental spoorking in the history of mankind and showed no signs of removing herself from it yet, although she was very happy and that's all that really mattered. Esmeralda couldn't wait till her best mate got down to some serious nesting and began breeding. However, her mate had already made Esmeralda promise to never put anything into the mouths of any of her children, which she thought was a little unfair.

"If you do the ground work in your early twenties then you'll have the time of your life in your thirties."

"I wouldn't be in my early twenties again for love nor money."

"Imagine what it must be like for women who have spent all of their lives worrying about what they look like or what men think of them? Their lives must be a slow torture from thirty onwards. How unbearable."

"Stop lezzing off at me."

"In your dreams, bitch."

Fascinating though they were, the men she surrounded herself with on a daily basis were complete arseholes.

"We're like square pegs in round holes," she told him.

Esmeralda did look forward to the next time she entered into another spoork with someone, but now wasn't really the right time. Although that's normally when it sneaks up and bites you on the arse...

Not only did she love the word vivacious, she made damn sure that she only surrounded herself with people whom she believed deserved the label.

"I think the way you should see it is that this is an opportunity for you to really concentrate on your listening."

You cannot travel on the path before you have become the path itself - Gautama Buddha.

She was tired. She was stressed. She was skint. She was "crass". She was pissed off.

Esmeralda wanted to be still. This is going to be a winter of peace and quiet, she decided.

Coffee had started to give her arthritis in her feet as well as her hands.

Someone had once told her their thoughts on war and women. They believed that women were as much to blame for wars as men, because they had brought the men up. At the time she had thought that this was a fair enough point, taking pride in her openness to give men the benefit of the doubt, but as she watched her brother grow up from a boy into a man, she decided that this just wasn't true. There was a point in his mid-twenties where he had rebelled against their mother. Although he was still inherently a good person, he had changed from someone who she didn't think could ever hurt a fly, into someone she thought that could.

Nothing is impossible, in my own powerful mind - The Levellers.

Esmeralda got on her bike and rode like the clappers to the studio. She picked up the money from her friend and then got a cab to the estate agents.

She really wasn't in the mood for that song so she skipped the track.

She loved songs that made her recall past love affairs.

Esmeralda sat up in bed and drew out a floor plan of the flat from memory. It had matched everything on her list of wishes bar three. It wasn't overlooking the sea, it wasn't in a Regency building and it wasn't in the same area that she was living in now. But it did have lots of light, it was dry and warm, had old features, there was room for people to stay, it was near to her friends and free from any pigeons. Pretty good going, really.

She dug out her book on Feng Shui. There had been no way of being able to Feng Shui her current room because the layout of it dictated where she had to place things. For example, the bed had to go in the alcove by the window or it would take up the whole room, which meant it was like sleeping next to an open fridge door in the winter and she regularly woke to sound of pigeons shagging right next to her head. Upon drawing out the floor-plan of her new flat though she was rather excited to discover that all of the rooms were laid out in such a way that they fitted exactly the right areas for good Feng Shui. *Excellent!* she thought to herself.

That night Esmeralda couldn't sleep, she was so excited about her new flat. She spent the whole night planning how she was going to decorate it and arrange everything. One thing Esmeralda loved above all else was the process of nesting. She didn't mind how disposable the nest was - she had lived in plenty of squats in her time and had shared scores of houses - but whenever she moved in anywhere, she would always enjoy making it into her own little sanctuary.

Her body had gone into shut-down.

I'm so tired - I wonder if I'm a manic depressive?

Every other word he said was "fucking this" and "fucking that". She wondered if it was really good for her well-being, hanging around with someone like that. At the same time, though, there was nothing she hated more than insipid people.

"If I was a famous celebrity, then I'd almost certainly think that I was a cunt."

The guy in front wore a grey hoodie. As they had walked towards the queue in the post office, he had turned to look at her for a moment and she saw in his eyes the haunted look of a skag addict. *Poor fucker,* she thought to herself. Those eyes had peered back at her from more than one of her dearest friends. The temptation to go that extra leg had never enticed Esmeralda. It was a boundary that she did not feel compelled to cross. Even though she wanted to try everything life had to offer at least once, she thought it was wise to put heroin and crack at the bottom of her list, so that she could get everything else done first. If her children put her in an old people's home, she'd take up a hard drugs habit.

The poor boy in front of her was shaking like a leaf. He was waiting to cash his Giro and the unmoving queue was torturing him. She wanted to wrap her arms around him and make it all better. Suck out the poison and set him free. When he finally collected his money he asked politely what the time was. As she left the post office she saw him sitting on the steps of a closed pub, drinking a banana-flavoured Yazzoo, waiting for his saviour to come and absolve him of his suffering.

"He was incredible to work with. He wants you to be amazing." Esmeralda was cooing over her most recent director.

"I'm not trying to be anything. I am whatever I am."

"How many people have you slept with?"

"It's not appropriate for a lady to discuss numbers. I'll tell you one thing, though: all those cocks never filled my hole."

I used to be the tight one, the perfect fit. Funny how those compliments can make you feel so full of it. - Dresden Dolls

Do I belong? Thought Esmeralda.

She looked at herself in the mirror. *Is that me?* She asked herself.

Another word she was fond of was "cuttlefish".

"What does idiosyncratic mean?"

She looked up "idiosyncratic" in the synonyms tool. It told her that it meant "characteristic". She then looked up what synonyms meant, but there were no results for that word.

She woke up and knew that she needed magic mushrooms.

"They're not in season yet," he told her.

"But I thought the season is from the end of September to mid-October?"

"I know, but my mate went out two days ago and said there was nothing. You should speak to him, he knows what he's talking about."

"Apparently they grow near silver birch trees."

"Really? That's interesting. They're really magical-looking trees."

"I hate boys," moaned the tired lady.

"Still? God... Get over it."

Esmeralda told the girls at the party about the theory of creating your world through your relationships with other women and that the men who enter into your world from time to time, do so only with your permission. They were impressed. The rest of the evening was passed having the most intense and enlightening conversations with her female friends. They hadn't talked like that in years. The men tried to woo her with a tirade of anecdotes about her misdemeanours. Even though this topic was her favourite in the whole wide world, it didn't manage to divert her energy away from the women. Suddenly the power of womanhood made sense to her in a way she had never got her head around before.

All that you know and all that you don't know -Jonathan Kay.

"Get out of your box!" shouted the young man.

It was a new moon and everyone had gone mad. Two of her friends separately returned to the house having had a huge row with someone. One had fallen out with a friend over whether women were smoking before the 1920's and if they had only taken up the habit because they saw men doing it and had thought it was cool. The other had been arguing about the chances of anyone doing anything to turn around the environmental disaster we are facing. Once they had all reconvened in the living room, they then spent the rest of the evening arguing with each other over whether Sonic Youth had been an awesome band or not.

"It's true that people can only intimidate you with your permission" – over a cup of coffee the next day – "but it's also true that people are only more powerful than you with your permission too. That's where the activist movement breaks down. I'm behind them one hundred percent in theory, but the pitfall is that they are acknowledging the brick wall and banging their heads against it. Whereas if you don't acknowledge the existence of the brick wall in the first place then you can walk right through it and piss on their parade."

She still hadn't got her period. It was nearly time to do a test.

The next day she got her period. "Wooooo hooooo!" she shouted in the toilet, "I'm not pregnant!"

"I had to quit my job as a lollipop lady because the drivers didn't take me seriously," she moaned.

The papers said that the eight-year-old had hanged herself because she had got the idea from a film. The judge had said at the hearing that it must have been impressed upon her somehow because an eight-year-old was too young to have a proper understanding of death. Esmeralda thought about this. She remembered fearing death when she was five or six and had first asked her parents about their religious beliefs. They had told her that they had asked Jesus into their hearts and that they believed this meant they would go to heaven. She had run upstairs and woken her brother up and told him that they had to pray to Jesus now and ask him into their hearts, or they wouldn't be with Mummy and Daddy in heaven when they died.

"Now that you've left Mummy and you're in love with someone else, what will happen when you die? Will you still be together in heaven, seeing as you were married in the eyes of God?"

Not only did she lose the sanctuary of her family when her Dad had an affair, but she also lost her faith in God. And her belief in unconditional love. But she did gain overwhelming respect for her mother, who chose daily to be an amazing human being.

"I first snogged someone when I was eight, I started smoking when I was nine, smoked dope when I was eleven and took acid when I was twelve. By the time I was fifteen I'd given up drugs and had got engaged," she confessed.

"And I had a born-again experience when I was eleven. I was walking through Colchester town centre when I saw an older guy that I had seen around the place and who I had made up this ridiculous story about in my head, that he was a Satan worshipper. He had red rings round his eyes and a piercing stare, but when I eventually got to know him years later, it turned out he was one of the loveliest guys on the planet. Anyway, it triggered me to start thinking about Jesus and what it must have felt like to sacrifice yourself for the good of others and how awful it must be when people don't appreciate what you're doing for them: both the physical pain of being nailed to a cross and the emotional pain of being persecuted. I burst into tears and stood still in the street. Then I felt as if someone had turned on a tap in the top of my head and mineral water started pouring through my body, cleaning me, all the way down to my feet. It was so overwhelming that I couldn't move. After the sensation had passed, I felt like I was glowing. I told my parents about it and they said it sounded like a born-again experience."

To practise a religion is a beautiful thing, but to believe in one is almost always dangerous - Tom Robbins.

"I'm in love with you but I don't think that you're too sure about me." The gentleman said to her.

"The King would dress as the Fool and the Fool would dress as the King. Everyone knew that the Fool wasn't really the King, but they had to obey him because the King was in the same room dressed as the Fool. This is the twin aspect that we all have inside of ourselves. We have a physical power and a more spiritual power, but these are both disguised as each other and the real power often lies in the opposite aspect to the one that is being directed at the world." The new director had inspired her greatly.

"I think you've been floundering for the last two years, trying to work out if you're doing the right thing or not, but recently something has clicked and now you're more sure about the choices you've made and are clear about what you're doing," he told her.

The writing on the wall screamed: NIGGERS OUT!

Underneath someone had written: BUT WE'LL BE BACK IN FIVE!

"You will find the silent you by addressing the silent aspect in other people. By seeing everyone as the same creature, rather than their hierarchical role, or the colour of their skin, or their gender. Instead, talk with their concerns and fears, essentially that which is beyond the defences, and

71

you will find that it is the silent you, the one that comes out when you are alone, that will be communicating with them. Then you will meet somewhere half-way and really talk with each other," shared the director.

The Composer cooked her dinner.

She lay back in his arms on the sliding futon.

"You make me nervous because I think that you're very talented and I admire you. I get scared that at some point you're going to realise that I have no talent and that I'm a fraud," she admitted.

"My only talent is not having any talent," he replied, making her laugh. "Seriously, I'm very talented at making people think that I know what I'm doing, when really I haven't got a fucking clue."

He stared into her eyes and stroked the hair from her trembling face. "Promise me something," he asked.

"What?"

"That you'll stop being nervous around me."

"I met this amazing African midwife who told us this incredible story about a woman living in Africa who, because of the culture she lived in, would give birth on her own, naturally, at home. Unfortunately she kept going into labour prematurely and giving birth to still-born babies. This happened so often she grew used to it and would dispose of the bodies herself. One time, she gave birth to a baby and it wasn't breathing, so she placed it in a box and left it on the doorstep to her house. After a while her sisters came to visit her, to see how she was doing and to comfort her in the loss of yet another child. When they came to the doorstep, they found a long trail of ants crawling up and into a box. They looked inside the box and found a newly born baby, and it was wide-awake. The ants, who had been carrying away the placenta, bit by bit, to their nest, had crawled across the baby's face and stimulated its breathing. The baby had been resuscitated back to life. And it turns out that the woman telling us the story had been that very baby."

"We've decided," shouted Esmeralda, "that in an emergency, we should all eat Bob. 'Cause you know he's only going to be a liability anyway, so it will save on rations and will help curb future disaster... So remember; in an emergency... eat Bob."

She spent the most amazing week with the Georgians. They truly are a race of such raw emotion, depth and artistic wealth. She felt like she was simmering in a rich beef stew of cultural yumminess.

"I'm angry with you."

"Why you angry with me?" he asked her with a big grin on his stupid face.

"You never told me you have a new wife and a young child," she yelled at him.

He dropped his grin. "How you know this?" he asked her.

"It doesn't matter. What matters is that you didn't tell me!"

He sighed deeply and rubbed his hands across his face. "You never gave me the choice. If you had given me the choice, then I wouldn't have done it."

"You are strong woman."

"I know."

"Last night felt like something strong feelings with you."

"I felt it too.'

He was a great big hairy bear of a man. He looked like he could kill her with his bare hands. "You are the kind of girl I could easily fall in love with."

The man on the stage said 'My only talent is not having any talent.'

Esmeralda felt like she had been tricked. His good friend had written the play and the character was based on him, plus he was the director of the play. Had the writer stolen the line from him or had he stolen the line from the play? Either way, did it matter that he had then used the line on her?

"I'm no boo-hoo-er."

She was very proud of her friend's writing, it was incredibly brave.

"You're very brave"

"Are you taking the piss?"

"No seriously, you are very brave!"

Somehow she had managed to have an affair with three men under the same roof for a whole week, but she had conducted herself in such a way as to avoid offending any of them. Maybe they hadn't even noticed, but she assumed that they must have.

His performance was incredible. He was the most amazing actor she had ever seen.

They left to catch the plane. She walked out of the station and her heart was singing.

Her mentor had the most stunning bright orange eyes.

He played her pussy the way he played the piano, delicately composing her orgasm like a piece of music. At first he circled her clitoris, using her own moisture to lubricate his finger, so it glided over the nub of nerves. Her mouth and nose filled with a metallic taste, as if she had placed her tongue on the end of a battery. She didn't normally like her clitoris being touched, the sensation was too much for her, and she would butt off any clumsy trespassing fingers. But his fingertips stroked with such precision and delicacy that she relinquished her strength in his arms, which were gripping her body tightly. Slowly, methodically, he wound up every nerve in her body like a tightly coiled spring. Her muscles were aching and her head was beginning to throb, but still he circled his fingers round and around her. Then he decided it was time. Like a conductor's baton he plunged his powerful finger deep into her vagina. With absolute certainty he fucked her hard and fast with his finger, playing out his crescendo, orchestrating her bucking thrusts, her screams and her moans.

Then, when she had finally spent the last drop of kinetic energy he had twisted up tightly inside of her, she curled up in his arms, feeling a complete sense of safety. His competence reassured her deeply. "Thank you," she whispered. "I've fallen in love with you a little bit."

"I love you, little one," he whispered into the darkness.

"Have we ever had sex?"

"No."

"Have you ever? Had sex?"

"Rest assuredly"

"So, why haven't we had sex?"

She failed to catch his answer. In that moment she saw that their lives were inexplicably and irrevocably linked.

How many people can you be in love with at the same time? Is it possible to be in love with more than one person at a time? How many different types of love are there? What is love?

"Did you know that a group of bears is called a sleuth?" asked Esmeralda.

How had he managed it? He had somehow tricked her into telling him that she'd fallen in love with him. It was true, she did, but it didn't need to be said. He agreed it didn't need to be said. But it had been said now. He confessed he was a little bit in love with her as well and then they spent the next few days wondering what the fuck was going on. He told her he was trying to work things out. He was sorting things away into the filing system in his head. She understood: this was all a bit unexpected, besides she was also in love with a few of her other lovers at the same time. They'd had the sense not to mention it to each other, though. Just because he'd tricked her into saying it, didn't give him any rights over her.

"Don't call me," he said.

"Don't worry," she laughed, "I won't."

His text read, *I'm covered in bruises.*

Good, she replied.

She felt funny that she had told one of her lovers that she loved him and not the others. It felt like she was treating them unfairly suddenly, that she ought to tell them all that she loved them, because she did love them all a bit. She cared for them in their own different ways. Telling him she loved him had upped the ante. She was now dealing with bigger and deeper emotions. This was all new territory. She had been "in love" before, in the normal exclusive sense of the word, but here she was in love with several people at the same time and she didn't understand what that meant. How long would this situation be able to go on for, before problems arose? Was it possible to avoid the problems? Unlikely.

The lack of exclusivity was not due to an inability to commit. Rather it was a clear understanding of the pros and cons of each lover. She was divided from one, whom she adored, by a gulf in years, one that would not be remedied for a decade at least. Her other lover was a complete eccentric whom she couldn't quite picture having a full-blown relationship with, but whom she felt inexplicably and irrevocably connected to; she could imagine him being in her life for many years to come. Another lived in Georgia and was married. Another had never left Essex. Another was nothing more than a floozy. Another she just simply didn't fancy enough. Then there were the ones that she wasn't in love with at all, but whose company she enjoyed. It may mean that she hadn't met the right person yet, but she suspected that really it just wasn't the right time. When it was the right time, she would fall in love and be ready and willing to spoork. Maybe this would be with a new person, or maybe with one of her current lovers. Who knows? Her only concern was that she wanted to avoid hurting the feelings of any of the people she was involved with currently. She cared deeply for everyone in her life and was not in the least bit interested in spoiling anybody's fun.

Her housemates could have been a little less excited about her moving out.

"It's great she's going to take my room. It covers my back and they all like her more than me anyway."

The move was obviously the right thing to do. It all happened like a fairy godmother's spell. Everything she wished for clicked into place.

Her mother very kindly came and stayed for a few days and helped to get the "room of one's own" sorted out. Mothers are such generous creatures. She knew that her daughter was shifting a gear by braving this new challenge and she wanted to do everything in her power to help ease her passage. This is a mother's love.

Within a few hours of her mother leaving, a shelf fell off of the wall and smashed its way through a plug socket on her wall. Esmeralda became wracked with fear. Was the place going to burn down? Or was she going to be found, weeks from now, fried to cinder from an electrical shock?

The huge pipe of pollen she had just smoked certainly didn't help matters.

It was going to take a little while to get used to living in a room of one's own.

"There are two things to worry about in life..." warned the shaman, "and these are fear and ego."

What if the place burns down?
What if I lock myself out of the house?
What if I fall and hurt myself?
What if I leave the cooker on?
What if I drown in the bath?
What if I go mad on my own?
What if the place is haunted?
What if the ghost takes a dislike to me?
What if I get lonely?
What if I've made the wrong decision?

"One thing I get really annoyed about..." said Esmeralda.

"Only one thing?" he interrupted.

"Shut up and listen," she said. "One of the things that really annoys me is that the English are always being accused of being repressed. Every time I go on a workshop I'm told that I'm repressed and that I wouldn't know what to do with freedom if it came up and punched me in the jaw. But it's becoming ridiculous. How many workshops do I need to go on before someone says to me, 'You know what? You strike me as a really liberated person'."

She had suddenly lost the desire to suffer fools gladly.

For a week after moving into her new flat, her inner dialogue was rife.

This was by no means the first time in her life that she resented the fact she had to spell out to her friends that she needed their support - friends she felt that *she* had supported, without being asked to, on so many occasions. She also guessed, though, that we've all felt like this from time to time. Sometimes we are the best friends the world has ever seen and sometimes we are the worst. Sometimes we need the support of those that we love and sometimes we forget that they even exist! At the end of the day, we are all a bunch of cunts.

She cried and cried and cried.

"Do you want to Christen my flat?"

"Really?"

"Well someone's got to."

Casting your pearls before the swine. Watch your back or he will suck you dry.

Life was getting a little bit on top of her. She was in a world of pain.

"It's time to get back into integrity."

They went to *Lost Vagueness* at the Coronet for Hallowe'en. He was there too. She had been looking forward to seeing him so much. She had not seen him for a couple of months now. But he had not come back to the flat with her. She had lost him along the way in a drug-fuelled stupor. It had been a fun night, but she couldn't remember anything. It annoyed her. It was a waste of brain cells. Apparently she hadn't been making any sense by the time he had left her, which was embarrassing, especially because he didn't take drugs.

Sometimes naked,
Sometimes mad,
Now the scholar,
Now the fool.
Thus they appear on earth:
The free men - Hindu Verse.

79

JAGUAR BLOOD

"So this is my story. It made me really ill when I had it done. There was never a doubt in my mind that it had to happen, I had just finished university and had just got out of a four-year relationship. It had been an unfortunate accident. I had come off of the pill and hadn't even had my first period when a condom split. I assumed it would be all right. As it turns out, you're especially susceptible to getting pregnant when you first come off the pill because you've been tricking your body into thinking that it's pregnant, so it's all geared up for it. Of course no one thinks to ever warn you about this.

"I was certain about my choice not to keep it, but the way it was dealt with by the doctors really fucked me up... And then there was also the spiritual side of it.

"I was twelve weeks pregnant when the NHS could finally fit me in. I had to sit in the antenatal clinic to get checked up, with posters showing all the stages of foetus development stuck on the walls and happy couples stroking protruding bellies. There was a Thai girl at the clinic with her boyfriend. He was very involved in what was going on and insisted on coming into the examination room with her. He had brought her a giant cuddly dog as a present. On the day I arrived at the hospital I found that she was in the bed next to me: she wasn't having a baby after all. She too was having an abortion.

"We were put in a dark corner of the ward, out of sight of the other patients, and were left there for hours. As we were going under general anaesthetic we had been told not to eat after 8pm the night before and some cruel bastard had put the canteen next to the surgery waiting room, so all I could smell was food and my stomach was rumbling. I could tell the Thai girl was really upset, so I was extra brave for the two of us. We had some suppository thing inserted into our vaginas, that made things up there go a bit gooey and helped with the process of sucking it all out. Eventually they came and collected her and then I went in soon afterwards. They administered the anaesthetic and my last memory was being wheeled down the hall towards the theatre. No one asked me if I'd changed my mind. No one ever offered me any counselling or support.

"After the operation I came to and I was back in the ward and felt an enormous sense of relief. It took a little while for the dizziness of the anaesthetic to wear off, but as soon as it had, I got up and went to the toilet. Blood poured out of me and as I stopped urinating my muscles tightened up in the most excruciating pain. The operation had given me cystitis. I burst into tears immediately. I had suffered from cystitis for the last eight weeks and had worked really hard at detoxing so that I'd get rid of it for the operation. The doctors knew that I was regularly crippled by this god-awful affliction and had told me that they would put an antibiotic in me during the operation to stop it from coming back for a while. They'd obviously forgotten. I was doubled over in pain.

"I went back to the bed in floods of tears. The nurse came over and drew the curtains around me so that I wouldn't upset the Thai girl recovering next to me. She never asked me if I was all right. She bought me some toast and told me I could leave whenever I felt ready. I waited until the tears had subsided and left the building. I didn't say goodbye to the Thai girl. I've always wondered if she kept that cuddly dog.

"After the operation I embarked on a year of promiscuous hedonism. I moved into a household full of powerful women. We were all single and we were all up for partying our little white socks off. We once emerged from a fortnight of having it large and realised that we had thrown three huge fancy dress parties during that time, without sobering up in between any of them, and found the whole house and our own outfits were a mish-mash of the themes of the different parties. I'd been so out of it that at one point I had been chatting away to one of my housemates, before someone pointed out that she had gone away for the weekend. I had got laid so many times I'd stopped bothering to put clothes back on and was wandering around the house naked, wrapped in a pink curtain.

"It was a powerful time in terms of sisterhood solidarity. We were nicknamed the Sirens on the Hill. We explored all our powers as women. Some of us became pole dancers. Some were finishing degrees. I set up and ran a feminist magazine. But it was a self-destructive time in terms of our own well being. I kept catching chlamydia. I developed a condition that meant I bruised if you touched me, to the point where friends would write their names in my leg by pocking me with their fingers. I started getting abnormal smear tests and I felt like I was rotting on the inside. Something was not right.

"Eventually a friend of mine offered to pay for me to see a Columbian shaman about my condition. He had been in the Amazon making a documentary about a magical medicine called ayahuasca. It's a strong hallucinogenic brew containing DMT and is prepared using several powerful plants that have extremely strong healing properties. He very kindly paid for me to go to an ayahuasca ceremony in Amsterdam. The drink sets you back to zero and purges you of all of your toxins, physically and mentally. You puke, you shit. Whatever needs to come out, does. It wasn't a bad trip. It was a complete expression of all that needed to be expressed.

"I actually ended up going to two ceremonies in a row and drank ayahuasca both evenings. The first time, I hallucinated what it must feel like to be ripped from the womb. How it was the seat of safety. The home of all homes. I felt the terror and pain that my child had gone through at being ripped out of me, knowing it was me rejecting her. But then I made contact with the spirit of my child. I saw her (and I knew that she was a girl) and I saw her floating in eternity. She looked like one of those spiky balls you used to get on rave flyers, with long tentacles that disappeared off into the universe. When my baby had been inside of me, those tentacles had been caught up with my own energy, forming slowly, so I hadn't noticed that they were there. But when she had been ripped from me, I could feel that an energy separate from my own had left my body. I felt like an old envelope. Flat and empty. She was absolutely beautiful. Her spirit was an iridescent blue shade of purple. Purple is a very spiritual colour and blue is a very calm and wise colour. She would have been a very special little girl. A little shaman.

"Then I saw God. He scuttled into my mind sideways like a crab. God looked like a Chinese dragon, but was covered in eyes of different sizes and displayed a great flaying tongue. With perfect comedy timing, God stopped and stared at me with a look of surprise, before the multitude of eyes blinked at me and then he scuttled away. I burst out laughing. God's such a joker. What a character.

"The next evening I really got hit by the emotions I had been suppressing. I began to literally throw up tears of guilt. I could feel them rolling up my body in a ball that came blasting out of my face. The shaman, a beautiful little being of laughter whose totem animal was the jaguar, spoke with me when he saw how upset I was and he reassured me. 'Children are a gift from Mother Nature,' he said, 'but they are not always a welcome gift and so sometimes we have to send them back. But it is important to acknowledge that they are gifts and that we have returned them, because the spirit of a rejected child can be a very irksome creature and it will come back to haunt you if you don't make peace with it.'

"He told me that the next day I should go and make an offering to the spirit of the child. It was up to me what I offered and how I did it, but I should concentrate on making peace with the spirit by asking for its forgiveness. He told me that the spirits of our dead children often end up being some of our most supportive and loving spirit guides. We just need to nurture our relationship with them in the same way that we do with the living. He also told me that the next time I had a period, I should make a blood offering to Mother Earth and that this time I was to apologise for returning the gift that she had so kindly sent to me.

"He did a healing ritual on me and sucked out all the pain and demons that had been affecting me. He spat water over me and lightly hit me with spiky holly leaves for what seemed like an eternity. I was cold and uncomfortable and I started getting very angry. I was about to flip when he took a giant quartz crystal and opened up my chakra points. Then out of the top of my head he sucked out all the demons and puked them up, into the air. I could feel the negativity being dragged out of me. When he felt that all the crap was gone, he sealed me back up again with a smudging stick, allowing the strong-smelling smoke to wash over me.

"The next day I was glowing. People stopped and smiled at me in the street. I went to a park and buried a crystal that a friend had given me to protect me at the ceremony. I felt that my heart had been crystallised since the operation, so by offering the crystal up to the child, I felt that I was thawing my heart. I dug a hole in the ground and made a prayer to the child and buried the crystal. I could feel her spirit on my shoulder, nuzzling up to my neck, like a dove. I can still feel her there now.

"A few weeks later I got my period. I caught the train out to Lewes because it is a village with a strong magical presence and I went into a field and sat on the grass and bled. Whilst bleeding into the earth, I thanked Mother Earth for the gift she had sent me and apologised for giving it back. As I sat there a raven landed on a post opposite and watched me. 'Hello, Odin,' I said. The raven squawked back at me. When I got up and left, the raven flew from tree to tree following me for a while, before finally squawking and flying away.

That was three years ago now. My health is completely back to what it was. I haven't had cystitis for over a year, my smears are back to normal, I'm less bruised and I feel well in myself. I've learnt to no longer feel uncomfortable about insisting on using a condom. I feel like I'm ready to have children now. If I got pregnant again I'd keep it, even though I'm still on benefits and not with anyone. Something inside me is ready for a child now, nonetheless. But I wasn't at the time and I don't regret not keeping it. And I'm convinced that the ayahuasca ceremony helped me to deal with the guilt, which then got my health back on track."

"Thank you," he said and switched off the dictaphone. "That was great. When I've typed this up I'll send you a copy to proof. Then if you're happy with it I'll make it into a chapter in my book."

"A whole chapter? Really?"

"I think it's an interesting story. I will call the chapter *The Blood of the Jaguar and the Spirit of the Dead Child*."

"I like that," she said.

SAMHAIN

Esmeralda knew that winter had finally begun. The sea had cast off its summer sheen of sapphire blue and had donned her winter coat of frothy jade.

Esmeralda was the luckiest girl in all the world. She just didn't know it yet.

Her school tutor had once asked her father at a parents' evening whether Esmeralda was really intelligent or just good at talking. When she had heard this, she'd been furious. She was always beating him in arguments and thought this was his way of getting his own back on her. She thought differently now, though, because she realised that her disinterest in retaining details or facts, and her inability to spell - or grasp grammar properly - or complicated maths, meant that she probably didn't have a very high IQ. She was a grade B or a 2:1 kind of a girl.

But she was very good at seeing the bigger picture, making links between events and their consequences, both emotionally and spiritually. Since the day she was born she had possessed a wild imagination and an articulate way of communicating. She had always been very brave and knew that whatever time in history she had been born into, she would have been a little fighter, manipulating the status quo, like Boadicea or Moll Flanders. People often called her an old soul and she felt as old as the universe. She was a little shaman, a witch, and a healer.

"You're a big person," said her Principal. "You can't walk into a room without people noticing you. You're good-looking and have presence, which is great half the time because it gets you noticed, but it isn't so great when you don't want to be noticed. It can often take quite some time for people like you to learn to deal with being big."

Esmeralda woke up in the snug pitch-black darkness of her "sex cupboard", as her friends had labelled her new bedroom. It was only just big enough to squeeze in her large double bed with its deep red bedcovers and her dressing table at the foot with its large strategically placed mirror. She had covered the walls with fairy lights and had replaced the doors that opened into the living area with heavy red curtains. It was like a luxurious little nest and an ideal sex den, although she hadn't seen any real action for months. The heating had been on for half an hour so the flat was lovely and warm. She pulled back the curtain and let the bright morning sunlight pour in generously through the thin white curtains that dressed her large living-room windows. Her main priority when choosing a flat, after two years of being caged in by damp walls and pigeon faeces, had been that it received plenty of light. Her new home enjoyed the morning sunshine through the living-room window and in the evening she was presented at her kitchen window with the full splendour of the setting sun over a panoramic view of Brighton. There wasn't a pigeon in sight, just the sound of seagulls, and the serene sight of dancing clouds made up of starlings swooping past on their journey to the West Pier twilight disco. She was happy and her plants were happy.

Saddam Hussein had been sentenced to death.

Apparently Investors in People have discovered that "management jargon" is detrimental in the workplace because people find it irritating. They surely didn't have to "think outside the box" to work that one out, did they?

"You know, I actually worry that one day the words that I write will maybe be used against me. That in my lifetime, freedom of speech may become a thing of the past and that the thought police may use this work to bring about my demise. Yes, I am self-obsessed, I am a true child of our times."

"Is that a photo of you on your laptop?" he asked her.

"Yes."

"Do you not get embarrassed about how self-obsessed you are?"

"It's a cool photo."

"I think it's fabulous the way you celebrate yourself, free from self-consciousness," his girlfriend piped up.

"It's a cool photo of me in China. It reminds me of what an amazing time I had over there with my family and it's a really good picture. I don't see what's so wrong with me looking at a picture of me enjoying myself."

She had a shower. There was an instant boiler in her new flat, so there was always hot water. The bathroom was clean and her floor was free from dribbled piss. It was amazing. After she had cleaned and primped herself, she put on her dressing gown and slippers then shuffled into her kitchen. To the background noise of Radio 4, Esmeralda cooked herself a bowl of porridge and filled a chintzy teapot that she'd picked up from the Sunday Market with Rooibos tea. She laid the dark oak butterfly table in her living room with a teacup and saucer, milk jug and glass of juice, then sat down to enjoy her porridge with honey, sunflower seeds, and raisins. It was such a fucking pleasure. Her breakfast was now enriched with sunlight and peace, rather than shrouded in botulism and farty male gazes.

"If fighting for peace is like fucking for virginity, then the war on terror is like shitting on arseholes," Esmeralda suggested.

"I don't think that works..." replied her friend.

Esmeralda realised she was practically living in a surveillance state, having just read *The Unbearable Lightness of Being* which had disturbed her somewhat. When CCTV first came into being it had pissed Esmeralda off immensely, but then she was a teenager who was drinking cider on the streets, so the last thing she wanted was for some cunt to be watching her. Then one evening, after drinking vast quantities of cider in town, a man began following her home. The route back to her house meant that she would have to cross the old recreation ground or make her way through a maze of quiet streets, so she decided to shake him off before she left the town centre. She kept turning corners and trying to lose him, but he was right on her tail. Just as she was beginning to panic, she remembered that CCTV cameras had been recently set up all around her and were peering down at her through the large black domes, just like badly disguised Martian Attack Ships from *The War of the Worlds*. Esmeralda decided to take advantage of this all-seeing eye and began to wander up and down the street in front of one, waggling her arms about and clucking like a chicken, to be sure that it noticed her. It worked... the guy quickly buggered off. For a time she decided that CCTV was actually quite a good thing.

As she got older though, she began to learn more about CCTV. She learned about how bad the picture quality was, that not all of them were manned 24 hours a day so could only be used as evidence after the event had happened, and that more often than not they failed to capture any images of the criminal. It ended up working more as a deterrent. She went back to thinking they were a bad thing. What had really saved her from the prowling man that night was not the protection of the camera, but her own initiative. If the camera hadn't been there then she would have had to come up with something else, and really the lesson had been: Always act like more of a nutter than the nutter.

"And that's the problem with a government," explained Esmeralda in the pub, "that is too controlling of the people. It stops them from using their own initiative. It stops them from taking responsibility for their own lives and responsibility for society as a whole. In this country we have all this street furniture which is set out to control where we walk and where we cross roads, but all that happens is people climb over these railings or bollards and put themselves and others in more serious danger. In Germany they don't have any railings at all and everyone waits at crossings and doesn't move till there is a green man. Then again, it is illegal to jaywalk there, so I guess that screws the argument up. Although I think I'd prefer a law that keeps everyone in agreement than actual obstacles impinging on my everyday psyche, because that's when your brain gets lazy and it stops you being present. Blah blah blah… God I get bored of the sound of my own voice sometimes."

It had been an interesting few days.

He had taken her hand and they had run through the streets of Edinburgh, out of the city and up Arthur's Seat, where he scooped her up in his arms and kissed her passionately over the edge of a cliff.

In the space of a week a Muslim woman had been told that she couldn't wear her veil at work, whilst a Christian woman was told that she could wear her cross. Something about this scared the shit out of Esmeralda.

"Is that a picture of you on your mobile?"

"Yes. But look... that's a snail on my face. My friend texted it to me the other day. I was at a party full of gay guys and I stuck a snail on my face to make them all squeal and they did. I'd forgotten all about it."

"Yes, but is that a picture of you on your phone?"

"Yes. I'm an arrogant cunt, all right? Now fuck off."

Hey you

Fate has brought me to London for a few days.

Send me your phone number or else contact me.

Her stomach turned as she read his email. It had been ten years. He was currently in love with someone else. That took the pressure off.

What makes someone a terrorist? Am I a terrorist because I don't agree with the government? Are you a terrorist if you're an anarchist who wants to upturn the current system? Are you a terrorist if you live in Iraq and you don't appreciate the presence of the UN armed forces? Are you a terrorist if you are a guerrilla soldier in Argentina, who was trained by the Americans to be used as pawns against the Russians? Are you a terrorist if you are suddenly feeling rather marginalised by the culture you live in because you are a Muslim and suddenly, since this new word "terrorism" came about, everyone has been looking at you a bit funny? Or is a terrorist our new answer to the bogeyman invented by America to excuse their never-ending pursuit of money, oil, power, land, and control, through a tangled web of fear and lies?

I can't stop typing. I feel like I'm throwing up words and I'm starving and I need to eat.

"When I was on auyahuasca I asked it to show me the spirit of my granddad. It showed me a tide of rolling

94

coloured balls, like a sea of billiard balls. I thought it was a bit weird. Granddad was a darts player. I had never ever seen him lift a pool cue. Then a bright star came flying into the vision and as it passed by it flared up, becoming brighter, and I heard my granddad's laughter and I could smell him. It was magical."

Her childhood could be summed up in one image and that was the morning that Esmeralda opened her Christmas presents in search of the Barbie bed she'd asked for. As she peeled off the wrapping paper she discovered the most beautiful four-poster bed. Her mother had made it for her out of a shoebox and those green canes used for supporting growing plants. She had covered it in luxurious material and sewn the pillows and duvet together herself. It was made with love, was completely original, and creative. All her friends had wanted one. They didn't have much money, but still they were the richest people in the world.

She slowed down her pace as she came under the archways of London Bridge station and saw the great spike sculpture come into view. There he was, still as stone, with his back to her, leaning against the wall.

She tried to sneak up on him by calming her energy and walking normally so as not to arouse his attention. It did not work. At the last moment he turned around and caught her. He pulled her straight into his arms. That smell! That's where it came from... For the last ten years Esmeralda had stopped dead in the street the moment she had passed a man wearing that cologne. She knew someone significant from her past had worn it but had never known who that someone was until now. It was him. Of course it was him.

They caught up on a decade of separation in four glorious hours. She was surprised at how well she remembered him. How his lips did not bow, that those fleshy pillows slipped at a sharp angle inwards. How much they deserved to be bitten. His eyes were a darker, more hazel, shade of green than she'd remembered. Otherwise she recalled him perfectly. And he was more *him* than she could have ever hoped for. Although unfortunately he was a him who was in love with another.

It all turned out perfectly, though. Lightness was introduced to their encounter, a lightness that would not have been possible if he had been single and she had been wrapped up in thoughts of possible romance. As it was, his commitment to the love of another allowed her the space to realise that she had been shackled, by a chain that she had not realised held her, ever since she had met him. He was her open backdoor. Her excuse to not trust, to not give her all, to not allow herself the right to experience the love that had been offered to her. He was her measurement by which all others were judged, and with whom they all invariably failed to compete. Whilst he was in love with another he could be no more than a friend. They walked arm in arm around Borough Market. Each street and landmark became painted by their very own songline. Like a musical score, its notes will forever after hang in the air. She would not be able to ignore its notes whenever she henceforth traversed those streets.

Although they may become friends she was not going to pooh-pooh the depth of her feelings for him. He was her true love. And she would stand by that. Because to not stand by that would just be creating more willynillyness in the world.

"I waited for you for an hour at Liverpool Street Station. What happened to you?"

"I drank a bottle of tequila, passed out and smashed my head against the bathroom sink. I came to at 7pm and realised what had happened. I couldn't believe it. I felt awful." she turned and looked him in the eye. "I'm so sorry."

"All these years I've been angry with you, not knowing what had happened."

"I really am sorry."

"You sabotage yourself."

He didn't look back.

My love sprung from my only hate... the bullshit of my brain rather than the beauty of my truth. How heavy my heart beats in my stomach for that which I can only dream of. I want a beautiful man in shining armour. I want to stroke my hand across the plates of cold steel rippling down his strong chest and arms. I am realising that the only person who will not allow myself this palpable pleasure is... me.

They met across a crowded fish tank.

"Say that you love me."

He didn't look back. He meant it when he said that he was committed. She didn't text him and he didn't text her. Which at least meant that his feelings were still as deep. He didn't trust himself.

An inordinate amount of her time and energy was wasted on thoughts of love. Always had been, always would be.

That's the way things lay, then. She would have to be resolute or else suffer at her own expense.

The rain beat against the window making the kitchen incredibly snug, just like the inside of a tent when camping.

When she was a little girl Esmeralda used to lie in her parents' big double bed with her daddy when it was raining and they used to pretend that they were cuddled up in the cabin of a large, old wooden ship and that the storm was thrashing around all about them, but that they were perfectly safe. One time when there was a particularly ferocious storm her daddy had taken Esmeralda and her brother downstairs into the living room and in the darkness he put on *Riders of the Storm* by The Doors. He had turned the stereo up full blast then slid back the patio doors and they sat together getting drenched by the rain watching the wild display of thunder and lightning playing out over the garden.

It was cold enough for the butter to be hard even though it was left out on the sideboard.

She was a size eight. *How exciting,* she thought.

"Stop playing small!" scolded her mother.

"He told me that he loved me and that he would be coming back to the country regularly."

It wasn't the right time for them to be together. First she would have to become a famous actress so that she wasn't struggling to grow in his already great shadow.

She knew her mood was a tad sour when she caught herself planning her suicide note.

Esmeralda had only felt suicidal twice in her life and they had both been this year. Of course she used to think about suicide all the time when she was a young teenager, before she had gained a full grasp of her fear of mortality (which she realised contradicted her previous thought that one does fully grasp the concept of death as a child) but since she had grown to understand the value and fragility of life, she had never considered cutting hers short until this year. There is no way in a million years she would actually go through with doing it. Two of her friends had committed suicide and it had blown her away how angry it had made her feel. It is such a selfish, self-centred, castrating thing to do to all the people in your life who love you. Until recently she had never understood why anyone would want to do it. Then she discovered why.

The first time had been at the beginning of the summer. She had slept with someone whom she really cared for and thought of as a good friend but who called her "disgusting" after they had finished shagging and it had been like a blow to the guts, leaving her feeling hollow and worthless. Waiting for the train on her way home she had stood on the platform and felt like throwing herself in front of it. The second was this term at drama school, which had challenged her whole personality down to its fundamental roots and had filled her with fear. A proper gut-wrenching *Oh my God, I'm pointless* kind of fear. A fear of not fulfilling the expectations that she had of herself and the expectations she believed others had of her. Because if she didn't live up to these expectations, then nothing in her life would have made any sense.

She had been brought up to believe that anything is possible. It was the principle that her whole life had been based on. It was what she stood for in the world and it was who she was for other people. But if she couldn't manifest this stand in her own life, then what the fuck was it all about? What the fuck had she been going on about all these years? Had she just been spouting bollocks? It would have all been a big fat waste of time. She could have been travelling the world, living on beaches, and sleeping in hammocks. Or had a simple nine-to-five job that meant she had the money to spend on clothes and pampering herself rather than getting in debt at university and living on £40 a week benefits for the last six years. Or she could have taken up skag after all. How long could she continue to find the faith and strength in her own convictions? How long till she had to admit that she was just a joke? That's what turned her mind to suicide. It was her fear of being a worthless joke. At least if she died now there would still have been some possibility.

Will this book be the story of my success or an excruciatingly long suicide note?

Of course all she had to do was appreciate how brilliant her life was right this second, that it was already fulfilling all of her expectations. She just wasn't looking at it in the right way.

Does art reflect life or life reflect art?- Andy Warhol.

"Well I thought you should know that my father is a pensioner," said the composer.

He wasn't your archetypal Prince Charming, but he was fucking funny.

Fuck. She would have to sleep on this one, or with this one. Depending on how you looked at it.

She sat drinking a fine glass of red wine whilst going for a dump with the door wide open. She loved living on her own.

Her gorgeous new friend stomped into the dressing room.

"Hey honey, how are you?"

"I'm really angry, actually. I've just been fucked around by the trains. I'm always getting fucked around by the trains."

"They're so annoying, aren't they? I'm actually writing a whole book about just how shit they are."

"Well if you need any help…"

Of course, the other really annoying thing about trains is those blasted announcements. Although Esmeralda could understand the need for audio information so that the visually impaired amongst us knew what was going on, and that it had to be loud so that the partially deaf could hear what was being said; but she didn't believe that each announcement really needed to be repeated on such a regular basis. It was as if someone's sole purpose in life was to press the buttons that set off the vast array of pointless announcements they have at their disposal and, seeing as they have nothing better to do with their time, they mindlessly whittled their lives away, pressing the buttons all day long to keep themselves partially alive and sane.

The weather had taken a turn. She was fucking freezing.

Damn it. She hadn't seen the sea for a couple of weeks. She knew that would happen if she moved away from living directly next to the seafront. *It's funny how the things we love the most tend to be the things we are best at neglecting,* thought Esmeralda.

"I've stopped having sex."

"You what?" he asked her in astonishment.

"It's true," she replied. "I have only had sex once since I moved in. I didn't think it was possible to fall in love with an inanimate object but it appears that I'm having an affair with my new flat."

"I don't believe it!"

"Well, I don't want it smelling of boys, you see. And I don't like going back to the guy's place. I mean... it seems so much more like you're expecting it. Don't you think?"

"I was thinking about you last night," her Principal told her at the feedback session, "about this meeting, before I went to sleep. And as I was dozing off I suddenly saw an image of the Chariot tarot card. Now the Chariot represents fulfilling an ambition and realising your dreams. However, it is careering around the corner very fast, with loose wheels and the driver is not looking where he is going, so it's a positive card because it shows success and movement in the right direction, but is also a warning for you to slow down and enjoy the ride."

"Isn't it amazing having a Principal who's into tarot and astrology?"

"Definitely," he agreed. "We are very lucky."

It had been a tough term. She had discovered that she was out of control, crass, rushed things, wasn't paying attention to the ride, did everything with an added push that wasn't required, didn't speak with her own voice and hadn't been bringing anything to the table. It was good, though, to be aware of all these things and therefore begin the work needed to overcome the obstacles. In fact, it was an absolute blessing. Esmeralda saw life for humans as similar to that of sharks. The shark has to continually swim or else it will drown. Although this must be tiring for the shark and he must find himself feeling jealous on an almost daily basis of the content star fish, basking on the ocean bed, it only makes life harder if he tries to resist his situation. If he accepts the state of play and embraces it rather than trying to resist it, then he finds that life is a slipstreamed path of ever-changing pleasures.

It was hard to enjoy the ride, though. Here she was, nearly twenty-eight years old, and she wasn't yet a famous, rich, successful actress. Why wasn't she? Was it because the celebrity cult was a sham and she had more integrity than that? Was it because the journey she was on was going to enrich her in many more interesting and diverse ways before she knocked on the gates of success? Was it all just luck and she hadn't yet been in the right place at the right time? Or was it because she was a waste of space with no discernible talent?

It felt like life was slipping away from her.

Trust.

Esmeralda forgot her lines. Her mind had gone completely blank. She looked out across the half-empty theatre, at the horrified faces of the audience. What a painful experience. She could hear their sphincters shrivelling up, like the key rings she used to make as a child by putting crisp packets in the oven. It was crunch point, though. She managed to pull it together and get through the speech, even though she missed out half of it. What she did manage to get out, she got out well. Afterwards she reached a point where she had had enough of the self-flagellation game. It suddenly dawned on her that her integrity had been out, left right and centre, because she had stopped being honest with herself. That, yes, she was asking for the moon on a stick and, yes, she did think that anything was possible. So there!

One of her old housemates called her to see if she was going to London for her brother's birthday. She wasn't, which was a shame, but she was right royally pleased that they were mates again and not bickering over the hot water.

"All right, gorgeous?"

"All right," replied her brother.

"How was last night?"

"It was hilarious. Everyone in Jefferson Airplane was so old! It was like being at a Spinal Tap concert. All the equipment kept blowing up and the female session vocalist they'd got in obviously thought that she was working for a country and western band."

"Did Dad have fun?"

"Yeah, we had such a laugh."

She was very pleased that her father was in their lives again and that he and her brother had developed a good relationship. It had been a rocky road but they had all worked very hard at getting through it.

It's a strange thing when a daddy's girl is forced to see her father as a real human being. He ceases to be this godlike figure and becomes one of the pack of bastards she has to deal with on a daily basis. No matter how much work they put into their relationship, he will never be able to return to that pedestal of The Father. And unfortunately, this means that the daughter's view of her father will always be tinged with a slight shade of pity. There is nothing more pathetic than a fallen idol. You only have to look in any kitsch shop at the gaudy flashing images of Chairman Mao, or the "Jesus Is Your Chum" action figures, to see what you amount to after your subjects cease to believe in you.

She had, though, discovered a new-found respect for her father over the years. A respect for him as a human being, one who could admit to his own mistakes and was open to listening to any that he had failed to notice himself. He had let them all express their hurt and anger at him, until the hurt and anger had run out. Then they had begun to rebuild their relationship again afresh. And by gum, there weren't many men in the world who would have the guts to go through all that. *So hats off to you, Daddy,* thought Esmeralda.

"Ha ha ha ha!" Esmeralda had discovered that she could sit on the toilet and still use the internet on her laptop!

"Hello."

"Hello, lover."

"That's nice. You used to call me lover."

"Oh, it's you. I thought it was my lover."

"Hi honey, how are you?"

"Oh my God, I had to ring you. I was just listening to the radio and, you know how *Nineteen Eighty-Four* we have got already?"

"Yeah…"

"Well, apparently the new plan is to put microphones in CCTV cameras so that they can record conversations!"

"What?"

"They're saying it's to record rows before they turn violent, so that it's easier to prosecute the right person…"

"Which I can understand."

"Yes, I can. But it's this thing isn't it, where it's all done in good faith, but it means the infrastructure is there if ever the government does become a dictatorship."

"It's all to do with surveillance and punishment, rather than prevention and responsibility."

"Exactly. It's scary. Anyway, how are you?"

"I'm good. How are you getting on? Still dumped?"

"Yes, but I'm enjoying the single life at the moment."

"Good. It's great when you celebrate it."

"And I want to come and see you soon. It's been ages."

"Sure has. That would be wicked. Look, I've got to go, I'm in the car with my mate."

"OK, just wanted to tell you that. Knew you'd be interested."

"Yeah, that's fucked up. Thanks for calling me about it. Love you lots, gorgeous, I'll speak to you soon."

"See ya."

"Wow, that was a profound conversation," commented the friend she was sitting in the car with.

"That was my ex. He's great."

They drove past Garboldisham.

"What a great name!" she said.

She caught a train.

"He's a player," claimed the thirteen-year-old girl to her friend, who was seated behind Esmeralda. "Seriously, he's such a player."

The girls left the train and they were replaced by a gaggle of toffs. One of them was actually called CJ and they all sported foppish hair and long scarves. Esmeralda loved a toff. She was like a magpie, eying up their naive sparkle, her heart dancing on the waves of their confidently ecstatic prattle. They smelt nice and they were drinking gift-wrapped champagne. *Oh, the joys of a train journey from Winchester*, thought Esmeralda.

"I always keep my phone on silent."

"Me too."

Me too, thought Esmeralda.

"Just give me a kiss for ambiguity."

What a great line, thought Esmeralda, *I'll use that*.

She went into Boots and asked if she could have a squirt of Joop on a stick. As soon as the check-out girl's back was turned she rubbed the stick dry on her gloves. Now she could smell him wherever she went.

He hadn't replied to her email. It must have been a bit of a head fuck for him though, being in love with someone else and all.

Esmeralda played her favourite game of listing her lovers and explaining to some imaginary person the current lie of the land with them all. The game was becoming increasingly complicated to play. Now that love had entered the equation things had become a bit murky and she was not clear as to what was murky due to the uncharted waters in which her relationships swam or if things were murky because she was not being true to herself? Actually that wasn't fair. She was being true to herself. She was single, living on her own, and didn't want a boyfriend. And she didn't have one. What she did have was a series of love affairs. She hadn't made any promises to any of them so she had hardly done anything wrong. She suspected, though, that at some point in the near future, she would almost certainly be asked some questions that would tip up the current status quo.

"I've realised I'm not going to be famous for what I do, so all I'm concerned about now is being true to what I do and being able to pass on what I've learnt," he said. "Like my brother. He's got two kids and he rang me the other day to say that he wanted to take up a hobby or something, because he felt he didn't have anything that he could teach his sons. I might only be a stencil artist, but I've been doing it for years now and his kids know my work and they love my work. I'm the cool uncle. I gave them some of my new stickers last week and the youngest one peeled the back off immediately and stuck it in the middle of the living room wall! They knew exactly what to do with it!"

"You look more relaxed."

"I could have watched you all night, but I wish you hadn't then added the politics. You didn't need the politics. I don't think art should have politics in it. Art is already political without you having to wedge it in there. You should just do art for art's sake and create something beautiful, without it having to deal with 'issues'."

She thought about how she'd quite like to sleep with him.

Then she realised that she probably would.

She didn't normally go for older men... But she did love Alan Rickman. His voice was like a violin soaked in honey.

She had accidentally found herself in Worthing. Whilst turning a corner on her bike she had discovered a stretch of shoreline that she had not explored before and, wondering what was at the end of the path, she had set off along it. It had turned out, after a good half an hour's cycling, to be a

107

little café at the end of an industrialised harbour. She tucked into a chilli con carne and then cycled back.

It had been nearly three months since she had last slept with him and it had been a while since she'd had had sex full stop, so she wanted to take her time, but she soon became aware of a niggling feeling that maybe he felt that she was using him. She didn't want him to feel like she was taking advantage of him. He was very young after all, even if he didn't seem it, and she suspected that he might actually be a bit disapproving of her behaviour. If it was the other way around, and she was his age and sleeping with a man her age, then she would think he was a bit of a slimebag. Although he was incredibly hot and the age thing was undoubtedly a turn-on, she really did love him, and she loved him because he was one in a million; someone who shone, who would always shine, no matter how old he was. It was just unfortunate that there was this great abyss of years between them.

"Hello, light of my life!"

That was the second time she had been called that this year.

She opened her window and the sound of seagulls came pouring through. It was so much better than waking up every morning to the sound of pigeons. The seagulls made you feel like you were on holiday, where as the pigeons invoked a fear of bird flu.

The bastard had committed suicide. He'd slit his wrists and bled to death all over her nice clean kitchen. Well she'd be damned if her Christmas was going to be ruined by him. She mopped up the blood with a tea towel and went through his pockets for his wallet. He only had forty quid, but it would do. She met up with her mate and went to the pub. Her mate had a load of pills on her and they ended up getting absolutely munted. Esmeralda tried a couple of times to tell her friend about the corpse in her kitchen, but it just never seemed like the right time. They were having far too much fun and she didn't want to put a dampener on things. They stayed at the party all night, rolling around on the floor with some guys they'd met, snogging and massaging each other into a fleshy pulp.

The next day, Esmeralda managed to deflect her friend from insisting they go back to her yard and instead they went to visit her mate's gran who lived nearby and they made her day by eating all her food and giving her a bit of company.

When Esmeralda got home, she cuddled up with the corpse of her lover and stroked his soft clammy skin. He had turned as cold as stone. After a few days he began to smell. She didn't know what to do. If she reported his death to the police there was going to be a whole hoo-hah as to how he died and why she hadn't said anything straightaway. Then, even if she wasn't arrested for murder, she'd have all his funeral arrangements to organise and would have to spend the next month publicly mourning his death. That simply didn't work for Esmeralda; she had plans.

So, donning a pair of sunglasses and an old pair of knickers, she dragged the body into the bathroom and sawed him up into pieces. She started with the limbs, slicing through the flesh with a carving knife and then, using a hacksaw, she cut through the bones. It surprised her how similar the process was to devouring a carcass over Sunday lunch. She guessed it made sense, really - we are all animals, after all - but as she wrenched and twisted the arm-bone free of the cartilage that kept it in its shoulder socket, she marvelled at how much it reminded her of ripping off the leg of a roast chicken.

There was a lot of blood and bile. Shit and piss oozed out of him, along with his last stinking breath. She was sick several times, just to add to the mess. In the end, Esmeralda found that she couldn't bring herself to sever his head from the torso. It seemed like the final violent act that would fully dehumanise him and turn him into nought but a pile of flesh and bone. He may have ruined her Christmas, but she had been very fond of him. She couldn't do it, so instead she stamped on his ribs to flatten him down a little.

After wrapping all the bits up in cellophane and stuffing them into a black bag in a rucksack, she cleaned the house from top to bottom. Forensics would have field day, but there was no reason for anyone to suspect her. He had no family and few friends. No one even knew he was there.

The next day, Esmeralda slung the rucksack on her back and went for a long walk on the Sussex Downs. She picked her way through barren winter-bare forests until she came to a hillside that was out of view of prying eyes. Luckily, the earth was still soft - there had not yet been a hard frost - which meant it was easy enough for Esmeralda to dig into the ground with a rather pathetic hand trowel. It took her all day to dig a hole deep enough to swallow up the stuffed full rucksack.

When she had finally covered the bag in a foot of soil and returned some of the sods to disguise the patch of disturbed earth, she ran around the field sprinkling the dug-up earth through her bleeding fingers, distributing it around the place so as not leave behind a pile that would undoubtedly arouse suspicion. When she had finished she ran over the Downs with her arms outstretched. She felt like she was flying. She was free!

When she got home, she looked again at his suicide note that he had typed on her computer. He had told her it wasn't her fault and to be brave. Well, she had done exactly as he had asked her! Beneath the letter was his manuscript for a book he had been writing. Attached were a list of publishers and a note asking her to send his manuscript to all of them. Esmeralda stared at the screen for some time. Then, lifting her fingers, she hovered for a moment above the keyboard, before finally deleting his name from the manuscript. In its place she typed ESMERALDA. She printed out the manuscript and began to send it out to the publishers... Not really. That was the plot from one of her favourite films. She really was writing her own book. Ha! As if a man could have written the monstrosity she was coming out with.

If you don't mind taking it as it turns out... it's a fine life! - Nancy in *Oliver*

Her breast fell out of her top whilst she was doing her singing presentation. That kind of thing was always happening to Esmeralda.

She wondered how long it would take for all drugs to be legalised. How long can a whole culture lie to itself about what is really going on within it? A very long time, it would seem.

It annoyed Esmeralda that they were still referred to as witch burnings. It's as if the education system is implying that five hundred years ago, there really were green-skinned old women flying around on broomsticks. Why don't they refer to it as the mass genocide that it really was?

Esmeralda woke up to the still of night. As is the norm on such an occasion, her brain began to run on overdrive and she found that she could do nothing to stop the tirade of loud and disproportional thoughts tumbling through her brain. However, a rather unexpected result emerged. After a series of processes of minor revelations, she finally came to the conclusion that she had actually made it... that she had answered her calling and was living the dream. Her life was exactly as she wanted it to be.

Two days ago, for a music video, she was writhing around in a paddling pool with an eighteen-year-old lap dancer, rubbing chocolate cake into her breasts whilst the girl poured champagne over their heads. Yesterday she was performing as Tiny Tim in *A Christmas Carol* in front of an enraptured audience in one of her favourite theatres. And here she was tonight, lying in her own little sex cupboard in a gorgeous little flat that she loved, cuddled up to a hot water bottle. In a few days she would be lying in the arms of her sexy-as-fuck eighteen-year-old lover, then heading to a Pogues gig at Brixton Academy with her brother and several of her closest friends; before heading back to Essex where she would get down to enjoying the festive period with her nearest and dearest, having the merriest time in all the world. She had settled into herself, that's for certain. She had stopped apologising for herself and had taken responsibility for who she was in the world. A couple of people had pointed out how she was talking differently. Someone commented on how she had really grown up lately. And others acknowledged the hard work she had been putting into her art and how it was visibly paying off. She felt very stable and very satisfied. Life is a bowl of cherries, she realised, and I'm one happy little fruit machine.

She noticed that people didn't like it when one told them that one thought that one's life was perfect.

The trick to directing is to make your performer cross a line, for them to discover more than what they think they are - Streetwise Opera Director

Esmeralda was looking forward to the start of the new chapter. But it wasn't time yet... The woman on the table next to her was a writer too. They kept trying to peek into each other's notebooks.

Esmeralda was very run-down and her poor, tired body was fighting off an assortment of germs and bugs. The skin on her face was bright red where she had tried rubbing Maldon Sea Salt on it in the shower that morning to exfoliate the dry skin she had accumulated from all the stage make-up she had been wearing, but instead it had scratched her face to pieces and made it red and blotchy.

Now the woman writer was writing about Esmeralda. She could tell. She wondered if the woman writer could tell she was writing about her too.

Someone she knew came in to the café. She hated bumping into people she knew in cafés. Cafés and trains, in fact. They were both times when she took the opportunity to reflect and chill out. She resented losing this time in the pursuit of small talk.

Tired. Tired. Tired. She had just noticed her arms were covered in little white patches.

Her friends all had the lurgies.

"The major lesson I learnt from this series of workshops," said Esmeralda, "was a respect for my work."

They explained how having respect for their work, their theatre building and themselves, had helped them to keep their sense of identity, their rights as individuals and as artists, throughout the conflict in their home country of Serbia.

"This made me realise that the artist's dignity is an abstract and delicate concept," she continued, "and that it is our ability as human beings to imagine the abstract that separates us from the beasts. It is the responsibility of the artist to elevate us into a shared concept of humanity."

"God bless us, everyone!"

Term had finished. She was on her way back to Norfolk. Into his arms.

Esmeralda lay in his bed and dreamed about her ideal funeral. She wanted a traditional service, nothing eccentric or wacky. She wanted to go out with dignity and style. Esmeralda, as is the case with most young hedonists, assumed that she would die rather young, when many of her friends and family would still be alive and so available for congregating into great flocks of distraught mourners on the day in question.

Esmeralda wanted to be buried. Ever since she was a child she had been struck with a fear of dying and time erasing her memory, not leaving a trace of her behind. The fear stemmed from a church graveyard that Esmeralda used to frequent as a child, when on outings with her family. This was a very old church in a very old village, inevitably resulting in it containing very old gravestones, two of which were tucked away in a lost forgotten corner. They were two little crosses made out of wood. Neither of them bore an inscription. One of them had even lost its horizontal axis and was now nothing more than a wooden stump in the earth. Their presence troubled Esmeralda. She would always leave flowers on these graves whenever she visited, to help somehow keep the memory alive of these nameless souls.

Thus began Esmeralda's fear of not leaving a mark behind her, hence twenty years of writing a journal, hence her continual creative outpouring, hence her ambitious drive to make the history books somehow. It was a tricky business, especially with this insufferable celebrity cult dragging things down for everyone else. Making the history books without looking like a cunt was becoming harder by the day. Esmeralda's perfect place of rest would be a burial in one of those eco-friendly coffins, on top of a windswept cliff top overlooking the sea, with a tree planted on top of her remains. She wanted the tree to suck her up into its belly, whilst the wind tore in from the sea, ripping constantly at its branches, pulling them back, the way it did with her hair.

She really, really was really rather fond of the young man.

"The women in the room are just waiting for you to grow up," said the comedian to the young man.

"Some of them aren't..." replied his father.

Esmeralda turned bright red.

"Like, I really love what we've got," he said. "We're not spoorking and at the end of the day we're really good mates."

"I love it too..." Esmeralda replied.

"I know I can take the piss out of you and that you can take it."

"And I'm better at taking the piss out of you, anyway," she retorted.

"Exactly..." He laughed. "Which is wicked."

That was the first time in the two years of their affair that either of them had ever mentioned what was going on between them. It was also the first time they had spent the day together, lying around in bed, just hanging out chatting. They had crossed a line. How exciting.

"So are you with him?" asked the teenage girl. She was a local girl and Esmeralda didn't want to stick a spanner in the works for him and any other affairs he may be embroiled in, therefore she responded with, "Sort of."

"I'm living proof of the pro-life argument," he said. "I was going to be aborted but Dad had a dream that told him not to do it, because I was going to be a special child. So they had me. And I'm the fucking best person on the planet."

"You certainly are special," she mocked.

Esmeralda thought about her aborted baby and she knew that she would have been a special person too.

The house was crawling with sleep-laden wasps. It was the warmest year in recorded history. It was seriously fucked up.

She had written a message to herself on her mobile, that read *Acting, made it, funeral, intuition. Crashing in my world,* but she couldn't recall why.

"Mum," he scolded, "stop trying to define our relationship." She had just given Esmeralda a framed picture of her and him laughing together, taken during the summer. "Our relationship is indefinable, isn't it?" he demanded, turning to Esmeralda.

"Yep," she agreed. *Thank God for that* she thought. *He finally defined it.*

So they were having an indefinable relationship. The ambiguities were the framework of their relationship and not the holes in it. It was perfect. Exactly what she wanted.

"My God, he's hot."

They had just had one of the best shags she had ever had. Not because it had been particularly adventurous, but it had been very intense. They were both passionate, hard and fast kind of lovers, and as their feelings grew for each other, so too did the intensity of their love-making.

She had covered him in blood. It was the weekend of the new moon and her periods had taken to coinciding with this. "I guess I've started my period then," she said. It's always a bit embarrassing the first time this happens with a new lover, but he never washed and didn't think women should shave, so even though he was a bit freaked out about it, she didn't really care.

She had the honour of meeting a very beautiful little baby boy. She had never been a baby person. She had been too busy trying to get the hell out of Essex to pay any attention to her friends' babies when she was at school and college, then the kind of women she had hung out with since university were the kind of women who had abortions, not babies. But last year she had met a lovely baby girl who was an absolute star, and it completely blew Esmeralda's brain away. She'd had no idea how much personality babies have. Just how pure, complete and perfect they are. It is the one time in your life that you are just you, a great big lump of personality, before you become aware of the world around you and spend the rest of your life trying to express yourself into it.

And this little laddie was such a dear. He was a musician, an observer and blessed with a very calm disposition. He wasn't interested in you pulling silly faces at him but was fascinated by you when you dropped the defences and showed your true self. There was something very magical about him.

The 18.15 train to London King's Cross has been cancelled due to a fire in a train on the track outside of Cambridge. There will be no trains to London King's Cross departing from this station.

"Ahhhhhhhhhhhhhhhhhhh!!!!!" screamed Esmeralda.

The cancelled 18.15 train to London King's Cross has been rescheduled. It will be departing from platform one.

They stood outside the train in the freezing cold, waiting for them to open the fucking doors.

We apologise for the delay to the 18.15 re-scheduled train to London King's Cross. The delay is due to problems attaching the two trains.

Everyone on the platform began to laugh. It was the festive season and the incompetence of the rail service had reached such a pinnacle of rubbishness that one had to find the situation amusing or else one was liable to have a little breakdown.

"If it takes them this long to attach two trains imagine how long it will take them to find the 'on' button," quipped a fellow behind her. Everyone on the platform laughed.

I love humanity.

It was almost time for the new chapter to begin. *How exciting* thought Esmeralda.

And the time was now.

KADESH

"Look at him," said Esmeralda's mother in a leafy park off Princes Street.

As she lifted up her eyes, they fell upon a form of such beauty, it was as if her innermost desires had leapt from her mind and formed themselves upon the grass before her. He was perfect in every way. Like a wild cat, he squatted amongst the dappled light and ate his fill from a pizza box. Long blonde hair tumbled about his shoulders, with two thick plaits framing his face. And what a face! Had Puck strayed from our shores and laid with Bast upon the banks of the Nile? She had never heard of such tale, but before her was living proof. He was dressed as a Viking. He wore leather boots and a leather jerkin over a white linen shift. His trousers were held up with a belt dripping in hanging pockets. He leant upon a heavy wooden staff. As Esmeralda stared at him in wonder, he looked up at her, and a bolt of lightning shot through her body. She began to shake uncontrollably.

"He keeps looking," her mother whispered.

Esmeralda could no longer finish the salad she was eating, even though moments ago she had been starving.

"Erm…" she said, "I'm just going to go over there to use the phone box. Erm… make a call…" and pointed obviously in the direction she was heading.

She walked over to the bright red phone box, the whole time feeling the intense pull that had formed between them, willing him to follow her. And he did, of course. She never thought for a second that he wouldn't. This was what one refers to as love at first sight. She turned around… and he was there.

"I think I have fallen in love with you," he said, "What's your name?"

"Esmeralda" she said "and what's yours?"

"Kadesh."

"Where are you from?"

"Israel."

Esmeralda stared into his eyes; they were emerald green. She wanted to touch his face, it was so soft and beautiful.

"Can I kiss you?" he asked her.

"Yes," she replied.

And he kissed her. He tasted of cabbages. His smell was sweet and slightly sickly, but at the same time deeply exotic. She never wanted that kiss to stop. She conjured the courage to reach up and stroke his cheek. He was as soft as a baby. They were only seventeen and he had not yet grown a beard. She ran her hands through his hair. It was thick and full of knots. She could smell his hair grease on her hand afterwards. They parted their faces and looked deep into each other's eyes.

"You're beautiful," he said.

"So are you," Esmeralda told him.

"I want to give you a present." And he opened one of his hanging pockets and produced a shell on a string of beads.

"It's from the banks of the Dead Sea," he told her, and hung the necklace around her throat.

"Thank you," she said.

Then he kissed her again quickly this time and walked away. She didn't look back; she was playing it cool. When she finally cracked and had to look behind her, he had already completely vanished and she was crushed.

For the next few days Esmeralda was like a woman possessed. She couldn't relax, she couldn't eat. All she could feel was that connection, pulling her towards him. She wanted him so much. Wherever they went, through the streets of Edinburgh, she searched for his face in the crowds. But it was during the Festival and bumping into him again was one chance in a million. Time dripped by like porridge until it finally came to the last day of being there. Just as she had given up all hope, she was coming out of Marks & Spencer's when all of a sudden she felt him; she could sense his gaze. Turning around she spotted him in the crowd, standing still in a sea of people, leaning against his staff and smiling at her. She asked her Mum if it was cool for her to go off with him and she said, "Of course."

Esmeralda walked towards him and he took her hand. They ran through the streets of Edinburgh, ran and ran until finally they were out of the city and were running up the side of Arthur's Seat. When they got to the top he swept her off her feet and kissed her passionately in his arms, right on the edge of a cliff. They sat there for hours telling each other stories. He was Kadesh the Dragon Lord and she was Esmeralda Queen of the Fairies. They told each other about their lands and the heroic deeds they had accomplished there. They spent the day in each other's arms, watching a kestrel hover on an air stream directly in front of them. Then, as the day wore on, he walked Esmeralda to the train station. She was going to stay with a friend for a couple of days. She boarded the train and it pulled away. He stood on the platform, waved her goodbye and returned to Israel.

They wrote to each other, sent each other maps of their worlds and told each other more stories. He sent her a box full of wonderful things, like a gorgeous sheathed dagger and a good luck talisman. He also sent a beautiful fairy wand that he had made himself, covered in rabbit fur, feathers and semi-precious stones. Then the day came when he flew over to England to visit her. He came to her home in Essex and that's when their worlds collided.

His visit had come at a bad time. A good friend of Esmeralda's had died horrifically in a fire at her mate's flat. They had been doing hot knives with a gas burner and somehow the cylinder had been punctured with a screwdriver and it had blown up in their faces. Everyone had scrambled to escape, climbing out of the smashed window, scattering glass everywhere, and in the process they had severed their hands and limbs. Half were badly injured, some even losing the movement in their fingers, and half had escaped unscathed. But one... he had caught the brunt of the explosion. They pushed him into the bath and poured water all over him. His flesh was bubbling and filled the flat with the smell of cooking bacon. The worst thing was that it made their mouths water. He was taken to hospital and died three days later of toxic shock. When they told Esmeralda he was dead, she couldn't control herself. She ran out of the pub and kicked in a dustbin. She was wearing sandals and smashed in all of her toenails, but she just couldn't stop kicking. She wanted to feel the pain.

Everyone was a mess. She spent weeks on end hanging out with the whole group of friends, smoking weed in silence whilst they shared in each other's grief. Sometimes they would sit around the flat where the fire had happened, which the council didn't get round to redecorating, getting stoned within the scorched walls, listening to *The Drugs Don't Work* on loop. The wounds on each person were a permanent reminder.

One of the pubs started doing happy hour from five till seven. She'd get straight off the bus from college every day and would go into the pub to meet the rest of the gang. They would drink themselves into a stupor. Then they'd go back to Esmeralda's garage and smoke lungs till the pain went away. They used her as a counsellor. She was one of the few girls in the group and they needed her shoulder to cry on. There were a lot of them and a lot of tears to deal with, so when Kadesh came to see her, she was unable to be Esmeralda, Queen of the Fairies. She was plain old Esmeralda, lost in a sea of drug-numbed pain.

He had gone through a change too. His long hair had been cut short and he had stopped dressing as a Viking. He looked gorgeous. But he was a virgin who had never even got drunk before, let alone taken drugs. His innocence was like a dagger in her heart. She couldn't be the person she wanted to be in her world in Essex and she really resented him for reminding her.

On the last day of his visit, she took him to a squat party in an old climbing centre in London. The floor was a trampoline and the walls were covered in fake rocks. It was like the inside of a great plastic cave. He drank some alcohol with them and danced at the party. He danced like a Native American and was a bit pissed. Esmeralda was embarrassed by his behaviour. The next day he went off to buy his family presents and she was meant to meet him to say goodbye. Instead, she went to the pub and sank four pints whilst Colchester kicked off the Premier League at Wembley. Then she returned to her mate's flat and polished off a bottle of tequila. She came to at 7pm in her friend's bed. Apparently, she had slipped and smashed her head against the sink in the bathroom and had been out cold all day. Kadesh's flight had long gone. She was so ashamed by her own behaviour and saddened by the state of her life that she could not bring herself to call or write to him. She knew then how imperative it was that she got the hell out of Essex. A month or so later, she finished her A-levels and moved to Australia.

Three years passed and he called Esmeralda at her house in Nottingham, where she was now at university. He had got her number from her mother. She was in love. She had never told her boyfriend about Kadesh - she had never told any of her boyfriends about him. Their conversation was short. She apologised for standing him up and admitted that his visit had come at a bad time. She had not been able to be the person she had wanted to be, the person who could be with him. He said that was what he had figured.

Another six years passed and Esmeralda found herself a single woman. She decided that she was not going to take second best in her relationships anymore, so she came to the conclusion that this would be a good time to get in touch with Kadesh again. She would normally have written to him, but they were now blessed with the magic of the internet, so she tried to track him down on that.

She couldn't work out how he spelled his surname, though. His handwriting was awkward and messy, obviously used to writing in Hebrew script. She tried a few different spellings but to no avail. In the end she tried the place name, as that would be easier to pinpoint. She found a place that could fit his spelling and found someone who lived there who could fit the spelling of his name. The address was for a healing master, which she felt fitted the kind of person she thought he was. She sent him an email.

Then she thought of typing that spelling of his name into Google. She couldn't believe it. Pages and pages and pages appeared! He had done rather well for himself. He was an actor and a model. There were millions of pictures of him, ten years older, but all the more beautiful. She found an email address for him and it turned out to be the same one that she had just written to. A healer and an actor - could he be more perfect? He replied soon enough, shocked to have heard from her. They exchanged some emails and then she laid it on the line, saying she wanted to go for it with him and try to be together. At first he was up for it too, but then he wrote to inform her that he had fallen in love with somebody else. That was that. She left it alone.

A year passed and Esmeralda received an email from him. He was coming to London and he wanted to know if she would like to meet up. It had been ten years since she had last seen him and she felt sick with excitement when she read his email. He would be arriving in just a few days' time. Due to a generous turn of fate his visit rather wonderfully coincided with a series of hardcore physical theatre workshops that Esmeralda was doing, so not only was she in top physical condition, but she was also feeling very present and inspired. Brilliant!

On the day, as she walked towards him outside London Bridge Station, she thought she was going to faint. She tried with all her theatrical cunning to sneak up on him, but at just the last second he swung around to discover her standing there and swept her up in his arms. He wrapped her up close and she couldn't bring herself to look up at him. Esmeralda felt old. Even though she was still so young, she didn't want him to look at her and think how much older she had become. And he had hardly aged at all, the bastard. But she probably hadn't either. The thing that overcame her the most, though, was his smell. It was he who had had that smell. For the last ten years, whenever she had passed by someone who had smelt like him she had swivelled around on the spot, her nostrils caught on the musical notes of his scent. Over time though she had forgotten where the smell had originated. Now she remembered. It was him.

They spent the day wondering around Borough Market. They had so much to talk about. Although they had spent no more than two weeks together in total, they knew a great deal about each other. Esmeralda had assumed that a decade of bigging him up in her head would have meant that the reality was going to be a bit of a let-down. But it wasn't. He was better than anything she had imagined. Gutted.

He was still in love with someone else and as much as she pretended to be OK with this, the reality of that knowledge was heart-breaking. He was of an age by now where he could feasibly settle down with his partner. This was probably it for them. Although, in his own words he said to her, "Fate obviously has plans for us". And the fact he was in love with someone else meant that there was less pressure on their encounter and they got to enjoy each other as friends. It amazed Esmeralda how well they knew each other. His mannerisms, his views, his tastes. They people-watched and told stories, just like they had on the side of Arthur's Seat ten years previously. And then he left again. And that was that. The next time she heard from him, he had got married and had a baby girl.

Both Borough Market and the streets of Edinburgh still hold the music of their encounter, though. Esmeralda catches the twinkling tune on the wind each time she passes by. And out on the streets from time to time... she can smell him.

YULE

Merry Christmas, you arsewipe, thank God it's our last

- The Pogues.

Esmeralda loved Christmas. She was a right old traditionalist at heart.

They had gone to The Pogues concert at Brixton Academy for the second year running. It was their way of staying in touch with the spirit of their Irish granddad and it helped them to stay true to themselves. Sean McGowan is one of the western world's last true poets. And look at what it's done to him.

They wept in each other's arms.

The programme showed images of animals in the womb. There was a bloody elephant foetus, floating blindly in its mother's womb. It was beautiful.

"It's not often nowadays that you see something you've never seen before, is it?" she said to her mum.

"That's true, actually," her mother agreed.

"I love lard, 'cause lard is hard!" announced her chum.

"I recommend being single to everyone," proclaimed Esmeralda.

"My husband was deeply religious," said the woman on the telly, "he'd even make us pray before we had sex. So how could I tell him that whilst we were doing it I always imagined that I was eight inches tall?"

"Does that mean your parents are married now?" she asked him.

"Yeah, they are."

"Aren't arses great?" she cooed. "A perfectly formed arse has got to be one of the greatest things in the known universe."

Esmeralda was going through a glamorous stage. Peroxide blonde hair, polka dot stilettos and rich red lipstick. She was feeling more like a woman every day.

Picking her nose was one her favourite things. Especially those flat ones that curve around your nostril and come with a sack of snot attached. After you've picked it, you can feel the cool fresh air of your breath again.

She wondered whether she was going to have to create a story out of all these words, but decided not to. It probably wouldn't be very good anyway, and it would end up being ostentatious (having only learnt that word yesterday, she was pleased that she had used it).

"I write the kind of books that no one reads," he said.

This thought made her sad. Out of the four people in the room, the two that were arseholes had written books that had sold and made loads of money and the two that weren't arseholes, hadn't. *The world's fucked up*, she thought to herself.

"I'm a radical feminist," she explained, "because I like men."

"I'm so glad I wasn't born in America" cried Esmeralda. "Thank you!" She shouted with her hands pressed in prayer to the sky. "Thank you! Thank you!" she said, with her hands pressed in prayer towards her mother, who sat on the sofa.

She had run far enough away from Essex to have no problem with the place anymore. She actually really rather enjoyed being back and was even considering moving to East Anglia again in the next few years. But, my God, she had hated the place when she was growing up.

Esmeralda really wanted to live in New York at some point in her life. She didn't have a problem with America as a whole, the place really got her juices going in many ways, but she did have a few problems with America - like hardly anyone having a passport, people living in gated cities and George Bush being elected to run it. These all scared the blue blazes out of her.

She was so excited, she felt like she was going to implode.

"She," replied her Grandma curtly, "is the cat's mother!"

"I like the word manifestation, but I hate the word botulism".

Does the full stop go before or after the quotation marks?

Esmeralda didn't have the Internet, so she couldn't check, but she guessed it was inside. *Grammar and spelling… They're not easy, are they?* She had to keep a Word document saved on her desktop entitled "Necessary" so she could use it when she needed to know how to spell the word, because the spellcheck was never able to work out what she was trying to do when she attempted to spell it herself.

Mum was chatting away to herself again.

Esmeralda never let her ineffectuality at mastering the English language put her off her love of books or her incessant desire to write, though. She knew the power of words and loved their spells. She was good at spelling in a different way.

131

He was really dyslexic and hated school, but had managed to overcome his unfortunate brush with the education system and teach himself to love books. He had only read a few so far, but one of these had included *Papillion*, so he had started well. There were so many amazing books out there, and he was getting to discover them all for the first time. She was so excited for him. And his personal endeavour to conquer any feelings of intimidation he felt, when faced with the great bastion of English literature, really turned her on.

Her father came to the door to collect her for a driving lesson. Esmeralda hated motorists with a passion, but she really wanted a van to live in by next summer, when she would be finishing school. She could see her dad coming to the door through the frosted glass. He was wobbling like a penguin from the cold.

"Have you seen that advert with the little girl?" asked her mother.

"No," they replied.

"The presenter is asking all of these little toddlers what they want to be when they grow up and they all say things like 'fireman' and 'spaceman'. But then one little girl says, 'I want to be a penguin when I grow up,' and she pulls down her sleeves and does a little penguin impression." Her mother then proceeded to illustrate the penguin impression for them. Esmeralda and her father glanced at each other's faces and laughed.

"So what happened to our legacy, then?" Esmeralda asked her mother.

She began telling Esmeralda how when she was a little girl she had helped work in one of the family shops. There had been three of them, selling bicycles, scattered around their home town in Essex. The shops were given the family name and everyone in the town knew both the family and the shops.

When televisions were first invented, her great-grandfather was the first person in the town to buy one. He set it up in the shop window, in the centre of town, right in front of the cattle market. Everyone flocked to see this amazing new invention and Esmeralda remembered seeing a newspaper clipping of her great-grandfather standing outside the shop with the TV looking proud, in a flat cap and braces. The shops began to mend TVs as well as bikes and for a time the family business was doing really rather well. But then Currys moved to town, and then Halfords moved to town, and both of them set about undercutting the prices. The family shops just couldn't hope to compete; so slowly but surely all the shops were closed down until there was nothing left of them, except a few old boys around town who remembered the family's name. When Esmeralda's grandad died, after working his fingers to the bone as a builder all his life, there was not a penny of inheritance.

"Well, that's what you call progress, mother dearest" responded Esmeralda coldly "We are all capitalists after all."

"Do you like Take That?" asked mum. Esmeralda stared at her in disbelief. Her mother dissolved into bubbly laughter, put the album on full blast and proceeded to do a silly wiggly dance in front of the TV, which Esmeralda was trying to watch.

"There is nothing better than a ghost poo. You felt it come out, but there is nothing on the tissue and nothing in the bowl. Perfect."

"I haven't had one of them in years," he replied with a tinge of sorrow.

"Isn't Johnny Depp gorgeous?" cooed her mother.

"He will be mine," replied Esmeralda.

"I don't think so, somehow," snorted her mother, which rather perturbed Esmeralda, as it was the first time in her life that her mother had told her she couldn't achieve something.

"I wish I'd got to know my nan better before she died. I was still a little girl. I would have loved her to have been part of my life as a young woman."

"She was taken too young," agreed her mother. "There were so many things she still wanted to do."

"The alphabet versus the goddess; who do you think would win?"

She took a moment to contemplate the question.

"Both?" she replied hesitantly.

"It would be nice to think so, wouldn't it?"

"But thirteen is an unlucky number!" he exclaimed.

"Not if you're a Bogwitch," she replied.

"What's a Bogwitch?"

"None of your business."

She also really liked the word "clement".

"I'm trying to engineer my life so that I'm drunk in a field for as much of it as possible."

"Let's get some cider," he said.

"I can't hear you!" she shouted to her mum, who was chatting away to herself again in another room.

"Can I buy your soul?"

"How much will you give me for it?"

"A tenner?"

"All right then."

"Haven't we brought her up well?" said her brother proudly, tapping their mum on the head.

They loved telling people the story of how the three of them had been on a family holiday having dinner together when the waiter had arrived with the bill and asked who was in charge. All three of them had said, "I am" at exactly the same time.

The concept of serendipity was making her heart sing. She couldn't stop squirming in her seat.

When a man died in Ancient Greece the only thing they asked at his funeral was, "Did he have passion?" - Serendipity.

"Welcome to the Orange answerphone. I'm sorry, but the person you are calling is not available. Please leave your message after the tone. If you want to re-record your message, press one at any time."

"You motherfucker! Answer your fucking phone! You fucking piece of shit! I fucking hate you. Answer your phone! I HATE YOU! I FUCKING HATE YOU! You fucking, fucking... CUNT!"

She pressed one.

Mir fallt ein stein vom herzen.

She had woken up this morning and decided that she needed to start earning some money soon. Artistic integrity was the most important thing in the world to her, but that did not mean that she couldn't earn any money. She would have to trust in her own vigour to run the course of earning cash for her art without losing the soul of why she was doing it. It was a tricky one though. The public sphere was absolutely littered with artistic zombies. Power and money inflict the same corruption upon the soul as time and air do upon a bowl of fruit.

If you want to improve, be content to appear both foolish and stupid.

"It's weird how some things are fixed in time, though," he said. "Like pop stars stay the same age, whilst we all get

135

older and older. I remember being mortified the day that I realised I was too old to play for England."

"It's true. I was mortified when I realised I couldn't enter *Blue Peter* competitions any more."

"Why? Did you use to enter them?"

"No."

"If ever I sell out, will you promise to tell me?"

"Do you mean to say you would turn down a job in *Eastenders*?" the mentor asked her.

"Yes."

"Don't be ridiculous."

Fuck you, she thought.

"I don't want to be famous whilst I'm alive, 'cause that would be hideous, but I'm terrified of being forgotten after my death. That's why I write a diary and why I love archaeology and history."

"I love *Time Team*. I can't get enough of those ale-drinking beardy types."

"Oh my God, elephants have got it right!" she and her mother piped up in unison. The programme explained how the females spend their time hanging out with each other and their cubs. When they come on heat they call out for a man. The men turn up and fight each other for a few days, whilst she stands around watching and eating. Whoever wins the fight shags her rotten and then buggers off in search of another female. Then she gets on with hanging out with her mates and children. Both parties are happy.

"The offal from the animal used to be called the 'humble' and these bits were given to the poorer people to eat, which is where the saying 'eating humble pie' comes from and being 'humble'."

Her brother bought her a T-shirt for Christmas that read *Never sell this woman anything – Ever!*

She went to bed fat. She hated it when that happened.

"One of the best things about Christmas this year was Pauline Fowler's death."

"It was a rubbish death, though. I wanted to see her getting ploughed down by a black cab."

"It's nice having you home for a few days," said her mum, for the hundredth time.

I wonder if she stopped talking, would her brain start working? thought Esmeralda.

Esmeralda met her best friend on Christmas Eve and they marched around the countryside, putting the world to rights.

Because I knew you... I have been changed for good – Wicked.

Then she went and met her old college friends for a drink in the evening. It was nice that they had all stayed in touch and one of them fancied the pants off her. She liked him too. He reminded her of Hugh Grant. They kept sneaking off to the toilets for a snog. Last year they had sneaked off to Tesco's car park and shagged on his long woollen coat behind a car. She had insisted he kept his leather gloves on the whole time and she had worn a hole into one of the fingers!

She had texted her Essex-based lover, but he didn't seem interested in meeting up. She assumed that he must have been getting it from somewhere else.

The best present she received was a lovely soft red and white pair of tartan patterned pyjamas. They looked like the sort of pyjamas a teddy bear would wear and were lovely and warm.

The little girl was very precocious. She and Esmeralda hit it off instantly.

There was a baby lying on the sofa next to her, gurgling in her sleep and gripping tightly to Esmeralda's finger.

Esmeralda's highlights had been when she hung out with the children over the Christmas period. She was definitely getting broody in her old age, but it was mainly because kids are so much more fun than adults.

The trouble with adults is that they are so full of shit. Esmeralda had a theory that the unpleasantness of adolescence was more to do with the shock of having the veil lifted on the bullshit of adults than it had to do with leapfrogging hormones. Her family, for example, all acted as if they were the ideal family. But in reality there were huge skeletons in the closet. They all wore big smiles and did a very good job of avoiding any reference to the let-downs or the lies they'd all endured. Her little cousins would have to pick their way through life, unravelling the stories and discovering the truth behind the smiles, until one day they knew as well as everyone else in the room what a bunch of arseholes they all were. And then they too would have to just smile and get on with it.

She loved them all very much though.

The magic tractor drove down the road and turned into a field.

"That's hilarious."

"Isn't it just?"

She was drowning in a sea of words.

"I've been set adrift!" she said, and she was right. He could see her disappearing into the setting sun.

"Will you be coming back?" he asked her.

"I don't think so," she replied.

She picked her way through the sentences, squeezing through the gaps between the words. *I know there is a meaning in here somewhere,* she thought to herself *some golden nugget of truth that has been hidden between the pages.*

"I will find you!" she shouted to the nugget.

"Hanging out with you two is like having a tooth pulled," she said to the brothers.

"OK then, think about how much stuff there is in your pockets, and then how much stuff there is in your bag. Then think about how much stuff is in the drawers in your room and in your cupboards. Then think about how much stuff is in the rest of your house. Then think about how much stuff is in all of the houses on your street, then in your town and in your county and then in the country. Then think about how much stuff there is in the world." She paused exasperated, before continuing, "And then you begin to realise why we all feel so stuffed. And that it really is fair to say that the whole world is stuffed."

"So… it's all just a bunch of stuff that happened?" he enquired.

"It's all stuff and nonsense," said his brother.

Sometimes she felt powerless.

"Apparently people who floss live longer," she read to him idly.

"Really?' he replied, continuing to leaf through the paper.

"That's what it says here." Then, having thought for a second she said, "But that's probably because people who floss are the kind of people who generally look after themselves."

"So, you think that on average, they are the kind of people who will live longer, rather than the flossing."

"Yes."

"Sounds plausible" he said, returning to his reading.

"I can't be arsed to floss," she admitted.

"Nor can I," he agreed.

She also liked the word "cathartic". She liked the feeling of the 'c' sound at the back of her throat. "Basting" is a good word too.

"Erm... so why hasn't anyone invented hover-boards yet?"

"Or self-lacing Nikes?"

There were gnats in the garden and ladybirds in the bathroom. It's December. It's wrong.

"The world's gone mad."

"Was it ever sane?"

Delight versus Delirium

She only got to see her fairy god-sister for a few minutes, which was gutting. This little lady was one of Esmeralda's favourite people. She was gorgeous and believed in fairies. For Christmas, Esmeralda had gone though every month of a fairy calendar and had written special messages to her. Esmeralda had learnt to read and write runes fluently when she was eight years old, after seeing the alphabet on the back of the brochure for the Jorvik Centre in York, which they had visited whilst camping at Robin Hood's Bay. Esmeralda had taught her god-sister to read and write them too and now they wrote to each other in secret messages, discussing the success of the spells they had cast to help her daddy's plants grow last summer.

She drank a gallon of whiskey with her brother and he taught her all the words to The Pogues.

The hangover was excruciating. She had flat brain. She felt sieved. But she did have a cast iron stomach and was never sick. The sunglasses were a lifesaver.

There were, in his opinion, drugs that diminished ego and drugs that engorged ego, which is to say, revelatory drugs and delusory drugs - Tom Robbins.

TABULA RASA

"The moral of the story is… move as far away from your mother as you possibly can."

"Do you not like your mother?"

"Of course I do. She's the most amazing creature I have ever met."

After the festivities had ended, she got on the train to Norfolk and back into the arms of her young lover. On the train she saw a photo on the front page of a newspaper. It was Saddam Hussein with a noose around his neck. He looked very dignified. It was the most shocking image she had ever seen.

Unfortunately he had got it into his head that he never wanted to fall in love. She hadn't picked up on this before; or rather he hadn't made it so very clear to her before. It was bollocks. He was in love with her. He had fancied her since the day he met her, he couldn't keep his hands off her and they got on like a house on fire. But he had decided to ignore his feelings and keep her at arm's length emotionally.

It was very childish, almost like a schoolboy saying "Girls... urgh!" But then, he was still a child. Part of her wanted to teach him how to love, to teach him that this *was* love. She was head over heels in love with him after all and didn't take rejection sitting down. But then she wasn't looking for a project. She had grown out of wanting to fix people.

"Why not get a coach up there? It will save us a fortune." She wasn't wrong. But they got the train anyway and drank all the way.

It was the best New Year's Eve and birthday of her life. She went to Manchester to spend it with her brother and her two best friends. It was the first time that all three of the best friends had been together in years. They were three incredibly powerful women. One of them was the most feline woman Esmeralda had ever met and was born to be the guiding mother of a fleet of beautiful children. And the other had been away for the last six years, at first selling capitalism to dictatorships, then settling into becoming the Jill Dando of Jamaica, before recently returning to England to work for a top press agency she had always dreamed of working for. It was great to see the wonderful women they were all growing into and to have time hanging out with each other again.

They went to a fancy dress house party. Esmeralda dressed as a sexy cat, with the features drawn onto her face in black kohl, cat ears pinned into her hair and wearing a really short puff-ball black glittery dress with a tail made out of a pair of glittery black tights attached to her bum. Her legs were covered in the sexy sort of black tights that you can see through and knee-high boots. Her journalist friend went as the Gallagher brothers' long lost sister, by drawing on a mono-brow and wearing a duffle coat. She told everyone all night that she had been locked up in a cellar all her life and was the veal calf of the family. Her other feline friend went as Jack Sparrow, but was horrified to find women were throwing themselves at her all night.

The party was brilliant. Everyone was incredibly friendly and men were going mental for all three of the girls. Esmeralda had one boy after another following her around. It was the most male attention she had ever received. One guy told her friend that he thought that Esmeralda was the most beautiful girl he had ever seen. Her friend kindly replied, "Really? Well... each to their own." Esmeralda was definitely getting sexier with age. But she didn't feel like pulling when she was on drugs and she was with her mates for the evening, and she had taken a lot of drugs. They didn't quite agree with her though, and she ended up projectile vomiting all over herself at one point, which was rather unpleasant.

After the sickness had subsided, Esmeralda and her remaining friend settled into causing some serious trouble. They danced their socks off, much to the drooling of many a man, and because the pills they were taking were really trippy, they also talked some very hilarious shit to each other. They perfected the Mancunian wave, where they put their heads together and did a Mexican wave with their eyebrows. Margaret's mono-brow linked it to Manchester. They spent the whole night showing it to everyone at the party and acquired themselves a choreographer and an agent. Esmeralda went around the party trying to buy people's souls for £1 and 1p. When she bought them she would drop the penny on the floor, so they could pick it up, and all day long have good luck. She managed to buy two. She also tried to buy people's dignity, but no one was up for that.

They were the last ones at the party, along with about five guys they had befriended, one of whom was claiming to be the King of Scotland and saying that he had invented everything. There was also a brilliant girl who absolutely wiped the floor with them when it came to being a potty-mouthed nutter. They blacked out the window to stop the light getting in and set up disco lights in the bar, where the decks were. They drank ten tons of booze, took more pills and her friend played the part of DJ.

By this point, Esmeralda's dress was on back to front because she had thrown up down the front of it, so the tail was now hanging at the front, and she had collected various bits of tat she had found around the place. She was now wearing a Christmas bauble of plastic holly and little presents hanging off her belt, a black silk tie, luminous orange braces that clung to her belt making it float away from her stomach like a magnet and a Status Quo-style hairband around her head with a plastic scabbard hanging off it like a Madonna-style microphone. The whiskers and black nose had faded quite a bit so it was less obvious she was a cat and when people asked her what she had come as, she told them that she was a squirrel with little hooves.

This inspired her to make the New Year's resolution to take up taxidermy. She would create a squirrel with little hooves and join two sausage dogs together at the bum and make a kingfisher with human legs. The friends also decided that when they got older they would start knitting a long scarf together that they'd never stop knitting, so the winner would be the person who lived longest and made their half the biggest bit of scarf. The space betwixt the two halves would be marked by a wafer-thin slice of ham, the sort with a teddy bear face on it. They were definitely feeling trippy.

In the end they got thrown out of the house as it was well into New Year's Day. They all got a cab to the pub. The first two pubs they tried were closed, which meant they ended up in a little Irish pub. At first the locals were not impressed with them at all, but they soon warmed up. A two-and-a-half-year-old boy fell in love with Esmeralda and kept giving her presents and the girl they had met at the party taught him to play pool, which really won over all the adults. All the old men kept eying up Esmeralda really provocatively and the girl made all of their nights by dancing with them. They dragged Esmeralda up to dance with them a few times too. They spent the day in there and had a real laugh, then they went around the corner to the pub that the guys they were with normally frequented and did a few shots before Esmeralda and her best friend returned to their other best friend's house. It was 8pm on New Year's Day by that point. She had just begun her 28th year and it had started with a bang!

Happy New Year, you blonde bombshell! She had never been called a blonde bombshell before. She liked it.

Her favourite character at the party was a wonderful down-to-earth Mancunian woman, dressed as Holly Golightly from *Breakfast at Tiffany's*. She was the most unlikely Audrey Hepburn ever - she was much more of a Shirley Valentine - but that's what made her so perfect. They instantly got each other's sense of humour and spent a pleasant hour or so at the party passing puns alluding to old school popular culture.

Holly Golightly came out of the toilet, fronted up to the rude bastard who had been banging on the door whilst she had been having a wee, poked him with her cigarette holder and delivered the immortal line, "I purse my lips at you, young man! I purse my lips at you!"

Genius.

Snot poured consistently from her nose. "I'm full of glug," she said.

Detox. Re-tox. Detox. Re-tox. Detox. Re-tox. Detox. Re-tox. Detox. Re-tox.

"God, I'm thirsty" whined Esmeralda.

"You're always thirsty."

Esmeralda listed her New Year's resolutions:

 - Learn to drive and get a van.

 - Start an inspiring acting career.

 - Learn to fly a plane.

 - Prophetess meets Prophet and they fall in love.

 - To find out when people's birthdays are and send them all cards.

 - Take up Taxidermy.

 - Be *über* fit.

 - Enjoy last year at school to the max.

She had already achieved "get a room of one's own" and "get *über* fit" from the list she had made earlier in the year and she had already started to learn to drive and was, so far, enjoying her last year at school to the max. Esmeralda was certainly a do-er.

The sea was calm like a silent mirror.

"I find it hard to breathe," Esmeralda explained to her friend. "It's like I'm holding myself back in some way. I remember once when I was tripping, I could breathe properly and it felt amazing. Like my lungs were these great big balloons and I was capable of sucking in all the air in the room. I knew then that my asthma was all in my head, that for some reason, I don't let myself breathe properly and that this stops me from expressing myself fully - as if I'm always holding back a little invisible part of myself."

146

"You talk about yourself a lot don't you?" she said to him.

"My work is all about narratives," he told her.

"Narratives about what?" she asked him, inspecting the pile of suitcases and walking sticks he was referring to.

"Nothing, you idiot!" he snapped. "I don't create the narratives. The audience creates the narratives themselves."

He turned and stormed away in exasperation.

"Oh," she replied quietly. "I think that's what I do too."

"I'm so angry..." she screamed. "I'm angry at the world. I'm angry at the powers that be. I'm angry that this is it!" she shouted, as she launched into kicking and punching an innocent wall, "This fucked-up, bureaucratic, concrete, health and safety-ridden, monstrosity that we call life!" Then, turning on him she wailed, "Where's all the fucking fairies they promised us?"

Once the guinea pigs had their veils lifted, their blinders removed by their unexpected collisions with the true nature of existence; once they gazed, unencumbered by dogma or ego, into the still heart of that which there is no whicher, they couldn't help but perceive the cowboys who bossed them, the Ivy League patricians who bossed their bosses, as ridiculous, and their missions as trivial, if not evil. - Tom Robbins.

The air hung heavy with remorse. Esmeralda sat on the train and played her favourite game. She set loose her Twisted Twin out of the train window and watched as it span and morphed into different shapes along her journey. She watched with delight as her twin wove into a long serpent that slithered in and out of the houses, trees and telegraph poles. They passed a medieval pageant full of knights jousting on steeds with distressed damsels waving their handkerchiefs. A giant high-octane fairy poured forth glitter from a golden goblet and a large furry tiger slept contentedly on the sun-baked roof of a car.

They walked hand in hand past a seagull the size of a dog.

"I always assumed that I would be rich by the time I was old.'

A jackdaw hopped, like a tightrope walker, along the rail track. Esmeralda hadn't known what a jackdaw looked like until she had met one with the highly original name of Jack, the week before. He had piercing blue eyes and rode on the head of a fellow with equally piercing blue eyes. They had both smelt of trouble, an observation that had turned out to be entirely correct. Watching the jackdaw hopping along now, she could smell trouble once again.

"The last time I didn't trust my instincts I nearly drowned."

"Let's have sex," he said.

"All right then."

Some words make you want to kill yourself, like… Eastbourne Motoring Centre.

As she swam back and forth through the hair-infested water of the local swimming baths, she watched through the cloudy chlorine as her Twisted Twin got up to all kinds of mischief; playing with the young men's todgers, chasing after cute babies as a bloodthirsty shark and showing off elegant manoeuvres as a beautiful mermaid.

"I've created a new super hero," he announced with great pride. "This is Dick Man."

And he presented her with a messy scrawling that vaguely resembled a fellow comprised solely out of cocks. "Now I'm going to draw Crack Woman," he announced proudly.

I love kids, she thought to herself.

"I fucking hate trains!"

It's lucky I didn't do a shit, she thought, as she noticed the toilet roll holder was empty.

"So who is your Twin?" he asked her.

"My Twin is everything that I'm not doing or being at this moment in time," she explained.

"Like… being a successful writer?"

"Correct. And unlike me slapping you over the head," she said, clubbing him with her bag.

Her favourite punctuation mark was an ellipsis…

The book she was reading had taken a turn for the worse. Esmeralda wasn't in the mood for an unpleasant twist of fate, so she put the book down and went to sleep.

I have my gods, but I make my own way - Cat Empire.

She wanted to dive into that forest and lose herself there forever.

She never wanted to forget the smells of those she had loved.

Thoughts were slipping through her mind like dead fish.

"I want to forget all the times that I have felt jealous, powerless or disgusting. I don't like the word disgusting. I can't think of a single instance when the person using the word disgusting isn't the person who is behaving like a pig. You only call something disgusting when it's something that you can't handle the existence of. Like paedophiles, raw sewage, or sex. But all these things do exist and if you can't handle their existence, then get out the fucking kitchen."

"Life is like a good curry. There are many flavours and it's generally quite painful, but the results are amazing"

"That's a crap analogy," he said.

"It's not one of my better ones," she agreed.

"I met a black guy in the street who was pilling out of his face and asking for directions to a party. I said I didn't know, but I'd bum him if he wanted me to. He said go on then, so I dry-humped him and it gave him a hard-on. So I told him that I didn't fancy him but to drop his pants anyway. I had to be dragged away."

Esmeralda looked at her friend's face. She was not amused.

"I think it might be time for a detox," suggested Esmeralda.

"I think you may be right," her friend agreed.

She desperately needed the toilet. "You always need the bloody toilet," he said.

Everyone went outside for a fag. Esmeralda hadn't touched a shred of tobacco since last May. She thought back to how indignant she used to be towards her parents, having the audacity to suggest that maybe she had been smoking when she was a teenager. Now, as an adult, she realised how much the stench of smoke clung to you. Note to all teenagers out there: you have no idea how much that shit stinks. You would honestly have to shower and wash all your clothes to get rid of the stench. No amount of deodorant or self-belief will counteract that smell. It really does stink. Your mum is in denial if she hasn't mentioned that she can smell it. She can really. She is waiting for you to do the decent thing and confess. And it's a horrible smell - the squalid stench of addiction.

"My perfect man is a footballing hippie."

Her heart pounded in pain. She knew it was over... or at least, that it was never going to really happen. She was absolutely gutted. He was one in a million. Goddamn age gap. Goddamn men and their stupid love issues. There was nothing she could do about it. Or there was, but she just couldn't be arsed.

The origin of love? In the minds of women?

The novelty of being single had worn a little bit thin. She had made the deal with herself to be single for two years. Since the age of fifteen, when her dad had left her mum, she had only been single for nine months, and after her last relationship turned sour she had realised that her relationships had been security blankets, protecting her from having to face the world on her own. Esmeralda had therefore cut a deal with herself to be single for at least two years, just to see what happened. What had happened was that Esmeralda had discovered a strong, driven, opinionated little so-and-so. She had discovered what a sexy motherfucker she was. She had found her boundaries, her tastes and had put all of her energy into making her dreams come true. And they were coming true, unfolding before her excited eyes like a magnificent flower. But now she felt that she knew herself well enough to be able to commit to a truly incredible man with confidence and trust. She knew her worth.

She guessed that this feeling was really just a new phase in the evolutionary process of discovering herself as a single entity. *I'm dating people I can't go out with and have filled my life with a course that's all-consuming*, she thought. *He will come to me when the time is right. And it's not the right time just yet... And maybe you don't really want him to come? Maybe your life is perfect the way it is?*

"It's great when you think you're going to be late for something and then you realise that you're just a time-illiterate knob-end!"

Secondary school education is the root of all evil. Teenagers should rule the world

151

"Chavs are working class people who haven't given up the fight yet. They're working class people who aren't taking it lying down."

"Chavs are certainly useful for making train journeys more entertaining," replied her friend.

"The good old Greeks, eh? Where the fuck would we be without the good old Greeks?" he announced, as he entered the room.

She hadn't been on Myspace for ages. She fancied an ego massage, so she logged on.

Anal sex. It became very mainstream a few years ago, what with slackened porn laws and programmes such as *Sex in the City*, so now it seemed that every man and his dog was endlessly trying to shove something up her backside. It really annoyed her that it had become so expected and that it made her feel like a prude for not wanting to do it. There had been times in her life when she had really enjoyed anal sex, but it had only ever been when she was in a trusting relationship with someone. The more you trust and love someone, the easier it is to relax. The thought of letting a clumsy one-night stand fuck her in the arse really turned her off. She fantasised loads about having a threesome or a full-blown orgy and would be more than willing to give up her arse for that, but not for a one-night stand. When you don't have a permanent boyfriend you have sex less often and so you are more inclined to wish for a hard and fast orgasm than to let them give you piles for the next week. And sometimes anal sex could go hideously wrong, for obvious reasons, and she certainly didn't want to experience that with some random guy she'd just met.

It was surprising really that she had never had a threesome. That's not to say she hadn't tried to engineer a situation. But every time it had been on the cards, one of the guys did something that really put her off. Men are fairly intolerable creatures at the best of the time, without having to deal with two of them at once.

Her brother sent her an amusing email of an old American woman on a chat show discussing whether it was dangerous to your health to have rough anal sex. She said yes it was, and that it could give you a nasty abscess.

Esmeralda really needed some money. She started considering hostessing.

I really need some cash and am considering hostessing. Discuss.

I started to text you but my thumb fainted. Hold that thought. I basically think you're too amazing to rent yourself out to dull people, but I can understand why you're thinking about it. Let's have a proper chat about it at the weekend.

It's all very well being amazing, but it doesn't earn you cash on its own.

"I can't get up in the morning without my furry alarm clock," he told her.

Her feedback this term was brilliant. Woo fucking hoo!

"Do not worship false idols," advised her wise and intuitive Principal.

Tony Blair released a message saying he was officially appalled by the way Saddam Hussein was hanged. The phrase "chinny reckon" sprang to Esmeralda's mind.

"It's not that I actively dislike Tony as a person; I've never met the guy and he seems like a nice enough chap. I'm sure I'd like him if I met him. It's just that I don't trust politicians. I can't get my head around the whole politics thing. Everything they say or do is bollocks. It's not really their fault, it's just that the whole system is built on lying or at least ignoring the truth: 'We'll just ignore climate change and hopefully it will go away'; We will imprison all the bored-out-of-their-skull poor kids who get caught with dope on them but turn a blind eye to our darling daughter's coke habit'; 'I will go to war for all the wrong reasons 'cause the big boys have told me to, even though all my peers and the people who elected me to represent them are quite clearly saying, 'no, it's wrong, can we not do this please?'"

"I guess it's nothing new. All over the world, the powers that be have had one set of rules for us and another set of rules for them, but (and it's not often I sing the praises of these guys, either) thanks to the media and consumerism, never in history has it been so transparently apparent that this bullshit is going on and never before have people been so utterly disinterested in the world of politics. The whole system might actually collapse from people's lack of interest. It's boring and it's bollocks and everyone knows it is... God, I sound like Nathan Barley sometimes. I do apologise for being such a twat."

Esmeralda took her strap-on with her into the bath. It was in need of a really thorough wash. Then, of course, the easiest way to wash it was to put it on and give it a really good rub down with the shower gel, like she used to do for her boyfriend's cocks. Thoroughly amused by the situation, she got her camera out and took a photo.

The vivacious young lady had never heard of the expression "It's just not cricket" before.

Esmeralda believed that actions spoke louder than words and she was rather excited to note that the sum of her actions revealed she was starting to attract exciting men with big personalities, who had already made significant movements towards achieving their dreams. She had met at least half a dozen in the last week. 2007 was already proving to be an exciting little number.

Her period pains were excruciating. She didn't mind too much though. They had been practically non-existent for ages after a decade on the contraceptive pill. She was relieved they were becoming a little heartier again.

"What a great collective we are!" he said.

"It's wicked, isn't it? Everyone is doing so well."

"It's brilliant. We are all successfully doing our own things, but we can all call on each other whenever we need to. I have a very talented director, cameraman, sound engineer, editor and actress at my disposal."

"And we all have a talented artist," Esmeralda smiled, squeezing his knee.

"And… we did it our way!" he sang, in the style of Frank Sinatra.

"We certainly did," she laughed.

They had worked so hard and had made so many sacrifices. But it had been worth it.

"Genius is mainly a matter of energy. It's all about the journey, not the goal."

Esmeralda still loved her ex very much. They sat in the pub with their laptops, showing off their recent work to each other.

The next morning Esmeralda had an epiphany. For the very first time in her life she had caught herself thinking about what she was going to do next, after she had achieved her dreams, because as far as she was concerned, they were pretty much in the bag. Now she could begin to think about what she would do with herself after she had realised her goals.

"I love Phillip Pullman's work. Since writing his books, he has opened a drama school in Oxford and does loads of inspiring stuff for teenagers in the city, unlocking their creativity and opening them up to all kinds of possibilities. That's what I'd like to do."

As she left the train, she became tangled up in a gang of rowdy teenage boys who were shouting, swearing and destroying things as they tore along. Rather than feeling intimidated by them, or annoyed by them, she found herself slipping into their energy stream and becoming one of the gang. Anyone watching would have been convinced that she was one of the of the school friends. By joining the pack, she was then able to calm them down, by slowing the speed at which they were walking and, by acting all sexy and confident, daring them to try and impress her. She could feel her control over their energy as if it were the volume dial on a stereo. It suddenly occurred to her that this is what makes a good teacher or leader, someone who can control the energy of a room without words, but by engaging on the same energy level as everyone else in the group, then manipulating the atmosphere. Throughout history this skill has been used for both good and evil. Not that Esmeralda believed in good and evil. Binary opposites are bullshit.

Esmeralda was about half-way through her book when she decided to send it to one of her friends, an older woman who had been a mentor to Esmeralda over the last five or six years and a huge support. She was Esmeralda's patron, paying for her to train and develop her skills as an artist, even though the woman wasn't the least bit interested in the kind of art that Esmeralda produced. At the same time Esmeralda didn't agree with anything the woman had to say. What they shared was a respect for each other's guts to play big. Esmeralda imagined them as being like two large garages. They were both impressed with the other's size, but totally at odds with the choices of what the other had filled their space with.

But this is the important thing about the next generation. We will never agree with or understand them, because the details would have changed. I'm sure if Esmeralda had grown up at the same time as her patron, the contents she'd have chosen would have been very similar. But she had grown up in a different world and although they were creatures from the same mould, their view of the world was at completely opposite ends of the spectrum. That is why details are irrelevant, in Esmeralda's view. Although she and her mentor had fallen out on many an occasion over details, sometimes almost to the point of no return, she knew that their hearts were coming from the same place. And this place concerned itself with the forest and not the trees. It was the web of womanhood that their friendship sprung from. She was one powerfully intelligent woman giving a leg up to the next. One day Esmeralda would do the same. And there they both stood, on a great pyramid of dangerously deviant women, each with their large voices and strong opinions, most of them disagreeing with each other. Sounds like a fucking nightmare, actually, but Esmeralda was proud to be part of it nonetheless. However that was also why Esmeralda was very nervous of sending her mentor a copy of her book. She was scared that her mentor might not appreciate the content.

"I've only read the first few pages, but I think it's fucking excellent. I'm sending it to my agent now." Esmeralda read the email and screamed with excitement. The thought of possibly earning some money out of her art made her head swim.

She gave him a blowjob for breakfast.

According to the computer, it is incorrect to spell blow job thus. It is apparently one word. This means it is a noun and not a verb. You use this as a name, but don't actually do it, as to blow would be wrong.

They had enjoyed a divine evening with tapas, great quantities of red wine and then back to hers for a good old session of hide the bishop in a turtleneck. The condom split, rather annoyingly, but it was the last day of her period, so Esmeralda decided not to take the morning-after pill.

"I like to frottage, it makes me cheese."

"My God, woman, I will never have sex again."

But later, he whispered in her ear, "Every time you come near me it gives me an erection."

"That makes me very happy indeed," she whispered back.

The next day, after talking to her friend about it, she decided to take a whole pack of the normal contraceptive pill... just in case.

"When are they going to get that male contraceptive pill out on the market? I'm fed up of making myself fat and messing up my cycles just so those bastards can sling it up me."

"I wouldn't fucking trust them to take the pill."

"No, I wouldn't either."

"That's so shit. How come half the human race is allowed to get away with behaving like irresponsible teenagers?"

"'Cause we let them?"

"'Cause it doesn't really affect them in the same way. We're the ones who have to go through the pregnancy."

"It makes me really angry."

"I bet you'd be the same though if you didn't have to have the baby. Think how often you're willing to take the odd risk as a woman. If you're a bloke you're going to be up for taking more risks 'cause it doesn't affect you so much. I bet you'd be the same."

"But we're not the same, and we do have to suffer the consequences of our actions, and I don't see why we can't all take responsibility for the world we create together. All right, women might be forced to be responsible, but if men think they're so great, why aren't they capable of doing it too, off their own friggin' backs?"

"I think they did used to assume the moral high ground, describing women as having weak minds and weak moral fibre. It was called the Victorian era and it was ghastly."

"That was bullshit. During the Victorian era there were two brothels to every one church in London. The only contraception they practised was using a prostitute instead of the wife."

"They must have had some sort of contraception; otherwise Protestant families would have had as many babies as Catholic families."

"Maybe Catholics just have more sex. All that guilt can be quite a turn-on." She had to learn all about Catholicism for the new part she was playing.

"It was lovely to see you at the weekend, but I feel like a real cunt. Did you get hold of the morning after pill? I'm sorry you have to put your body through this."

"What a lovely young man. He's one of the good ones," her friend observed later.

Doctors bothered Esmeralda. It was very rare for her to go to a GP with a problem and not leave the premises in tears. They always made her feel stupid. And she didn't believe it was necessary for them to behave the way they did, as if they were the guardians and gatekeepers of her body, as if she had nothing to do with it. Why couldn't they be straight with her about things?

A doctor had once told her that there wasn't really any need to take the morning after pill because her period had just finished. She could do it for peace of mind, and because there was a slim chance of getting pregnant, but the morning after pill was really bad for your health and if you could avoid taking it, then you should. OK, so how is the morning after pill bad for you? How likely are you to get pregnant straight after your period? And if you take a whole pack of the normal pill, will it have the same effect as the morning after pill, thereby saving you £25? It infuriated her that these answers were not readily available, not even on the internet, and that each practitioner gave you a different answer, each giving you a look of disdain for asking such a stupid question... which was based on the information the last doctor gave you. Apparently there are no symptoms for chlamydia; however an STD doctor knew that Esmeralda had it the second she looked between her legs. Why can't we be trusted to learn how to inspect our own fannies?

Esmeralda had once joined a feminist health group, whose intention was to practise mutual inspection so that they could learn for themselves what to look for. As is so often the case with brave young things nowadays, though, they didn't get round to doing it. Apathy? Laziness? Embarrassment? Fear? Alcoholism? Hectic lifestyles? Dossers? Programmed? Controlled? Disenchanted? Disillusioned? Disinterested? Castrated? Answers on a postcard, please...

As she rode her bike down the hill, she saw a fat, red-faced, tattooed skinhead in a wheelchair sitting by the side of the kerb with the most unbelievable expression on his face. It showed torture, compassion, fear, and deep heart-wrenching sadness. As she passed by she saw that he was desperately holding onto his fat, red-faced, leather-clad girlfriend who was shitting in the gutter. He held onto her tightly, with what faculties he could muster, so that she didn't fall into her own shit. They were not far from the methadone clinic. This image disturbed Esmeralda deeply and branded itself onto her memory for life.

Her male friends were having an interesting email debate about Intelligent Design and the Second Law of Thermodynamics. This was an area of discussion she found interesting, so she tried to join in, but was scared of sounding stupid... and as it turned out, she didn't feel like she particularly wowed them with her intellectual prowess.

Teenagers of the world, don't long for lucky breaks. They're bullshit. Even when they do occur, most of them only lead to a brief flash in the pan. Have pride and belief in what you have to offer the world. Execute your time on this planet with dignity. Enjoy the adventure, because that's what it's all about - the process, not the result. The ultimate result is death. The ultimate process is life. Fact.

If she was completely honest, the thing that scared her most about writing a book was the opinion of all the clever men, whom she respected and admired. She was scared of them reading it and thinking it was shit. Like Stephen Fry.

I just made my first loaf of bread and it tastes amazing! It's a tad on the heavy side, but impressive seeing as I don't have any scales. Mmm... yummy!

Um, I'm so, err, proud of you! Post me some toast! X, replied her brother sarcastically. Nevertheless, he had replied instantly.

I am very impressed. I've never made bread because it's difficult. U is a proper mama X x, replied her best friend.

She had eaten too much bread in a fit of self-congratulation. She went to bed feeling like she had a bun in the oven.

"On average, how many months a year do you reckon you spend worrying whether your period will come or not?" asked Esmeralda.

"Depends on how much sex I'm getting."

She hadn't heard back from the agent yet.

Esmeralda couldn't sleep. She was full of bread.

They were having an email rant about grunge music...

I seem to remember a similar argument a few months ago in someone's living room. It was a full moon and everyone had returned from evenings out, having argued with the people they were out with about all sorts of random things, only to continue arguing with each other over the merits of various grunge bands. Don't mention Sonic Youth, it proved to be a bone of contention.

I believe all the Nirvana albums were relevant at their point of release to the different stages of the grunge movement. In Utero had a much more polished feel, with provocative videos that had a bit more of a message incorporated into them than, say, Teen Spirit. *The album was a synthesis of the band's growing confidence as musicians and as cultural icons. It's a confident album and deservedly so.*

But Nevermind *was a landmark event that changed the lives of thousands of young people all over the world. I will never forget the first time I heard it, at my mate's house in Bury St Edmunds. She played it to me on her cassette Walkman because her parents had banned her from listening to it and had already destroyed one copy. She had one of those T-shirts with the acid face on it. Her older boyfriend, who had just returned from America, had given both artefacts to her. The album hadn't even been released in England yet. I looked and looked for it on the shelves of the music stores throughout Essex, but it didn't show up. Then on a school trip to Paris in my third year at school, I found it in a music shop and spent all my pocket money on buying it and listened to it on loop all the way back to England on the coach. People in my year couldn't understand it. I didn't care who I sat with on the coach. I wasn't desperately trying to join in with the back seat antics and prove myself a cool kid. The penny suddenly dropped. They had lost their control over me. I think youngsters all over the world had similar experiences and that means, for me,* Nevermind *will remain the most influential and significant album released in my lifetime.* Bleach *was just the cherry on the cake of the whole rebellion factor. It didn't do much to prove their worth as musicians, but it did prove their worth as a rebellious movement."*

Eloquently put, replied her brother.

Grunge led to techno. Techno led to burlesque. We're all into corsets and cabaret now.

Esmeralda rushed to the toilet feeling sick. *Shit!* she thought. *Is this morning sickness?* She had woken up feeling really ill, as in flu-type ill, so she wasn't necessarily pregnant. She had been worrying about it, though. All the contraceptive pills she had eaten had turned her into an emotional ping-pong ball all week. She had also grown the greatest spot in Christendom. There was no way she could keep it if she was up the duff. Esmeralda had already sacrificed one baby and three love affairs to get where she wasn't today, so she daren't throw the towel in now. What a bleedin' waste of time and manufacturer of tears the whole affair would have been otherwise.

"It's perfect that you live in Brighton and I'm here," announced the Composer down the phone.

"And why's that?" asked Esmeralda.

"Because if I lived in Brighton I would never talk to you."

"If you lived in Brighton I would never have snogged you" laughed Esmeralda.

Esmeralda remembered an interview with an actress who had just won an award for Best Newcomer. Esmeralda remembered how the actress had laughed at this title. It was as if she had just popped up out of nowhere, even though she had been working as an actress the whole of her life. Esmeralda imagined being interviewed as a celebrated newcomer and how no one would know the journey she had gone through to get there. But one thing was for certain, nothing and no one was going to stop her from getting there.

It was great, though. The two most significant men in her life were extremely fond of her but neither of them were in the least bit interested in spoorking. They liked things just the way they were. The woman in her was stamping her foot, demanding to know why the bastards weren't completely hypnotised by her. But the Popess in her knew that this was exactly how she had created things, and that this creation of hers was absolutely perfect.

"For lunch today I had some organic cheese on top of some organic chicken leftovers from a roast that I cooked on Sunday, both on top of thick slices of wholemeal bread that I baked myself in the oven! It's amazing, Mum, I've turned into a domestic goddess!"

"You've really shifted a gear since you've moved into your own place haven't you?" replied her mother.

Esmeralda got up and went to Sunday Mass. She really rather enjoyed it. It was the same feeling she got from dragging her sorry carcass out of bed to go to the Sunday market. It made her feel wholesome. Probably what it feels like for most people when they manage to get themselves to the gym.

January had put Esmeralda on her arse again. It did this every year. She had been ill for a whole week with the flu, had decided that no one liked her and had been desperately lonely. Got herself into a right old tiswas, she had. But then she remembered that at the same time last year, she had been gripping the railings on the seafront, sobbing great hordes of blubbery tears at the poor old sea, for exactly the same reasons. And she had realised then, as she was realising again now, that January was the problem, not anything else. It's a miserable old month. *Boo! to you, January... Sorry, January. It's not your fault really. It's us who should learn to hibernate or something. You just carry on with your chilly bleakness; you're doing a grand job.*

Actually, this January had not been itself at all. A programme on the radio had been listing all the sightings of animals that shouldn't have been around at this time of year. Frogs and hedgehogs, both hibernating creatures, and half of the migratory birds hadn't bothered going on holiday this year. Global warming was no longer a wacky lefty idea. It had finally become fact, but probably far too late for anyone to do anything about it. Not that anyone was.

"Although this is wholly inappropriate, considering the magnitude of what I'm about to speak of, I feel compelled to say it anyway. I am so sorry for the irresponsible, irrational and selfish behaviour of my time. We have behaved like a pack of morons. We have buried our heads in the sand, pushing our luck, so that we can have just a few more seconds in our own self-absorbed movies, before we have to pull ourselves together and take responsibility for clearing up the mess we've made and begin behaving ourselves. We still haven't done it. And it looks as if we may have pushed our luck too far, anyway; that no amount of cleaning up is going to bring to a halt the runaway train of damage that we're doing. So, children of the future, we do not deserve your forgiveness. What we have done is inexcusable. It's unimaginable. But for what it's worth, I am sorry. I wish we had listened and I wish we had acted. We have let ourselves down, we have let you down, and we have let the whole world down. All I can say is that I hope you are better people for our mistakes.

"I'm not looking forward to being an old person. Everyone is going to hate us and no one is going to want to look after us. 'Fuck you, old people!' they're going to say. 'You fucked up our planet man... Now we're gonna fuck you up!' Maybe."

She was so bored of having a nose full of snot. She hadn't been able to smell or taste anything for a week.

Esmeralda was meant to be going to Sunday Mass, but she couldn't be bothered.

"When I was a little girl we were asked what we wanted to be when we grew up and I said that I either wanted to be a nun or a stripper. When I became an actress my mother said (in an Irish accent) 'Ach, I knew I should have been worried when you said you wanted to be a stripper.'"

"I've discovered two new heroes. It's really exciting," Esmeralda answered.

"Living heroes?" asked her vivacious young friend.

"No, of course not: Nell Gwynn and Mary Robinson."

"Why, what did they do?"

"They were two of the earliest actresses in England. It was illegal for women to perform on the stage until Charles II changed the law. He had returned from exile, after Cromwell and the Puritans had run their course, and he brought about a time of tolerance, debauchery, celebrity and decadent hedonism. Not that dissimilar from now, really. Suddenly women had a lot more freedom and could become actresses, which meant that women like Nell, who had been brought up in a brothel, could earn her own wage in a fairly legitimate way, whilst rubbing shoulders with the wealthy and the elite. She soon became the mistress of Charles II and a celebrated wit. Mary Robinson was a bit later, but there was still the same vibe. She came from a broken home and a world of debts, but ended up becoming a mistress of the Prince Regent. She was in a tragic accident, though, which left her crippled and meant that she could no longer perform on the stage. Even this didn't stop her: she became a successful author and part of the early feminist movement. Not that any of us have heard of her now."

Her friend snorted in disapproval. "It's mad to think that there was this time of liberalism before the Victorian period. It just goes to show that the pendulum keeps swinging. We may have a lot of freedom at the moment, but if we don't watch our backs then we are going to find ourselves under moral lock and key again."

I think men find it easier to re-marry after their partner has passed away. The woman's voice from the TV resounded into the living room.

"Of course they do!" shouted one of her best friends from the sofa, with utter indignation. "Because men can do whatever the fuck they like!"

Behind every great woman… is a man who tried to stop her.

She slobbed around the living room of her friend's house with the rest of the gang, watching wildlife programmes and sniffing.

How unbelievably amusing. Esmeralda had gone to her friend's house and discovered that he had disappeared for the day to meet a date that he had found through a very respectable internet dating agency. Esmeralda and the housemates went on to the same web site to have a nose at his profile and check out the talent on offer. Much to Esmeralda's horror and delight, she found herself drooling over half of the members, before uploading her own profile and then paying a small fortune to subscribe to the site. Suddenly she was writing emails to complete strangers she had sourced from the search engine. She couldn't believe she was doing it, but it was hugely compelling.

Aren't you meant to be doing some work, rather than trawling the internet for cock?

You bastard! I'm meant to be doing my tax return...

She got home from school and logged on to her email to see if any sexy new men had made contact with her whilst she was out. It was a complete addiction. There were three messages. She went and scanned their profiles to see what she thought of them. They were all nice enough: in their late thirties, active outdoor types who used to party hard and had gone on to do fairly well at pursuing their dreams. Esmeralda was absolutely shattered, though, so she decided not to attempt replying with intelligent and witty emails until the morning. Then she logged on to her Myspace site, to see if any of her young boys had replied. One had. She had known him since he was fifteen, but he was seventeen now and becoming an attractive young man. There were lots of photos of him playing in bands and in compromising drunken poses. You only have to write short "comments" on Myspace, so she knocked out one full of innuendo that would have him wanking for a week, and then went to bed.

"Do you know the reason why we can't mention the 'Scottish play' in any theatrical building?"

"No," answered the wide-eyed girls in unison.

"It's because," imparted their majestic teacher, "part of the spell cast by the three witches is taken from an actual Satanic Mass that was commonly known in Tudor times. Shakespeare shocked his audiences by using it and ever since, the play has been plagued with bad luck."

"Is it really though?" braved the sceptical amongst us.

"When I was younger I thought it was all superstitious nonsense so, being the obstinate little thing that I was, I shouted the name repeatedly in the theatre where we were rehearsing. Moments after, the power in the building went off. Everyone made me go out the front door immediately and turn around and spit, to reverse the curse, and we all had to leave the building whilst the technician found out what was wrong. When we got back, the power was on again but he didn't know why. He said none of the fuses had blown and everything had just come on again after we'd left. I've never said the name again since."

Esmeralda looked at the faces of young women sitting around the table. Such was the power of this woman that she would wager none of them would ever utter the name in a theatre again. Even though it was superstitious nonsense.

"I'm so disenchanted," said her workmate. "We've had a few good years of funding for the arts, but now we've got the Olympics coming up, all the money is going to be sucked out and everything we've worked for is going down the pan."

RIP Gardner Arts Centre

You illuminated the darkness, but now your light has gone forever.

In the last week, Esmeralda had found out that nearly every area of her work to date in the arts was about to be irreparably damaged by funding cuts.

Dear Wandsworth Council,

I am writing regarding the change in funding and rent that has been proposed by Wandsworth Borough Council for the Battersea Arts Centre, which will inevitably result in the closure of the centre.

I'm going to be frank. It is news like this that makes me want to leave this ridiculous country. How can anyone justify such a disregard for the arts? It seems to me that this country no longer understands what the point of the arts is.

Every step of the way BAC has supported, challenged and stretched me as both an artist and as a human being. The major lesson I have learnt from my participation in BAC is to respect myself as an artist and to respect my work. The way BAC is run and the kind of artists that they support have illustrated to me how having respect for your work, your theatre building and yourself, helps you to keep your sense of identity, a sense of your rights as an individual and your rights as an artist. I recently worked with a company from Serbia during a master class at the Nightingale Theatre in Brighton, and they told me how during all of the fighting and upheaval their country has suffered, the one thing that they fought long and hard for was to keep hold of their theatre and their daily routine of working as artists. This made me realise that the artist's dignity is an abstract and delicate concept and that it is our ability as human beings to imagine the abstract that separates us from the beasts. It is the responsibility of the artist to elevate us into a shared concept of humanity. Even through conflict and dark times, we keep our dignity and respect by believing in something beautiful, something creative, the possibility of a beautiful and creative future. It is more obvious in the hard times to see how much we need the arts to keep our heads above the water, at times when the world has gone mad and people are behaving like animals. People understand the power and strength found from the singsongs during the Blitz or the graffiti on the Berlin Wall, but here in England during this wonderful time of peace, the Arts are still JUST as important. It's imperative for a sense of community, for forward thinking and a sense of the individual's identity. Creativity was a landmark point in our evolution that came hand in hand with conciousness, perhaps even IS conciousness, and for us to evolve we first must imagine the future we hope to evolve in to. We CREATE our futures.

Throughout the whole of my life, BAC has had a huge impact on me, and I don't even live in London. The effects of BAC permeated its way to me even as far as Essex, where I grew up. And its effects are also felt here in Brighton, where I live now.

And that's just my story. I am one of thousands.

BAC is a light in the dark. I cannot believe that someone would ever consider extinguishing it. Most councils would give their right arm for a centre like this. It ticks every bleedin' box you could throw at it and it does so in a non-patronising way. It is so unique to have outreach work that is diverse AND good. It's an inspiration I tell thee and the decision to cut its funding is inexcusable. It's a rude slap in the face to a whole community of artists who have sacrificed so much to make this world a more interesting and vibrant place to live in. A world where the question mark is our crucifix and where we are working towards a future in which anything is possible, and here you are, with the power to wipe it all away in one fell swoop; how very dare you.

I have never written to the council before because I've never believed that politicians listen to you anyway, and I doubt very much that you will prove me wrong, but I can not see BAC disappear in the sands of time without letting you know how much I detest those who have chosen to bring about its demise. Without BAC, Wandsworth is nothing to me.

Yours truly,

Esmeralda

"What was it, now? A bunch of cells held together with toxins, I believe," said the Composer down the phone.

"Did I really call you that?" she laughed.

"I believe so," he replied. "Yes."

"That's hilarious..." cackled Esmeralda "My God, I'm funny."

Esmeralda dragged her feet along the pavement from the shop around the corner to her house. *I'm not going to meet a new man here,* thought Esmeralda, I know everyone in Brighton. Then she realised that she was being ridiculous. You don't know everyone in Brighton, you fool. You don't know who lives in any of these houses. And she swung her arms around, looking like a nutter.

Curious and exciting! Esmeralda had randomly decided to set up a profile on an internet dating website and within the week she was on her way to a bar in town to meet with an extremely intriguing older man.

I expect you in your Juliet attire, he texted her.

I like being told what to do, she replied cheekily.

He was just as fascinating in the flesh. He was a writer who had returned from a year of travelling, researching random little communities for his new book on Utopias. He was an extremely attractive fellow with a gentle and self-assured spirit who put Esmeralda at ease. She was soon telling him everything there was to tell and he was doing the same. At one point they even got on to the subject of fetishes and began revealing to each other their deepest, darkest fantasies.

"So you like being told what to do, do you?"

At the end of the evening, when he had taken her home and they were adjourning to her little sex cupboard, he began to do just that. He ordered her to strip, tied her hands behind her back and teased her for hours. He spanked her with her hair brush and whispered in her ear "It says on the dating site that you should never let anyone tie you up on your first date", which had scared the living shit out of her, and at the same time had made her wetter than a January morning. She came so hard she ejaculated, which wasn't a common occurrence. The next morning, before he left, he ordered her to be at his house at 6.30pm on the dot on Sunday. He told her to be in an outfit that she thought would please him, and if she did then he would introduce her to his collection of toys.

"How was your date?" asked her mum.

"Not what I was expecting."

It turned out that he lived just round the corner from her house, not far from the shop where she was swinging her arms around in exasperation the day before.

Sunday came and Esmeralda spent the whole day desperately counting down the seconds. He had ordered her not to masturbate. Her pussy was throbbing. She slept as long as she could, to make the time pass quicker. She took a long hot bath, she cleaned and moisturised every inch of her body, applied make-up, painted her nails red and then dressed. She had plumped for the secretary look. A tight black A-line skirt, over fishnet hold-ups and black and white polka dot stilettos, with a frilly white blouse over a black lace bra. No knickers and a pair of secretary glasses to finish off the look. She looked hot, but she doubted she would be dressed for long.

Whilst he had been plunging inside her, he had whispered his intentions into her ear. He was going to strip her, put her on a lead, then bind her to his bed and unleash his toys upon her. The game was for her to relinquish all control - the complete absolution of ego. There was a code in case she felt anything was going too far. Amber, if she was uncomfortable and red if she wanted him to stop.

It was 4pm and Esmeralda was dressed and sitting on her sofa, counting down the seconds. The only other thing she had done all day was go to church in the morning. The sermon that day had been on unclean mouths. All she could think about was the blowjob she had given him for breakfast the day before. Her head had began to swim until eventually she thought she was going to be sick and she had to sneak out from the pews to quietly escape. Her stomach was tied up in knots; no one had ever done this to her before. A whole new world of delights had opened up to her, one based on liberation and trust. "Who does not contain within them worlds unimagined" was scrawled on the mirror in red lipstick, overlooking her dishevelled bed - a quote from the Sandman comics. Her wrists were bruised from the bindings he had tied her in. She was scared of the world he had introduced her to, but already she was addicted to it.

5.45pm. Her heart was pounding.

6.00pm. She was panting. She couldn't breathe. He didn't live far from her. Five minutes' walk, tops. Time was trickling away so slowly, like treacle through a needle. But she liked this game, very, very much.

6.27pm. Having found his house, she realised she had been too eager to get there and still had three minutes to go before she was allowed to knock on the door. Waiting in the cold night, standing perfectly still, she enjoyed the freezing air biting at the soft ends of her fingers and lapping at her chilly wet pussy, naked beneath her tight black skirt.

6.30pm. Esmeralda climbed the steps to his house and knocked on the door. He opened the door, fastened a collar around her neck that was attached to a lead. He then ordered her down onto all fours and welcomed her into his house.

11.00am. Esmeralda's stilettos clicked on the steps as she trotted down from his front door and back onto the street. Her make-up was all gone, her hair was a mess and she was covered from head to toe in black and blue bruises. When she reached the bottom of the steps, she turned and gave him a cheeky wave goodbye. He smiled gently back at her from the doorway.

The first thing she did was phone her mother…

"It would appear that I've accidentally become somebody's sex slave!" exclaimed Esmeralda. "He made me lick soup out of a dog bowl, under the table, whilst He sat eating his dinner. I can't believe I only met the guy on Thursday."

"Look at my arse..." Esmeralda pulled down her trousers and showed her friend.

"Fucking hell! It looks like a Mike Leigh film down there."

"I almost fainted at one point."

He looked deep into Esmeralda's eyes and softly stroked up and down her arms.

"You look beautiful." He whispered.

"Thank you, Sir," she replied.

"Now..." He said, softly licking his lips, "I want you to go upstairs, follow the candles into the bedroom, where you will find some clothes on the bed."

He slowly stroked his hands up her body and placed them on her shoulders. He gripped hold of her and peered deep into her eyes.

"I want you to put on the outfit..."

"Yes, Sir," she replied.

"Then, I want you to put on the ankle restraints."

"Yes, Sir!" she accidentally gasped.

"Then I want you to put on the wrist restraints."

"Yes, Sir."

He nonchalantly plucked some fluff from her shoulder before returning his gaze to her eyes.

"You put on the collar, attach the lead, then you come downstairs. I've made you some soup. Are you hungry?"

"Yes, Sir."

"Good. Now do you understand what I've told you to do?"

"Yes, Sir."

175

"What do you say?"

"Thank you, Sir."

"Good slave. Now go on."

Esmeralda was smug to discover that the outfit He had chosen for her was exactly the same as the one she was wearing, which she had chosen to please him, though his one was made from latex and satin.

Esmeralda had become someone's sex slave. She hadn't even known the fellow a week ago and now her every waking second was consumed with thinking about Him. Now He was defined in her thought and speech by the capital letters that she mentally affixed to every mention of Him. Him, He, Sir, Master. He had taken up the empty throne in the middle of her inner world, the one that had been vacated by Dad and God years ago. What a bastard. How the hell had this happened?

"You'd forgotten that I was planning to come down?"

"Yes. I'm sorry. But something rather unexpected has happened." She told her friend all about the bizarre series of events which had recently unfurled. Her friend was a very special friend, a gentleman who understood her implicitly.

"Well, it was only a matter of time," He replied when she had finished explaining. "Congratulations."

She decided not to tell anyone else about it. From now on this was her secret. As a firm believer in the theory that one creates one's own world, she knew she had created this for a reason. It thrilled the fuck out of her, obviously, but there were all sorts of issues being played out. She had embarked on a voyage of discovery that she hadn't realised she'd been preparing for. But she had been. This was clearly necessary. She was excited... and absolutely terrified.

"I won't fall in love with Him I don't think. This is a sex thing."

"No, you will probably fall in love with him in a purer and deeper way than you've ever imagined," replied her friend.

"Fuck!" exclaimed Esmeralda with sudden realisation. "I'm going to get really hurt, aren't I?"

"You don't know that. And it's better to get torn apart quickly and learn from it, than rot away slowly in a dysfunctional relationship. This is beautiful. You're going to discover so much."

"I guess you're right."

"You address me as 'Sir'. Don't forget. Otherwise next time you will faint."

The train didn't have a train driver, so it was cancelled. She was going to miss school. But she didn't care. She didn't care about anything any more. How far would she go? How far would He make her go?

Serendipity was coursing through the veins of this affair. She had worn exactly the same outfit to his house that he had bought for her to wear; He had really liked the secretary look on her. She knew he was going to like the glasses and he did. She felt like she understood Him. He had her favourite book on his bookshelf, one that was out of print and which she had been trying to get hold of for ages. He also had a copy of one of her favourite films, another rare find. Then, just now, she had switched her phone on after recharging the batteries in case He was trying to contact her. As soon as the phone came on she received a text from Him. He had only just sent it. The text read *Goodnight, slave. Sweet dreams.* The only other man she had ever experienced this kind of synchronicity with was her true love, the Israeli. The planets were in motion over this one, that was for certain.

£350 on sex toys was a wee bit excessive though.

"He has the most brilliant blue eyes and He smells divine… a sensory feast."

"You know we all have that question; 'Who's on top, who is on the bottom, who's in control?' In S&M, they say the bottom is in control."

She spent the weekend in Florence and Rome with her mother and brother and returned feeling wonderfully relaxed. It had done wonders for her constitution. She had been bedbound for most of January and completely lacking in energy, but now she felt reinvigorated, fortified in body, mind and spirit. They had eaten delicious food, drunk fine wine, walked miles around some of the grandest architecture in the world and had seen some of the most beautiful works of art.

"I've got Catholicism coming out of my ears. I went to the Vatican in Rome and about six different churches in Florence, including Sunday Mass at the Duomo. I bought rosaries from a nun and saw all the religious paintings of Michelangelo, Da Vinci and all the other Teenage Mutant Ninja Turtles. In the end I had to go to the Coliseum in Rome, just for a taste of the heathens. I couldn't take any more of that God stuff."

Although there was, and always would be, a dark corner of her heart entirely devoted to religious perversions, like her desire to give someone a blowjob in a pulpit, or to be screwed by a priest in a confessional box, she really had got over God. He was like a long-forgotten lover who no longer made her heart jump. And so, finding that she was in need of her own kind, she caught the train to the Coliseum in Rome.

There was no unrelenting self-flagellation, no guilt-ridden nonsense to be found in its powerful columns, just bare-boned, honest pain and pleasure. She would have loved to have seen the place in its original splendour, before the Popes throughout the ages had encouraged the local citizens to slowly tear the place down. It would have looked incredible, towering up in white marble, contrasting beautifully with the red blood spilling about the arena floor. Outside the walls of the Coliseum, the Republic had created a world that had order, peace, education, and any number of logically organised working systems. But inside the arena, chaos reigned. Blood, pain, heroes, theatre and all the many varied colours to be found between life and death played themselves out for the public's viewing pleasure. She had a huge respect for her heathen ancestors. She found honesty in their world, an honesty that she felt was lacking in the modern world around her. And it was this same honesty that she had found residing in His world… her new Master. He had become her Coliseum, her realm of chaos, pleasure, and pain, and one that gave meaning and structure to her world outside.

Esmeralda and her family always had fun, wherever they went. They were all a little bit hopelessly in love with the world.

"We're like a family of squirrels."

"How's that?" asked her mother.

"'Cause we're so highly strung we can't sit still. We have to run around exploring every nook and cranny."

"And we like to collect things to bring home with us," laughed her mother.

"Exactly!" exclaimed Esmeralda.

She rang the Composer to put off him staying with her. She explained that she was currently involved with someone and it didn't seem appropriate for him to stay. He was an absolute darling about it and understood perfectly. She adored him. He was such a wonderful man. "You're seeing someone too?" she screeched at the Composer through her drunken haze. She had wondered why he had kept hiding his phone and had just now seen the photo of a blonde girl on the front of it. "I can't believe you've been playing the wounded soldier all day and making me feel guilty," she laughed, before proceeding to repeatedly slap him. "You little bastard!"

Esmeralda had gone into confused mode, which meant that something was wrong. She was worried about whether falling in love with her Master was the right thing to do. At the end of the day, right or wrong doesn't really come into it.

Alarm bells rang in Esmeralda's head whenever people told her she wasn't being herself. Her sixteen-year-old best friend told her she didn't sound like herself on the phone and one of her closest friends had said, "That's not like you" in one of his emails.

She deeply regretted having told her nearest and dearest friends about her recent sexual exploits. She hadn't meant to mouth off about it; she had known at the time that she would regret it, but it was a protective thing, a way of belittling her feelings and experiences to try and rein them in. Now it looked as if He was becoming a permanent fixture. But her closest friends had already formed pretty strong opinions of him and were going to struggle to look him in the eye when they finally met him.

It was interesting to discover quite how prudish people are. She had assumed that everyone was a bit more interesting. That everyone was a little bit kinky and up for trying something new and unusual, but it wasn't the case at all. Mediocrity reigns, it seems.

"No, he's not into asphyxiation. Just role-play and textures mainly. And he doesn't actually want to be the

Dom: this is the first time he's played the role. Normally he's the sub. It's just that I'm loving being the sub at the moment and I've never done this before, so he's letting me have my fun. I tried to be the Dom the other day and was rubbish at it, mainly because you have to make such an effort. As my Dom he is thinking about me the whole time, making sure I'm constantly in a heightened state of arousal. When the roles were reversed, I just got him to make me dinner, massage my feet and then went to bed. The point is, the one being Dom has to be sexually engaging the sub the whole time for the game to work, which is actually very generous. Our games last for hours. It's all based on trust, consent, communication, boundaries and creativity.

"And that's the last I'm going to say on the subject. Having seen the gang at the pub tonight, I have realised that actually I think this guy is going to be a fixture for the time being so if you lot are going to meet him, which is likely, none of you are going to be able to look him in the eye as it is. So I'm going back to the world of having a private sex life... I can hear the cheers from here".

A new hero has been discovered - Elaine Morgan, who champions the Aquatic Ape Theory. "It's taken me 35 years to get over writing that book." The little grey haired lady was referring to her book *The Descent of Woman*, where she had first discussed the Aquatic Ape Theory. The book had been a bit of a coffee table feminist, pseudo-science knee-jerk to the Savannah Theory. This theory had only recognised males when looking at why the species had evolved into becoming bipedal and naked apes before evolving into humans. The book had been a huge success, but Elaine Morgan had got over the knee jerk and had found in her investigations that there was lots of evidence to suggest that the Aquatic Ape Theory may even be correct.

181

She deeply regrets ever having given it a feminist slant in the first place because spotty-nosed geeks the world over are still discrediting her work as coffee table feminist pseudo-science. She's not a scientist, she's an artist, and is the first to admit she has no qualifications to back up her work, but she has been investigating this for 35 years now and she thinks that there is enough evidence to at least warrant a look by the science world. Some scientists are finally beginning to agree. And David Attenborough supports her work, so it must be true.

Esmeralda had a dream about her first love. It was the first time she had ever done that in the ten years since they had split up. Dreams are such funny things. She could remember everything about him, his smell, the consistency of his skin, the way it felt to kiss him. She had enjoyed being in his arms again and cuddling him, but the second she had put his cock in her mouth and she had tasted a drop of his spunk, it had made her feel sick and she knew she didn't really want to be with him.

Esmeralda's mouth had never been used so much. Voice work, singing lessons, line speaking, and now it was also engaged in red lipstick-wearing, ball gag-biting, food and foot licking, lots of kissing and daily cock-sucking. She liked the taste of His spunk. She had given up her arse too.

"Master John was here tonight."

"Was he?"

"He asked me how I was doing and I told him that I had got myself a slave. He said that I didn't deserve one and asked who it was. I told him it's the little blonde girl over there and he said 'You bastard! I haven't been able to keep my eyes off of her all evening.'"

Esmeralda squealed with pride.

"What wondrous fun. Have just spent the last few days hanging out with be-speckled geeks from all over the globe who all share a passion for science. It's been very interesting and loads of fun. Geeks love it when a little blonde lady shows an interest in their work, and they have all spoilt me rotten. So this week I found out that...

"We may have descended from Aquatic Apes and not the plains of the Savannah. That bird flu really is something to worry about as they think the last outbreak may have been Spanish influenza and that killed more people than the First and Second World Wars put together; and that bird flu is the fault of pigs, not birds, because it's in pigs that the bird and human strains join forces.

"The reason your genes know which order to grow a little finger through to a thumb and that your head is at the top and toes at the bottom is a gene called the Sonic the Hedgehog gene. "Dowsing works. I had a go."

Her period had started. She had a momentary "phew". The cystitis was back, though. She hadn't suffered from it for two years, the whole time she had been single. That's the trouble with having a rigorous sex life again. It was time to get back into being fit and healthy. She had spent too much time in her brain of late, what with falling in love, and that blasted inner dialogue had gone off on one again. Time to get physical and hang up on the droning miserable bastard that was her head.

I want God,
I want poetry,
I want danger,
I want freedom,
I want goodness,
I want sin - Aldous Huxley.

183

GOD

Hello God.

Thanks for a wonderful holiday - for this quality time with my mum on her fiftieth birthday and quality time with my brother. Thanks for all the new and exciting things that are happening in my life, for the new man who is absolutely perfect for me at the moment and who is introducing me to all kinds of new and exciting things. Loving your work, God, as always.

She liked having someone to say thank you to. Esmeralda lit the candle and placed it alongside the other flickering prayers before a glittering casket encasing a statue of the Madonna and Child. She turned and absorbed the beauty and magnitude of the Church of Santa Maria Novella. The immortal words of her mother wafted through her head: "Look up, look back, backdrop and sniff!" This sentence had played out as a precursor to every room in every single art gallery, museum, stately home and castle they had entered during their cultured childhood, to ensure that they never missed a thing. The programming had worked.

Esmeralda automatically gazed up at the great domed ceiling of the ornate church with its delicately decorated forms and enjoyed the calming effect from the depth of vision. Breathing in deeply, Esmeralda drank in the ancient scent of worship with relish. She loved sacred spaces. Having managed to give her mother and brother the slip, Esmeralda had taken the opportunity to lose herself in her thoughts and relish a spot of God time, but now her mind had turned to deviancy. Facing Giotto's great golden crucifix, she walked slowly down the central aisle of the church towards the marble altar and took up residence upon the last pew, where she took out a pad and pen, and set about writing a truly filthy story for her new lover. After scrawling several pages on sodomy with the devil and wearing a butt plug to confession, Esmeralda sat back and surveyed the gilded S&M torture scene of the crucifix that commanded the whole space and the religion.

When Esmeralda was eleven years old she had experienced a sensation that she came to believe was a born-again experience. In one brief moment Esmeralda fully comprehended how it felt to be persecuted and deserted by those that you love and are fighting for, whilst they set about the motions of nailing you to a cross. It was like the feeling of vertigo or those flashes of the imagination when you think you're going to jump in front of an oncoming train, and for a split second your whole body experiences the sensation of being hit by a locomotive travelling at 90mph. Her whole body had suddenly experienced the pain and suffering of a crucifixion, but worse still, she had experienced the loneliness and magnitude of the sacrifice Jesus had made for those who were persecuting him. It had all happened in a flash, coming out of nowhere, whilst walking through the grey old streets of Colchester on a drizzly Saturday morning. It had glued Esmeralda to the spot for what seemed like an eternity, but had, even in reality, been for a good few seconds. After the vision passed, Esmeralda had felt as if someone had switched on a tap in her head, pouring out mineral water through her body, cleaning her blood, which had suddenly felt like mud. The water ran right down to her toes, until her whole body was full of crystal-clear freshness and she half expected to find that she was standing in a great dirty puddle. When she was finally able to move again, her body erupted into a convulsion of tears. She felt responsible for the way Jesus had been treated and responsible for continuing his torture through her actions in the present day.

Surprisingly, as she sat scribbling down the finer details of her fetish for part-man-part-cloven-hoofed creatures beneath the mournful gaze of our Saviour, this was still her attitude to this present day. Having revisited the experience of that morning in Essex through the eyes of an angry feminist, a critical atheist, a universally connected pagan and now, as an inspired artist with a sense of humour, she had never denied the event that took place on that day, nor watered down the significance of the message she had received. And now, as a 28-year-old sitting squirming on the hard wooden pew, moist from the episode she had just jotted down concerning her (as "Lucy") getting jiggy with a deviant Mr Tumnus against the lamp-post in Narnia, she still took responsibility for the world that she lived in, including the history that she was privy to and the perspective on it that she had taken, because she took responsibility for the world that she created.

Over the last decade Esmeralda had completely dismantled her reality. By this she meant her perception of it, her personal inner movie. She had torn down everything that she believed to be factual and tangible, dispelled the myths, threw out the stories, dropped the baggage and ate her taboos. It was an arduous task. Some things she didn't want to give up, some things seemed so intrinsic to who she

187

was or how she thought the world was that she didn't know who she would be or where she would be without them, but she gave them up anyway, just for the hell of it, just to see what would happen. And it was a task that will never be completed. The self is like an onion, layer after layer peels back to reveal waves of fresh tears and revelations; but rather than peeling layers away, reaching down into a deeper core of the self, what Esmeralda found beautiful was that the further in she went, the more she found that her journey was bringing her outside of herself, more into the outer world and less into her own film. She had reached a point where her life had become like a blank slate, a clearing in the forest, a newly-tilled, fresh plot of land in which she could choose to grow whatever she wanted.

So she set about creating her life, knowing that anything she chose to paint onto her blank canvas was purely a choice and not because it was true, right or of any value or worth whatsoever. It was there purely because she had chosen to put it there. Anyone else with a blank canvas would choose to put other stuff onto it and that would be their choice and that was up to them.

And, surprisingly, she had chosen to put Christianity back onto it. Not because she believed in the Christian God above all other gods. She didn't agree with the dogma or views of the church. She had simply chosen to include it because of the familiarity of the vocabulary and because of the awe inspired by the buildings of worship and the iconography. She had also chosen to put bits of all the other religions onto it too, cherry-picking the stuff she liked best from each of them. Christianity took up the most canvas space because it was part of her roots - the first road she had traversed into the Divine. She had felt like a fraud when she had started praying to "Mother Nature" and had felt a hole

188

in her life experience when she had point blank believed in nothing. Religion for Esmeralda was like the gravy on a roast. You can do without it and there is no reason to have it other than it holds the whole meal together with a unifying rich flavour. She liked wearing a cross, lighting candles and using the name "God". She also wished the Coliseum was still up and running, with its gladiatorial games and the amphitheatres with their festivals for Dionysus. She liked stone circles, churches, burial sites, old-fashioned theatres and forests. She collected the stories of all the gods, because they sure beat the stories of celebrities. And it all added to the flavour of her spiritual gravy.

When she was on ayahuasca, Esmeralda had asked it to show her God. This funny crab-like thing had scuttled sideways into her vision and had stared at her through a million different eyes. It was like a hybrid between a Chinese dragon, the monster "Ahhhhhhh" from the Quest for the Holy Grail and the God that appeared once in South Park. With perfect comedy timing, its multitude of gormless eyes blinked at Esmeralda and then scuttled off again sideways, with its tongue flaying. She had rolled about on the floor laughing. It was one of the funniest things she had ever seen. And then it had occurred to her... God has a sense of humour! Well of course he has, he invented the penguin hadn't he? And that was the God Esmeralda had painted onto her canvas as her God: a multi-eyed, side-scuttling, tongue-flaying, dribbling creature with brilliant comedy timing. He was a comic genius and she was proud to have him as her embodiment of the Divine and she was happy to give him the name of God, just for the hell of it.

IMBOLC

Esmeralda woke up requiring muesli, which meant that summer was on her way. The flat was a mess. She had taken her eyes off the wheel for a second and now everything was in disarray. Her laundry needed doing, bills needed paying and her nail varnish needed removing. She lay in bed on the dirty white linen, covered in porridge from some recent sex games, and wondered how best to tackle the day. She had run out of laundry bags, so she needed to bike to the launderette and buy some and then go to the shop to get some nail varnish remover. If she then took the laundry to the laundrette, she could clean the flat, collect the laundry and then have a bath. Sounded great in theory, but she couldn't be bothered to move.

People believe, thought Shadow. It's what people do. They believe. And then they will not take responsibility for their beliefs; they conjure things, and do not trust the conjurations. People populate the darkness; with ghosts, with gods, with electrons, with tales. People imagine, and people believe; and it is that belief, that rock solid belief, that makes things happen.

- Neil Gaiman *(American Gods)*

The rooibos tea was going down a treat.

"It's called Imbolc," she explained "'cause it's the time of year when Mother Nature goes to the garden centre and buys a job lot of plants and wildlife for the year. So she gets it all in bulk, you see?"

"You're such a muppet!" He said.

"It's interesting how things have gone full circle and now priests and vicars are seen as purveyors of evil superstitions and witchcraft."

February had been eerily warm and as she sat on the train heading out of Brighton station, spring sunshine gilded the wet roofs of the city. Esmeralda smiled. She was listening to a compilation album her Master had made for her. It was so goddamn melancholic! But it was full of humour and quirkiness.

She had made some rather exciting choices as she descended into this new relationship. Firstly she had decided that she was going to avoid putting her new lover in a box. He had made a sweeping statement a few days ago, telling her that He thought she would turn to religion at some point. He then also mentioned that He had lost the love of his life to religion once, their paths having grown in different directions. This hadn't sat comfortably with Esmeralda at the time, but she couldn't put her finger on why. Then she realised that in one fell swoop, he had inadvertently swept her whole body of work - concerning her spirituality and her exploration into what religion meant to her - off the table of discussion. She wasn't His ex for a start and maybe the relationship had failed because they had grown into different people, rather than religion being the problem. Esmeralda had lost her second love to journalism, after all, and her Master was practically a journalist, but it didn't mean He was going to suddenly run off to chase Britney Spears around America. Either way, she wasn't going to be put in a box in this relationship, and she would grant him the same respect.

Esmeralda saw people like the Hawkins theory on the shape of the universe: as an ever-increasing doughnut continually spiralling outwards, growing in all directions, with the past slowly dying behind it. If she treated him like a doughnut, then she believed He would be led by her example.

The second choice had been made because she had caught herself getting annoyed when her Master had started sermonising at her about one subject or another, when it was something that she already knew a fair deal about. Esmeralda had a very unpleasant competitive streak. She had done a good job of ironing out this crease over the last few years. The acting industry is not a fun place to be if you're competitive. She suspected it was a characteristic of all men to harp on as if they were the leading brains on a subject, even when they knew very little about it, but then Esmeralda was pretty good at doing this too.

Either way, Esmeralda decided that rather than sitting there stewing and slagging Him off in her head whilst He was imparting his knowledge, she would instead a) listen (she might learn something new) and b) enjoy an ownership over all his knowledge and experiences, like an external hard drive. He was her partner in crime now and over time, their rich cultivated worlds would merge and they would learn all about the things the other one knew and discover the things they had seen and experienced during their fascinating and varied lives. They had all the time in the world for this to take place. So until then, they were both storage units for all the wonderful facts and insights that would one day be booted into each other. And he was very clever and had made some genius choices along the way. It was all very exciting.

"I'm an actress, not a tart!"

Her dreams had been crazy of late. She had dreamt again about her first love. They had been in the honeymoon period of their relationship and she kind of knew it was a dream and enjoyed relishing the opportunity to wallow in the experience of him again. But then the same thing happened in a dream about her second love too, which was also fun to indulge in. Two nights ago she had spent the night as a fish, hanging out in the fish tank in her kitchen with her pet fish Moggers and Boggers. Then last night she had dreamt of her friend, who thought that she might be pregnant. Esmeralda had a feeling that she was. It turned out she wasn't.

She had also experienced two very strong cases of *déja vu* in the last few weeks. One incident had lasted for a whole sentence that Elaine Morgan had said during her talk on Aquatic Apes at the science festival. As Esmeralda was falling in love with her Master, long-forgotten rooms in her psyche were being unlocked and aired again.

All the hard work she had put in over the last two years of singledom was paying off. This love affair was unfurling with a smooth tranquillity. Esmeralda felt supported by the structures she had put in place and felt that she had played a large part in the creation of this beautiful flower. The universe had stopped happening by chance for Esmeralda; it had stopped happening *at* her. She took responsibility for the world that she created and she was loving her work.

She lay face down on the black satin sheets, wrapped in a white satin dressing-gown and stared at the black silhouette of the bare tree against the grey sky outside of His window. Her face felt puffy from the mascara smeared around her eyes and she could feel her bed hair was off on one. Her shoulders and ankles ached in their sockets where they had been bound to the bed all night. She twisted her wrists in the leather restraints, but it was no good. It was better to relax than try and find a comfortable position. He had gone to shower. She loved the smell of His room.

One of the songs on his compilation had given him away.

"I'm your little doll, to dress up and do with as you please."

"Is that what you want to be?"

"Yes please!"

I need someone much more mysterious…To be my Miss… To be my Mistress. – Red House Painters.

Esmeralda wasn't very good at being mysterious.

Esmeralda crawled back out from under the desk, where she had been revealing her bare bottom so that He could pour melted wax over it. As she stood up she banged her head on the table.

"Did you bang your head?" He asked her.

"Yes, but I'm all right."

"Of course you are. You're a sadomasochist." That was first time anyone had ever called her that, and yes, she guessed she was.

"I'm not very good with technology," He said over the microphone on the stage. "My girlfriend had to help me switch my new mobile phone on the other day."

But I helped him switch it on thought Esmeralda. *Oh… I'm his girlfriend!* She swooned.

"I hope you didn't tell your mother everything. We should have some secrets." He looked at her face "You're not very good at secrets are you?" She felt as if she had done something to displease her Master and she felt sick to the pit of her stomach.

195

The black water winked at her through the naked forest.

"I have made a lot of mistakes."

"I don't want to know."

"Don't forget who you're addressing, slave."

"Sorry, Sir."

She couldn't bring herself to tell the eighteen-year-old the first time she rang him.

"It's not the vast number of men I've already slept with who you should be worried about. They're the ones I've already had. I'd be with them now if it was meant to be. It's the men I haven't slept with you need to worry about. And there's a lot more of them."

Not that He really had anything to worry about. She would always be his constant, play His games, and be a vessel for his pleasure - she was the most loyal of creatures - for as long as He provided her with space in which to grow and be herself. *Put me in a box though and I swear to God I will tear it down and piss on the remains.*

"He is perfect," she told her friend gleefully. "He is perfect for me at the moment and we may find that we are perfect for each other for a long time to come."

Brutal beatings and name calling

To lose me to the spell…

…The attention I needed was much more serious. – Red House Painters.

He was trouble.

She liked trouble.

"Do you trust me?'

"Yes. Very much so."

"How far are you willing to go?"

"I don't know, Sir. Try me."

"Absence makes the heart grow fonder, Sir."

"Abstinence makes the heart grow fonder, slave."

"My orgasms belong to you now, Sir."

They kept manifesting things together for the fun of it. During their weekend away, He introduced her to bird watching and they kept manifesting rare birds. They spotted a Pied Flycatcher and a Dartford Warbler!

"So in the future we need to manifest a beautiful cottage in the countryside, with me pottering around writing all day and you whirling off to film shoots and theatres."

But she liked to write too…

He asked her how she felt about children. She had been dying to ask him, but had decided not to. She was over the moon that He asked her first. It showed that she was learning at least some degree of self-restraint.

"Manifest this museum being open."

"This museum is open!" she commanded, trying the door, but it was locked. They shrugged their shoulders and entered the pub. It didn't matter. They got into the warm and ordered a pint. Then He noticed that the entrance to the museum was through the bar. Not only was it open, but they could also walk around it with a pint of real ale in their hands.

The pub was full of colourful locals, all with broad Dorset accents and weather-beaten faces from a life at sea. They met Owen, a red-faced old drunk with skin like leather, who knew all about hats and kept mocking her Master on His inability to wear a trilby at the right jaunty angle. Esmeralda showed her Master how it was done, much to Owen's delight.

"You're adorable," exclaimed her Master. "Another thing I like about you is…" He spent the whole weekend listing all the things He liked about her.

The weekend away was amazing. Bird-watching and bondage, what fun. But towards the end, trouble struck as Esmeralda found herself becoming overwhelmingly intimidated by her Master. Not by the whippings or from being tied up, but by his intelligence and His ten-year head start down the road that she was on. Now she was feeling completely out of control, raw and vulnerable.

"I fucking hate falling in love."

"Why can't I just enjoy it?"

"Fun… Fun, fun, fun."

"Oh fucking bollocks."

"I've gone and lost touch with reality again."

She had a breakthrough. Waking one morning, tied up in knots about a) her Master and how much she hated falling in love as it made her feel powerless, and b) her forthcoming show in which she was singing and how, in her opinion, she couldn't sing for toffee, Esmeralda decided to manifest that both issues would be resolved that day. She wrote a long email to her Principal, explaining how scared she was about the singing. When she saw her later that day, her Principal told her to stop it. So she did. She saw her Master too later that day and decided to stop being silly about falling in love. Yes, it makes you feel vulnerable, but that's what is so beautiful about it.

"Your acting this term has vastly improved."

"Has it?"

"Yes," said her school chum. "You're so much more vulnerable and softer. It's really beautiful."

"Wow, thank you."

See? Falling in love isn't so bad.

Life was a highly amusing whirlwind. For example yesterday, Esmeralda spent the morning wallowing in her pyjamas, moping about the house making a compilation album for her Master. She had gone off on a "He thinks I'm stupid" trip again over the last 24 hours, so her choice of songs were all about broken hearts killing off their love, themselves, or their lovers. She was really pleased with the CD when she had finished it though and felt it was a job well done and she knew that He would really like it. Then she went to school and finished off a database of all the agents and casting directors in the country, so they could send a mail-out about their next show. She then nearly managed to finish off her accounts, before having an amazing opera-singing lesson with a brilliant singing teacher.

After the class the girl she was singing with needed a good old cry to relieve herself of all the stress she had been under at school with the show coming up. Esmeralda gave her a hug and an absorbent shoulder to cry on. Esmeralda then found herself on the receiving end of lots of hugs as people arrived saying thank you for doing the database.

The rehearsal went well and the director told Esmeralda that the character she was coming out with was really delicate and quite lovely. She spent the evening on her knees as a Catholic schoolgirl in floods of tears as she confessed to a priest that she had been forced to do impure things by a boy. When she finished rehearsing, Esmeralda found a text on her phone from her Master, which read "Your Mistress requests you attend tonight at 10.15pm. Let yourself in, lock the door, get undressed and come upstairs."

She got to the house and let herself in. She took off all her clothes and made her way into the bedroom. Her Master was dressed in pink satin underwear, a leather pencil skirt, fishnet stockings and a pair of black PVC high heels. He dressed Esmeralda from top to toe in rubber, gagged her, bent her over a chair, flogged her and filled her holes with vibrating toys. She sucked his cock till he came then they curled up together in his black satin sheets. Esmeralda gave her Master the CD, which pleased Him immensely, and they went to sleep in each other's arms listening to the tunes she had chosen for Him.

It's an interesting conundrum, whether to talk to your partner about your concerns or not. Considering how 99.99% of people's concerns are their own nonsense, there is the danger that by voicing these concerns one is physically creating the concerns out in the world whereas, on the other hand, one could work through the nonsense oneself, while it was still a flimsy concept, rather than trying to deal with it once it has turned it into a hard-boiled issue.

Esmeralda had got it into her head that her Master could talk for hours about His own artistic discoveries and developments of the day whereas when she began talking about her work He lost interest and changed the subject. Whether this was true or not Esmeralda had developed a filter on how she listened to her Master so that no matter what He said to her, she translated it all as "I think you're stupid" and "I'm not interested in your art" which meant that the poor sod didn't stand a chance. The choice for Esmeralda was to either talk to Him about her concerns or simply remove the filters herself and start hearing what he had to say without them, thus avoiding the manifestation of her concerns out in the world. She was pretty sure he would be devastated if he knew that this was what she had been thinking about Him.

Not that He was necessarily completely innocent. He was a man, after all, and whether true or not, Esmeralda's opinion was that all men thought that the world revolved around them and that their career and path through life was of far greater significance than their female partner's. She didn't know any woman who didn't feel the same way as her on this subject. Men simply think that they are more important. But again this was her own nonsense and her own filter for how she listened to men, so this view was also to be taken with a pinch of salt. All in all, Esmeralda needed to address the situations in which she felt powerless and look at what needed shifting in herself to allow her power to flow freely again. And this would not happen by pointing fingers, making up stories, or deciding on facts about the world. It's only by shifting ourselves that we discover new realities in which we can express ourselves powerfully.

The sea bobbed frantically like a can-can dancer cheekily flashing her white frills at the beach.

"My book is about space and time. I've just realised."

Sitting in a café, people-watching, is the greatest pastime known to man.

Esmeralda's favourite book was *Fierce Invalids Home from Hot Climates* by Tom Robbins and her favourite film was *Amelie*.

"My mate got his face smashed in by this guy, and it left him looking so rough that people would cross over the street when they saw him coming 'cause they thought he looked like a psycho. He told me that if he ever saw this guy again, he would kill him. His life has already been ruined, so he doesn't care if he goes to prison."

"People are so prejudiced." Person. Judgement. Person. Judgement. Person. Judgement. Person. Judgement.

She loved the smell of her own body odour. She went to the party without washing, because she still smelt of him.

A painfully large piece of cereal got lodged in the back of her throat.

"OK, so the game is that each time you say 'Wicked' or 'Fucking' you're not allowed to touch yourself for a day. Agreed?"

"Yes, Sir."

She couldn't shake the feeling that he was trying to change her. She kept feeling judged and that he didn't think that she was good enough.

LOVE

After Esmeralda's last relationship, it occurred to her that she had been traversing from one boyfriend to the next without ever spending any time on her own. She began to suspect she had been using relationships as a security blanket, ever since her dad had left them and had broken her little old heart. Boyfriends had become her replacement daddy who would give the unconditional love that her real daddy had cruelly taken away. Those poor men. She had been asking them all for the moon on a stick - unconditional love - whilst at the same time projecting all of her distrust of the very concept at them, along with her fear of it being taken away again, because she believed at some point it always would be. The poor bastards never stood a chance.

Three long-term love affairs so far, with three different slogans:

Forever After

Eternal and Unconditional

You Complete Me

No more slogans, she decided. After three "The Ones" Esmeralda realised it was time to give up on that idea and to

203

take people on with a continual open generosity and enjoy each day as it comes.

Esmeralda had conjured up this inspiring specimen of a man she was now seeing, through developing and training herself in the belief that she was always creating her own world.

"Let's look at the facts. I cast the spell that I wanted to be single for two years and exactly two years later, I meet this man. I was flinging my arms around saying how I knew all the men in Brighton and that it was impossible for me to meet the man of my dreams here, right outside where my new fella lives."

The concept of unconditional love is dangerous and the world is a better place without it. Conditions on love equal a love you take responsibility for, rather than a love you can happily take for granted, because you believe it is never going to go away. All experiences of unconditional love had scarred her deeper than anything else in her life. Father and God. The day she realised that the love of both of these fallible creatures was in reality hung with conditions, like translucent baubles, it ripped her world asunder. The deepest wound inflicted. The first and deepest cut. But from this grew the deepest respect for love and for those who conduct themselves through the stormy course of life with dignity and integrity. Like her mother, who had sailed like a mighty galleon through all the storms that life threw at her and kept her cargo - Esmeralda and her brother - safe and warm. And her father, since his indiscretion, had spent a lifetime making amends. He was human, but he was a good human after all, just an impulsive and selfish one.

Love is a garden. It needs constant attention for it to grow and flourish. But it is too much work for one person to do on their own. Both people need to look after it together or it's no fun for the one doing all of the hard work.

My dream love is a wild secret garden that grows freely and appears effortless, because the labours of the gardeners are totally equal and both are joyfully self-expressed.

OSTARA

Esmeralda hired a suite in a boutique hotel for His birthday. It cost a fortune. He was her slave for the evening. They had reached a happy medium, taking it in turns to play the role of slave and Master. Both were subs at heart, but they had fallen in love and were happy to play the Dom for each other.

It was delightful to see how many different ways they could express their pleasure of experience and depth of feelings for each other, without resorting to the age-old "one sentence fits all" of saying "I love you". They hadn't said it once yet and the electricity continued to build up between them. You could light a cigarette off it. By waiting to say it, they had set the bar far higher.

"I'm not nervous, but my head is full of thoughts which I would normally muddle through on my own, but then I thought to myself: I've got someone in my life that I can sound off at now! So I thought I would."

"I'm glad you called."

She sat before the brightly-lit mirror in the theatre dressing room. A great gold ball formed in front of her stomach, between her up-turned and down-turned hands. Once the ball had fully formed, she spun it out, so it flayed outwards like a Catherine Wheel, filling the room with gold, sparkling light. Now the ball filled the entire room, extending out from her stomach, like a huge great glittering bubble, so that when she moved, the whole room moved with her. The auditorium had become a flight simulator, with Esmeralda at the controls, spinning out the yarn they were telling.

"Once a Catholic, always a Catholic. Those are the rules."

"But I'm still a virgin!"

The play went down a storm.

Sometimes Esmeralda had to just stop and laugh. She had just thought about how, since meeting her Master, she now regularly ate food out of a dog bowl and off His feet.

"Are you falling in love with me?" He asked her, stroking His thumb across her cheek and smiling deeply into her eyes.

She blushed. "Is it that obvious?"

"Well… I'm falling in love with you too," He said.

She had stopped writing. She had fallen in love and she had stopped writing. He had stopped writing too. Love is an irksome fellow. She had heard a talk a few days ago from a scientist and performer, one of the brains behind *Spitting Image*, who explained love from a scientific perspective. He said that falling in love released little bursts of endorphins that made you feel euphoric and kept you in a state of deluded distraction. Love is a state of madness. Until you have got over the falling in love bit and settle down into a deep friendship, the image of them will remain branded onto your retina and your mind will insistently wander down the garden path of their memory. Nothing else will be as important to you. People you have known all of your life and who mean the world to you will suddenly pale into insignificance. Pastimes that have previously absorbed you suddenly leave you cold. You would rather sit on your own, replaying conversations that passed between the pair of you, than create fresh conversations with the people around you. All is obsolete apart from them.

"That is what has happened to me."

"My brain has petered out."

This book has petered out.

"I'm happy though."

She had fallen in love. We couldn't hold that against her now, could we?

IT HAPPENED
OR IT DIDN'T
HAPPEN

I'm lying here feeling sick with grief, mourning the love that, only a week ago, was the most beautiful love I had ever known. Something crept out of the darkness and killed it. And I'm sorry, but you let this monster out.

"I am 100% convinced that things have changed because of the answer I gave you in the bath, when you asked me if I thought I'd ever get bored of S&M. I gave the wrong answer. You retracted your love from me. And now I'm in pain. I know you have been hurt before. By the sounds of things, all of your previous girlfriends have revealed that they weren't really that into S&M after you split up. I understand that everything has felt like a lie to you.

If I may be so bold, having experienced what you're like to be with, I suggest that you have created this situation. This is your pattern. In the time I have known you, I have felt like I am being continually tested, having to always prove to you that I'm game.

211

You have not allowed me to own my own sex life. It's all about you. I fell in love with you and I really enjoyed our sex life; whereas I feel like you fell in love with me because of the sex life. The second you feared that the sex life might go away, you froze on me. Do you have any idea how much that hurts? I completely opened myself up to you. Every step of the way I was terrified. But you mesmerised me and you made me feel brave, so I lowered my defences and revealed my vulnerable ugly insides to you. And you thought they were beautiful. I thought yours were beautiful, too. But you continued to test me. Always there with the questions: 'Do you think you will always like S&M?' 'Have you practised S&M before?' 'Are you sure you are really enjoying this?' Then one day I didn't give the right answer and you stuck a knife into me and now I'm in agony. You are breaking my heart in two.

You asked me if I ever thought I would get bored of S&M. I said that I would get bored of anything if it was all we ever did. And that is exactly what I meant.

The ridiculous thing is, I do like S&M. I hadn't practised it all that much before I met you, which is why meeting you blew me out of the water. I've never felt so turned on. I want the butt plugs. I want the restraints. I want the whippings, the satin, the rubber, the pleasure, and the pain. If we split up I will still want these things. I will go out and look for a new Master. One who is firm but gentle, one who will also let me play the Dom. I want a Master just like you. So why can't I just have you?

This is such a tragedy. I was falling so helplessly in love with you. We were the architects of the most incredible creation I had ever known. We could manifest anything together. A life with you thrilled me and offered me everything I had been looking for. You are everything I want, S&M and all.

But I can't go on like this. You have cast me out naked into the cold. I have been banging on the door asking you to let me back inside again for days now. I need to start thinking about finding some clothes and making my way back home. All you have to do is let me back in and we can return to basking in the bliss that we knew only a week ago. We could have it all. We are both such passionate, powerful creatures. Nothing will get in our way. The only things that could hold us back is ourselves. And you're holding yourself back, over the same issue that your other relationships have caused you pain from. Break the cycle. Be fearless and let it go. Stop testing me and start trusting me. Let me have ownership over our mutual choice to be in an S&M relationship. Let me be a pervert like you.

You might say that this is not the problem and that you're just tired. Well I don't believe you and even if it was true, then I'm afraid it's just not good enough. If you are torturing me over some sleepless nights and giving up smoking, then you're not the sort of person I want to be with anyway. I don't mind if sometimes you need time to yourself - I do too. I'm a firm believer in having time to oneself to keep a relationship healthy. But this is more than that. You have shut down on me. Last night was a little bit better when we got home, but only marginally. I don't feel safe anymore. I'm not present to your love. Besides, everything changed the second I gave you my answer in the bath to your eternal unanswerable question, 'Do you think you'll get bored of S&M?'. My answer was simply, 'I will get bored if we always do the same thing'. What did you make that mean? Can you please give it up and let it mean what I meant it to mean, which is what I said: 'I will get bored if we always do the same thing'.

There are many ways to skin a cat, my dear, and I'm well aware that you can't come unless it's a bit kinky. I've still chosen you though, knowing that this is the situation, without any delusions that I can change you. Sure, the female in me would like it if you fell so hopelessly in love with me that one day we could just make love in the missionary style and you would look deep into my eyes, weep and come hard inside me. But that would be it, wouldn't it? A one-off. Then what? I wouldn't then want to just do it in the missionary position every time we had sex. I wouldn't want you continuously weeping on me, either! I can't think of anything worse.

What's great about this S&M malarkey is it keeps things fresh, thoughtful, balanced, honest, open, fun and adventurous. That's why I like it. That's why I want to practise it in my relationship with you. You're not making me do it. I feel under constant pressure to prove to you that I want to do it, but it is still my choice to actually do it. I'm telling you now that your girlfriends were lying to you if they told you they were just doing it to please you. They were enjoying it too. They just told you that to hurt you, because they knew it would hurt you, because it's all you ever go on about. And to always go on about it is selfish. It's all about you. Change the fucking record. I like S&M. I want an S&M relationship. I would like that relationship to be with you. That is the last time I will ever tell you that.

Please think about what I'm saying. Don't just dismiss this ramble as not the problem. Maybe I'm wrong, but what if I'm not? If this is a pattern then think about how liberated your life would be if you were to break it. How amazing life would be if it were free from the control of your sex life. How much fun your relationships would be if you weren't worrying the whole time whether your partner might go off of S&M. Sex would be pressure-free, worry-free, harmless fun, rather than the be-all and end-all. Think how amazing it would be to feel fully self-expressed without having to label yourself with the S&M title. What would your life look like if you weren't so attached to it?

I've had the most amazing three months with you. Knowing you has nourished and enriched my life. You've made me unbelievably happy and I was in the process of giving myself over to you completely. I still want to. But I can't go on like this - the way things have been this last week. This isn't inspiring. The connection between us has to be made again or what is the point? This is my last bang on the door. I want to be with you, but you have to let me back in now or I'm off. I'm cold and lonely out here. You're hurting me. This isn't fun anymore. Please let me back in.

It took three days for Him to reply. He wrote that he was just depressed about being back at school and from giving up smoking. She tried to believe him. But as the days turned into weeks and the weeks became a month, her faith ran out.

BELTANE

"The fucking honeymoon period has come to an abrupt end," she moaned. "He got ill, tired, gave up smoking, then decided to move back into his castle of defensive bullshit, which he had temporarily vacated just long enough to convince me that he was special and different from all the rest. He tricked me into falling in love with him, when he was actually full of the same old bollocks as everyone else." She wasn't quite sure what to do. How the tides can change. She no longer felt the need to capitalise. In any sense of the word.

She looked at him across the breakfast table, over the top of the book she was reading; at the funny little man that she knew less now than ever and whose nose was buried in a book, as it had been all holiday. They were together in Rye for two days and had only engaged in one conversation. And that had resulted in tears. They had been bird-spotting together and had tied each other up in sex games. But they had done all of this in their own separate worlds. They had hung up on each other. All connection had gone.

Esmeralda was empty. She had lots of new and exciting "stuff" to play with, follow up and explore, stuff that she had been introduced to since meeting him, but her soul was

216

deeply sad and she had become a great lumbering, uncoordinated mess. Things had fizzled out between them. Here she was again, wondering what on earth she was doing. Love gone wrong is always a messy and unpleasant business. She was strung out and ready to cry at the drop of a hat. Why had it gone wrong?

Bird-watching and bondage. She had loved all the things they had done together.

He had bruised her internally and this hadn't been an agreed part of the game.

CODE RED! CODE RED! CODE RED!

I've heard it said that people come into our lives for a reason, bringing something we must learn, and we are led to those who help us most to grow, if we let them, and we help them in return. Well I don't know if I believe that's true. But I know I'm who I am today, because I knew you. – Wicked.

Thank you, sir, for the good times.

"Are you glad you split up with my son?" asked the mother of her significant-ex at her best friend's wedding. It was the first time she had seen her in many years. The wonderful woman had been like a surrogate mother to her when she had first left home and they had loved each other very much.

"It was definitely the right thing for me to do at the time," answered Esmeralda, looking over at her current man. "But after all these years, I've come to realise that they're all pretty much the same."

"What do you mean?" asked the mother.

"Well the grass isn't greener," replied Esmeralda, turning and looking her straight in the eye. "They all come with their own bag of nonsense."

He had inadvertently taught her one very important thing. He had taught her to stand by her own convictions.

The relationship looked like it was coming to an end and it was because she was not willing to settle for anything other than the very best. He was an amazing person with a great wealth of personality, who described himself as an eligible bachelor, but he did not see Esmeralda's worth. She had decided to leave him. And she was proud of herself for doing so.

Esmeralda dumped him. Her friends were wonderful. She couldn't believe she had been willing to sacrifice their genuine love for her, warts and all, for his deeply conditional love.

"Oh no, what a shame! I thought you said he was perfect?"

"He was."

"So what happened?"

"He wasn't in love with me."

"Oh…"

Every day, wherever she went, men were paying her far more attention than she had ever had in her life. She was getting better with age. And with every drool that greeted her she thought of her recent ex: *what a fool.*

A good friend of Esmeralda's split up with her long-term boyfriend and was distraught. It was like she had been sawn in two. They all took her out and got her twatted. They necked piles of MDMA at a party and by the time it was light they were playing on the swings in a kids' park.

"Do you want a jaw massage?"

"I haven't had a squidgy MDMA session in years."

They pulled out the sofa bed, all got into comfy clothes, and lay around cuddling each other and telling each other how proud they all were of them all. They drank gin till 2pm and then finally passed out.

Esmeralda woke up face down on the sofa bed, on her own, in an empty living room. Her phone was out of battery and she couldn't hear any movement. She peeled herself off the floor and took the walk of shame home.

When she got back to her flat she was nicely surprised to see it was nine o'clock, which meant she had the whole day to nurse her come-down and still had time to meet her friends to watch a film at 5pm as promised. It left plenty of time to get into bed for a little nap. She woke up an hour later and to her surprise it was dark. It had been nine o'clock at night, not in the morning.

"I was having a good old think as to whether Bali was really a possibility or not, but as much as I try to make it seem plausible I'm afraid it just isn't. However... I am up for meeting you still and if I buy tickets now for some later date then they will be much cheaper. Where are you going after Australia? And when will you be getting there? I think we talked before about meeting in South America? Now I'm well up for that!" Esmeralda listened as her friend responded down the phone.

"Don't worry about me though. I'm not so disappointed to be single again. All boys are fucked up because they are emotional retards. The day I meet a man who doesn't need years and years of therapy to achieve even a fraction of integrity is the day I grow a cock myself and show them how it's done. Every one of us women is a self-harming pervert for going back to them each time for more. Not that I'm twisted and bitter or anything.

"I'm *so* bored with them, though. I feel like I'm either about to crack or make do with one of them whatever shit they come out with... or run away to a convent and become a nun. Can't we just put them all on a spaceship or something and tell them to go start a colony on Mars?"

219

That's right, honey, we'll be right behind you. You just make yourself comfortable and put up some shelves or something till we get there. We'll be along in a minute... Laters!' Bliss.

"Anyway, enough pasogony for one day (is there actually a word for women who hate men?). You let me know your plans and I'll come and find you. Then it's pina coladas all round!"

She was deeply disappointed with her ex. He had bottled out of love. What a wimp. Esmeralda noticed that she was increasingly unimpressed with men. She was aware that she was creating this in her life and she also realised that she would dearly love to uncreate it. But she was finding it harder and harder not to completely loathe them. One day she would have to make the active choice to burn all the evidence, but for the time being, she was deriving a certain amount of pleasure from compiling it all up against them.

Really! Everywhere she went, men were falling at her feet. As she sat now on the train, the man in a suit was eyeing her up across the aisle, the young chav sitting opposite kept awkwardly catching her gaze and even the conductor had lingered in returning her ticket. It was funny: the more she despised them, the more they wanted her.

She probably could make a fortune as a dominatrix, but there wasn't a chance in hell that she would waste her time and energy pandering to the fantasies of the unimaginative shits. The dominatrix really is the biggest sucker on the block. They are giving the man everything he wants: the fantasy, the desire, the erection, the chase, the brief fulfilment. Plus the promise of repeating those stages all over again. How? Because she never becomes real. He never feels her warm flesh, hears her twittering conversation, drinks her salt tears, smells her monthly blood. He never has to hug her after sex. He gets all of the fun without any of

220

the hassle. And that is everything that is wrong with men. They see the reality as a hassle. Well fuck them.

Esmeralda thought that maybe she would become a dominatrix. Might as well make some money out of her loathing for the opposite sex. She was only interested in the big league stuff, where you charge thousands of pounds and they're never even allowed to touch you.

It's not that she hated all men. On the contrary, it was because she had known some truly amazing men in her life that the bar was set very high in terms of what she expected of them and what she knew they were capable of being. Her granddad, for instance, was the most powerful and loving man she had ever met. He was a builder, built like a brick shit-house, and yet the most gentle and good-natured fellow you would ever meet. He drank like a bastard, told extravagant stories and had a makeshift office in his garden shed lined with nude page 3 photos. But he never swore in front of a woman, he never wronged anyone in her lifetime and when he got drunk, he laughed and joked like a toddler. And he had been there for them like a father, when her own poor excuse of a dad had bottled out on her mum. And her gorgeous, darling brother had inherited all of their granddad's greatness.

Like the guys in her friendship group. All of them big softies, who told each other they loved each other, forgave one another for their foibles and were great fun to get drunk with. Each and every one a shining ray of light. Then again... there was probably a woman out there for every one of them who thought he was a total bastard.

She was sure no man on the planet had ever thought that her mother had behaved like a bitch though.

"I'm going to move to London."

The country was becoming smoke-free. Esmeralda was over the moon. She only had to walk into a pub and her voice degenerated into a husky sex-line leer.

"How are you? It's hard not to think of you. I just saw a buzzard."

"Tell him to fuck off!" shouted her friend, trying to snatch the phone out of Esmeralda's hand, so she could write the reply. "Tell him you're my wife now."

The next day Esmeralda sent him a reply - *I miss you, sir* - just to test the water.

Do you still want to play?

Yes.

A week later she went to his house for breakfast. They talked. She told him all the things that she thought were wrong with him at the moment and getting in the way of his ability to love. He agreed with most of them, but they couldn't agree on why he had fallen out of love with her. In the end she suggested they close the door on the whole mess and forget about it. He thought that was a good idea. He asked her if she still wanted him to be her Master. She said she did. *Might as well have my cake and eat it,* she thought to herself as he led her upstairs. He stripped her, made her kneel down on the floor, stuck a dildo in her arse and one in her pussy and fucked her with them hard and fast until she screamed in orgasm. Then he put a collar around her neck, attached a lead and held her head onto his cock whilst he fucked her face. After three weeks of being apart, he hadn't wanted to put his cock in her pussy. *That guy has serious issues,* she thought to herself as she trundled off down the steps and back into her lovely life.

She didn't tell anyone. It was the first secret she had ever kept. She just carried on being a single, I'm-so-over-him, liberated woman.

"Have you got a boyfriend?"

"No."

"Can I have your number?"

"Yes."

The best thing was that she didn't want to go out on the rampage and sleep with loads of guys, because her sexual fire was being stoked. Which meant, for the first time in her single career since losing her virginity, she was putting a high price tag on her sexual self. And this was perfect timing for her move to London. She decided that when she went up there she was going to be a top catch, not an easy lay. This was a novel idea for young Esmeralda.

"Are you calling me a slag?" Esmeralda asked the author.

Esmeralda wasn't a slag. A slag is someone who has sex for the wrong reasons: because they think it will make them popular, or feel temporarily loved, or because they don't think they deserve to be loved. Whereas Esmeralda fucked because she liked fucking. She was a total slut and she was proud of it. And she was only a slut when she was in between men whom she thought were deserving of her love. When she met a man whom she thought was deserving, she was a completely monogamous creature, capable of the grandest emotions. But in between such momentous occasions she saw no harm in getting her fill from as many different cocks, and in as many ridiculous situations, as her troublesome little nose could sniff out. Equally, there had been times in her life when she had felt that not giving a man what he wanted was advantageous for one reason or another. There were certain situations where she didn't put out at all, because it would in someway diminish her power. For instance, she didn't sleep with people from work, housemates, or her inner circle of friends. She had an Elizabeth I sense of when it was a good idea to put out and when it was a good idea to keep her legs firmly locked.

She was playing Lysistrata in her end of school showcase.

"Our legs are locked together, so to speak. The peace will be concluded in a week!"

"What are they? Men. Are they a match for us?"

"No!"

"Come on, then! Follow me, girls, in Aphrodite's name. To death or glory... and enduring fame!"

"What is your book about?"

"It's kind of turned into a love story." *Or an anti-love story.*

Esmeralda opened her book and began to read. Marking her page was a bookmark she had bought on her trip with her mother to Bath. It read: *Someone loves you more than you know and will be with you where ever you go.* She had bought it for her master, but after dumping him she had decided to give it to herself.

She rang the eighteen-year-old. He had already booked her in for a whole summer of frivolity before she even had time to mention that she had split up with her fella.

"I realised that he was trying to change me."

"How can anyone change you, Esmeralda?"

"He didn't approve of my hedonism."

"What? What are you without your hedonism?"

"An empty shell..."

It's difficult to maintain a relationship in this day and age.

As she left the office, her adorable colleague told Esmeralda how his girlfriend was worried that they were stuck in a lovely but unexciting relationship.

"But they are all lovely and unexciting" exclaimed Esmeralda. "And being single is exciting but lonely."

"Yes," he said, "the grass is always greener on the other side."

"Love is the ultimate thing though," Esmeralda insisted. "If you can't let love into your life then your life really is a waste. That's why for years I put up with a boyfriend who let me down and cheated on me, but only three months with my last chap who was nothing but lovely to me. The first one loved me completely, but he was a useless bastard. Whereas the latter didn't know how to love, and I just couldn't work with that."

See you at 8.30. Bring condoms and vibrator. Dress for submission.

She could happily fuck him though.

By nine o'clock she was wearing a black rubber mask, an ankle-length black rubber dress that she couldn't walk in, black PVC metal-studded shoes, and a spiky metal collar with a heavy metal chain hanging from it. She was currently tied to a bed and being fucked up the arse. It made her chuckle. *What a shit, though,* she thought. *He is getting all the fun of the fair without having to deal with any of the hard stuff.* She was beginning to loathe him. But she was also still in love with him. There was no denying that.

She just couldn't understand why he wasn't in love with her. All right, so he had an issue with her hedonism, but really, in the grand scheme of things is that such a big deal? He'd never even seen her drunk, for God's sake! In which case, what the hell was going on? He fancied her, he liked her company, he thought she was talented, and valued her opinion on his work. He wanted to be involved in many areas of her life. But for some reason he just wasn't in love with her. You can't make someone love you. He really fitted much of what she was looking for, which was gutting. She wanted someone just like him, but who was hopelessly in love with her. And she deserved to be hopelessly loved. It just seemed so unfair.

She was very clear that she wasn't going to put herself out to earn his approval though. It was never worth it in the end. Never.

"It must be wonderful to witness, all this fitness. How we wish we were you watching us!" It was their last performance together as an ensemble and they went for it with gusto.

As Esmeralda stared vacantly out of her kitchen window over the grey bleeding skyline of Brighton, dressed in a shimmering veil of sea mist, she noticed below her the two seagull chicks she had been watching grow each morning over her breakfast routine. The parents had finally left them to it and they were desperately trying to strengthen their wings for flight, in search of breakfast. She felt an allegiance with the pair. It was time for them all to fly.

The daughter of the house kindly drove Esmeralda to the airfield. She had got on really well with the fiery young lady over the last week. They had been thrown together. She was recovering from an illness and a spat of life rearranging whilst Esmeralda had arrived at the commune to discover her now nineteen-year-old lover had his eyes on someone else and wasn't up for anything that might get in the way (He told Esmeralda this after he had slept with her, of course.) Although Esmeralda had laughed at the time and said she would have done the same, she was still gutted. Therefore Esmeralda and her lover's sister spent the week sitting around at a festival covered in mud and putting the world to rights. Now they were driving to the airfield together. One of Esmeralda's former lovers had offered her a ride in his glider. She couldn't believe it was happening. It had been one of her new year's resolutions to fly a plane and here she was, half-way through the year, and about to go and do it!

It was every bit as amazing as she dreamed it would be. She felt like a bird, completely free and in control. It was magical. He did a loop in the air and she felt her body pass through the G-force, then turn into weightlessness, and then pass back through the G-force again. She had kept her eyes open the whole time and had seen the world backflip before her. "Fuck me!" she screamed, "That was like the best orgasm ever."

SEX

She decided one day to address all her past loves, in chronological order

1. "I can't believe I am actually losing my virginity. I'm glad it's to you. Do you like the black lace basque I'm wearing, with my red suspenders and black stockings? Do you like my long red henna'd hair? I'm on the pill so we're safe. But the condom is still a good idea. I feel comfortable because this is all so well-planned. There is an engagement ring on my finger. The floor is littered with dinner plates and glasses of wine. The room is flooded with candles. You are a virgin, too, and are so nervous. It really is very sweet. This is beautiful and perfect.

2. "Your room looks just like a sauna. The walls are all covered in pine and we keep pouring with sweat from the blazing summer sunlight. The Smashing Pumpkins album blaring out of your CD player is setting the rhythm. This is your first time.

3. "Here I am in the centre of a covered, private, indoor swimming pool. It's like a giant waterbed. You're giving me head. I don't really like you that much but I want to get this out of the way as it's been nine months. But I do like your thick head of hair. I like running my hands through it whilst

229

you bury yourself down there. And I like that you're stinking rich. And your puppy dog eyes, most of the time. But sometimes I think they're insipid.

4. "I told everyone I'd pull you, Mr Bagel Man. You're like a local celebrity to us college kids. You are so much older than me. What a naughty boy. You are the first man I've seduced. I told you that I fancied you and you turned to putty in my hands.

5. "You're such an Essex boy, but I really fancy your footballer's legs.

6. "There are black bruises and scabs running down my spine. I have fancied you from the second I laid eyes on you. I'm falling in love with you. I love you because you have a big lopsided grin and dazzling green eyes. You are spiritual and brave. You wouldn't hesitate to jump across the roofs of two buildings. You're experienced, worldly, and would fit in to all social occasions. If someone didn't like you, then I'd hold it against them and not you. And here I am bent over with my skirt pulled up around my waist, surrounded by the staring eyes of antique mannequins in a stony cold museum of a basement in Prague. I love the feeling of your huge balls slapping against my arse."

7. "You look like the Wheatos Professor, but I like the way you keep your leather gloves on.

8. "It's all in the interest of international relations. And an Aussie in a bush is worth two in the hand… actually that's probably not true.

9. "Every time I open my eyes you come. It's great.

10. "I can't stop stroking the wall separating our rooms.

11 & 12. "I've just sobered up and you are doing me doggy style. I told you 'no'. I had also said 'no' to your friend, who apparently has also had a go. I curse you both.

13. "And an Englishman in a bush is never worth it. Even if it is in Australia. They're definitely bed men."

14. "You are lovely to cuddle, even if you think I sound like a seagull."

15. "You've got a broken leg, for goodness sake. Does the male libido know no bounds?"

16. "I was just told that I fucked you last night. I don't remember it, but everyone saw us. They told me that I was cackling, so I guess I was having fun."

17. "Your cock is so big and yummy I don't ever want to let you out of my bed."

18. "You're not what I'm looking for but your cock is like a magic wand and I think I may be addicted to it."

19. "I didn't want to have sex with you."

20. "It is hard to keep balanced on this slither of a bed, built above a toilet, and the water that keeps running down through the drain is putting me off. Hardly inspiring, and nor are the bright blue pants. But it is mid-winter in Berlin and the window to my room won't shut. I'm freezing."

21. "My head keeps banging against the ceiling. You built the bed too close to the roof. It's a good design, though. Good use of space. A lot of the folk in this squat have done the same thing."

22. "I only did it 'cause you were wearing a fox mask, but that's a good enough reason for me."

23. "Here I am gripping tightly on to the edge of your fairytale bed built out of tree trunks that are bolted together for a giant to sleep in. You are a giant. A great big ginger giant. I love you, my ginger giant. You fuck so hard and deep I think I might lose you inside me forever."

24. "God, your breasts are huge."

25. "I've always loved the Italians and your long black hair shines in the candlelight. But what a poser."

26. "I can't believe you are letting me do this to you. I've fancied you since school but I never in a million years thought I'd find myself licking your gorgeous little pussy."

27. "Don't worry if you can't get it up. You can wear my strap-on..."

28. "You're so big I don't think it is physically possible for our bodies to fit together... Oh, yes it is."

29. "I watched you playing the piano all night. Completely ignored the play. If I put on some classical music, will you play it for me across my naked body?"

30. "You androgynous angel."

31. "I love sucking your cock. It is so snug here under the cart, even if we have to be silent so as not to rouse the suspicions of the schoolchildren standing all around, with only a red curtain separating us. Luckily our comrades are making enough commotion as they perform the play of the *Seven Deadly Sins* above my bobbing head. You only left school yourself a few years ago, didn't you?"

32. "I've fancied you for fifteen years. That is one year for every minute it lasted. But I'm so glad it's finally happened. You'll always have a piece of my heart."

33. "Do you want to do me from behind whilst I read you *Where the Wild Things Are* and look like an eight-year-old? It doesn't matter if you're not a paedophile. I'm not really an eight-year-old."

34. "Come on then, let's go and get some coke, and whilst we're there we might as well do it."

35. "You really know how to wield that weapon. I can tell you're good at fencing."

36. "I don't trust you and you don't give head. But you do make me laugh."

37. "Pretentious twat."

38. "Christening my strap-on has set you up as a permanent member in my All-Time Favourite Lays, dear chap."

39. "You talk too much."

40. "Love the accent. But you're a lying fuck."

41. "What a coward. You are pathetic. But I also like your accent. Especially the fake Russian one."

42. "So that is what you look like naked."

43. "Sex on drugs equals fun."

44. "You are amazing. How unexpected."

45. "As you're banging me from behind in the shower I can see through the glass bricks as my friends jump into the hot tub. This festival has been such a wash-out, but this makes the whole weekend worth the effort. You stop a moment and rub your thumb over the tattoo at the base of my back. I feel like you have seen me. Through all the drugs and drink you have actually taken a moment to really see me. I can't believe how much that drives me wild."

46. "I like being on top and I like the warmth of the sauna. What a weekend it has turned out to be. Oh, and I'm loving the Viking horns."

47. "I love it in the hay."

48. "Having dressed you in pants, leather swashbuckler boots, hung a sword from your belt, and covered your shoulders in a thick black cloak… I would have been mad not to have taken advantage."

49. "I'm trying to decide whether I'm up for you taking a Viagra or not. We won't be having sex if you don't, but the Viagra is a huge time commitment. You'll be 'up' for hours. I've decided I want you to use your hands with your huge workman fingers instead. They were the reason why I pulled you anyway."

50. "You naughty little punk."

51. "You are the most amazing actor I have ever seen in my whole entire life. Didn't tell me you were married though, did you? I'm not impressed."

52. "I'm bent over the black iron bed where my wrists are tied. Sweat pours down between my hot skin and the rubber you have covered me in from head to foot. I can just about breathe through the gimp mask. My face is buried in the black satin bed covers. You are slowly and methodically ploughing into my arse. My pussy is screaming for attention. But you ignore her cries."

Is it ever satisfying? Nope. But generally speaking, it is a lot of fun.

HIGH SUMMER

Within an hour of arriving at the commune, she realised what it was that her master didn't understand about her. He didn't know what a totally filthy wrong'un she was. She realised that there would have been no use pretending that she wasn't. One can run, but one cannot hide from the devil. Especially when one is extremely partial to his company.

"You know I'm an unaffectionate bastard?" he asked her.

"Yes," she said.

"It's because there is this girl who I really like, and she is going to be at Eastern Haze."

"Oh," said Esmeralda.

It was the last thing she had expected to hear, especially as they had fallen into sweaty sex the second they had seen each other and he hadn't been any less affectionate than usual. "I hadn't noticed anything was wrong actually" she said. "It's cool, though. I understand."

"I like the fact you understand that I'm an unaffectionate bastard," he said to her later.

He acted like a twat all weekend. He wasn't just chasing one girl. He chased every bit of skirt that passed by. Esmeralda managed not to do the jealousy thing, which she

235

was proud of. But she finally got annoyed with him ignoring her. She was also acutely aware of how much she still fancied him, and that he fancied her, and how much they suited each other. Yet it was increasingly apparent how much the ten-year age gap mattered and that it would continue to do so for at least another ten years. So it wasn't worth continuing anyway. Not that she had a choice anymore. That ship had sailed. When they got back to the commune, their desires for each other were as evident as ever. But they didn't touch each other. They both needed to move on.

The next day she got on a train and met her master for a couple of days in Southwold.

"I've had an amazing time," she told him, "thank you!"

"Me too. I can't believe we saw a Bittern! You are a lucky mascot."

"So… are you going to come and meet me in Suffolk for August Bank Holiday weekend?" He didn't look enthusiastic, even though a few hours earlier at Minsmere RSPB centre he had been really into the idea. Esmeralda got the sense she had failed some sort of test again.

"Do you not want to see me?" she asked him.

"I do, but I want you to understand it doesn't mean you're my girlfriend or anything."

"Oh don't worry," she replied curtly, looking away to hide her upset, "I get that."

"How are you feeling about it?" he asked her.

"I'm fed up of giving myself to men who don't give me anything back in return. I deserve to be loved."

"Everyone does," he replied.

"I know!" she snapped angrily. "I love you…" She trailed off. She hadn't meant to say that. It made her eyes well up. He held her in his arms. "Why don't you love me?" she asked him. "We get on so well. What is going on? Is there someone else?" Silence. "There is?" She hadn't seen that one coming.

"I met someone a week and half ago," he said.

It was nothing to do with the girl though. Hours later they were both in floods of tears in his car, looking out over the moonlit pier.

"I'm still not over her," he wept. He was talking about his long-ago ex. "I've written a book, two albums, and a monologue. I've travelled all over the world and it's been three and half years. What am I meant to do to get over her?"

Erm… just get over it and stop being so pathetic? Maybe? Just an idea.

"I think you'll be an amazing actress," he said.

"I am an amazing actress." she snapped, before adding, "Actually I'm a pretty good actress. But seeing as most of them out there are shit, I'm happy enough with that." She curled herself up into a tight ball on the car seat and starred up out of the window and up at the stars. "I'm an amazing lover though," she wept. "I'm so good at being in love. I just want someone to come along who will let me love them." The tears poured out of her as she sent her wishes up into the universe.

"Your life is all icing and no cake. OK so you have a fun, varied sex life filled with kinky sex, but you're incapable of making love. You're lots of fun, everything you do is lots of fun, but you are incapable of loving or of being loved. There's no substance. It's all just icing."

They both lay awake all night. They could hear the other was not asleep. Esmeralda hadn't let him off the hook lightly. He had been forced to see the pain he had caused her. He had felt her tears. She never wanted to see him again.

So is that what this book is about then... an anti-love story? What has happened to all the big love stories? The old stories used to be about couples that fought alongside each other, against all adversity, just to be with one another. No man would do that nowadays. They're too preoccupied with working out how they can avoid commitment. They're never going to fight for commitment and get down to a really explosive love story. What are men so scared of? Are their lives really so much better without all the hassle of passionate and extraordinary love affairs? Are they really so much better off on their own that it's not worth giving us something sacred? Fuck them. Let them have their narrow little lives. They're nothing without us. As much as we try we cannot escape the merry-go-round of life. No matter how much you want to get off.

But the pain... The pain!

Hector says it's the only education worth having.

Hmm... I just wish there were marks for it. - Alan Bennett, *The History Boys.*

She lay there next to him and imagined climbing out of bed, slipping out of the hotel, and throwing herself off of the pier. That would teach him. Esmeralda was tired. An eternity lapped between their tense lonely bodies and the unwelcome dawn. First thing in the morning he drove her to the station.

"I will miss you this summer," he said placing his hand on her knee.

The tears bubbled up behind her sunglasses and she instinctively clutched the mineral water bottle to her like a teddy bear. She couldn't and didn't answer him, but sat in stony silence until he eventually removed his insincere hand.

Esmeralda sat in a muddy field surrounded by people who loved her. She hadn't been on Myspace for ages. She found a really lovely comment on one of her blogs from a girl who loved her way of thinking. Esmeralda had written the blog a year ago. She read it and remembered how empowered she had felt before she had met her master and was astounded at how incomplete she felt right now.

To Commit or Not to Commit? That is the Question. Current mood: productive. Category: Religion and Philosophy.

I woke up yesterday and decided that I wanted to write a book about the role of love and sex for young women growing up in the 21st century. Sex is my favourite subject. Not just in a gossipy titillation way - although I do love it for that reason too - but because it is a whole world in which we all play a part but that is kept hidden away behind the scenes. It's a horrible thought, but all of your mates, when they get the chance to, get naked and roll around in bed with other people. This is a whole side of them that you know very little about. Do your female friends shave off their pubic hair? Do your male friends insist on wearing condoms, or do they try and get out of using them? How often do your mates go for STD tests?

We live in a society that is rewriting the rules. The rules that used to keep what was once the norm in place have been torn apart by the modern pace and direction of life. We are free to choose the way we live our lives, probably more than any of the powers that be (or even we ourselves) dare to admit. And as women we are in an interesting point in history where our time-honoured roles in society no longer fit. We are no longer the trinity of Virgin, Mother and Crone. We now have many other roles, like the Businesswoman, the Diva, the Single Mum, the Promiscuous Woman, the Lesbian, to name but a few.

We are a generation from broken homes, brought up by single mums. We've had a Queen on the throne for generations and many of us recall a female Prime Minister. I'm now in my mid-twenties, many of my friends are now in their thirties and hardly anyone I know is settling down yet. They are still partying hard, going for their dreams, and living in shared houses without the money to buy their own.

I hear more and more women saying that they prefer to be single than in a relationship. I've heard a lot of older women saying this over the years: the ones who have done the husband-and-kids thing, got shat on, and now can't be bothered with the sacrifices that go with being in a relationship. But many women my age are starting to say the same thing. And I'm in that camp.

I can't be bothered with the compromises. I get everything I need from the other areas of my life. Instead of the main source of love coming from one person, I get love from everyone I know. Instead of sex with one person, I get exciting random sex as well as cosy knowing-someone's-body sex. I don't fear being on my own because I'm on my own and I'm not in the least bit lonely. When I was talking about this the other day, someone said to me,

'Yeah, but I'm a hopeless romantic and I still believe in the one,' so I asked her if the current fella she was with was the one and she said that he wasn't. 'Exactly,' I told her. 'If you met The One tomorrow, you wouldn't be available to fuck off with him. If I met my dream man tomorrow I'd be free to jump on the back of his white stallion and ride off into the sunset.'

I don't want to meet my dream man at the moment though. He'd turn my life upside down and I like my life the way it is, thank you very much. And that's how I came to my current theory. With the concept of Yin and Yang in mind, is your dream partner really a living breathing person outside of yourself, or is it an aspect inside, a balance between the male and female aspects within each of us?

The Greeks used to believe that we were beings with two heads, four arms, and four legs. The Children of the Sun were two men rolled up in one, The Children of the Earth were two women, and The Children of the Moon were part woman and part man. We never knew love because we were complete. But the gods were scared of our strength and defiance, so they sent down a shower of lightning that sliced through the flesh of The Children of the Sun, the Moon and the Earth. Then the winds scattered us across the Earth.

We are always looking for our other half and when we find someone that we think might be them, we have sex to try and put ourselves back together again. That's why love hurts. It's the memory of the wound. But what if we were to realise that this had never really happened? We hadn't ever been split in two? Could it be that the paths we have chosen throughout history have left us feeling divided from ourselves? We chose to embrace left-brained logical, linear thinking and turned our backs on our holistic intuitive right brain. Is it not possible that in doing so we have suppressed our ability to feel complete?

She couldn't believe how miserable she was feeling now. Esmeralda spent two weeks fighting back tears. She hadn't felt this much change taking place in her life since the year when her mum had gone into hospital with a tumour, her nan had died of cancer, her grandad had been diagnosed with cancer and her dad had run off with her drama teacher. Actually, the year where she had split up from her four-year relationship, got pregnant with her ex's best mate whilst finishing her degree, finished her degree, aborted her child, and moved to Brighton had been a pretty big year too. So had the year she had left her fiancé, her family, and her hometown, to move to the other side of the world where she lived for six months in Sydney without a penny to her name in a tiny flat with a guy who was in the midst of a mental breakdown. This one had been nowhere near as eventful a year as any of those, come to think of it, but everything had changed in all areas of her life, and she was currently mourning the death of the status quo she had known for so long, which was fair enough. As had been the case with all of these mental years though, they had made her who she was today, and had been the most valuable years of her life.

"I feel like Bridget Jones or something. I'm sitting at home weeping at soppy films. It is so fucking depressing," whined Esmeralda.

Flu and heartbreak coursed through her veins bringing with it a potent cocktail of tears and pain.

You heard of Proust? Well he gets down to the end of his life and he looks back and decides that all those years he suffered, those were the best years of his life, because they made him who he was. All the years he was happy… total waste. Didn't mean a thing.

- Little Miss Sunshine.

"Do what you love and fuck the rest!" she shouted to the sea, "I love acting, writing, reading, singing, dancing, flying, swimming, snogging, fucking, drinking, fooling, dreaming, believing, being, loving, laughing, and creating a life filled with tales of nonsense I will be proud of, or at least amused by, when I tell them to my grandchildren."

"Make it a good story..." advised her mentor.

"I'm not the best actor or writer in the world. I'm not a natural genius. I just love doing all of the things that I do and I'm never going to stop doing them. What's the point in comparing myself to other people? What's the point of worrying about whether I'm good or bad at doing them? I just do them because I love them. Because they make my life worth living." Only last week she had been saying to the now-nineteen-year-old how it was all about the journey and not the result.

She stayed in and watched soppy films. She was meant to be orchestrating a rendezvous with a young man whom she had been informed held a torch for her. But she didn't feel like it. She had lost interest in chasing cock. She was well and truly over cock for the time being. From now on, the cock could chase her.

"I really don't know what I'm supposed to do now" huffed Esmeralda.

"That's easy," replied her friend. "Whatever comes next..."

"I'm no longer looking for love," Esmeralda smiled, "I'm expecting it."

After cleaning the flat, she settled down and enjoyed her own space and her own peaceful company. She was very pleased to discover that, what with the MDMA comedown from the last two weeks having worn off, she was more over the boy and the master than she had previously felt. Huge changes were afoot. Huge fuck-off changes that meant that she was leaving much of the person she had been behind. The urge to sleep with lots of people had gone. She didn't regret sleeping with lots of people but she now felt like setting the bar higher. Very high indeed. She was also setting the bar high on her dreams, her life plans, and her goals. She wanted the moon on a stick and nothing less would do. She was ready to play with the big boys now.

He kept phoning her and asked her to meet him. She met him, just to see what he wanted, and it turned out, unsurprisingly, not to be worth it. It had left her feeling like shit. She wrote him the following email:

When you are in love with someone it feels like you are unable to be without them, that your whole life revolves around them, yet in the cold light of day when you really get over someone they disappear from your world and their influence over you vanishes into thin air. I feel like I can't be without you at the moment and that you will obviously keep featuring in my life forever. Yet less than seven months ago, I'd never heard your name and I know I can live a very full and well-rounded life without you in it, thank you very much. I managed it for 28 years.

The one thing I knew I had to say to you the last time I saw you was that I didn't want to see or hear from you ever again; then as soon as I saw you I wanted to accommodate your existence in my life and somehow make it work. That's because I want you to be in my life. The problem is the reason why I want you to be in my life is because I want you to be my partner and that isn't going to change until I have moved on, far on, into a future without you in it.

I can't see you or speak to you again for a time. That means I am going to delete your number from my phone and your address from my email and, after I have sent this email, I would appreciate it if you didn't reply to me or get in touch with me again. As for the shoes, boots and top you bought me, I know this has become a big deal in my mind because I can't stand the thought of anyone else using them, though in reality, if I'm getting over you then it really isn't that big a deal. I will leave that one up to you. I will just try to forget about the thought of you using them in your play with someone else. (Ahhhhh!)

I want you to know that I value the time we have spent together and I have grown so much from knowing you, but you know as well as anyone that if you stay in contact with the person that you are in love with when they don't love you, then it is a slow and arduous torture that really isn't necessary. All it takes is that last painful step of cutting them out of your life, then you are free to get on with yours. As long as you are in mine, I will always want you to be mine. So you can't be in it. It hurts like crazy, but nowhere near as much as wanting you and not being able to have you. Best of luck with everything you do.

But when she read it out to her mother she pointed out that Esmeralda still sounded like she was hoping he would change his mind and that she would take him back if he did. Her mother said it depended on what Esmeralda wanted to achieve. If she really wanted to be free of him using her, the way he had been, then she needed to put her foot down and tell him to bog off. For the first time Esmeralda realised that she was sick of being treated like she wasn't good enough for him, so she wrote the following...

I've finally realised what a merry dance you have been leading me on and have thankfully also realised that I'm not interested in you leading me on anymore. Because you don't love me, you have nothing to lose from enjoying my company, using my body, or sucking from my creativity. I, on the other hand, am losing everything from this arrangement and I've been stupidly giving it all to you free of charge in the hope that I would win you over again. Now that I have sobered up I've realised what a mug I've been. I'm really not impressed with you. I'm disappointed that you don't have the moral fortitude to do right by me. You say you'd do anything for me, but what in the blue blazers do you do for me? All you do is suck from me, judge, and test me, and then every time let me know that I have lost. Well cock off! I have nothing to prove to you. You're nothing. Not even a big fish in a small pond. If my life is a cold house, an empty bed, a job I don't really want, and a few unrealised projects by the time I'm your age, then I will be seriously disappointed in myself.

You haven't even figured out what love is yet. You may think you loved your ex, but she obviously didn't think that you knew who she was. And now you're dating the ghost of an idea of who she was, without taking any responsibility for the fact that you didn't really know her or notice that she had grown up and left you behind. But then, why would you? You're too busy thinking about yourself. Maybe you should just make a woman out of rubber? Then she could be whatever you decided she was and she wouldn't ever point out to you that actually she is far more than that. You are a sad screwed-up man and I'm well shot of you. I hope you continue to enjoy chasing all the things that are on the end of your nose. I can see you're getting a lot out of it. Bye.

Her best friend pointed out that this email was too angry and desperately wanted Esmeralda to abstain from giving him any more of her energy. "From now on I will only refer to him as the Unworthy One," declared her best friend.

One should always write in the green light of truth and not the red light of anger. - Virginia Woolf.

Esmeralda agreed that this one was a bit emotional and was showing him too much of her pain, so she sat on it for the weekend.

Esmeralda had gone a little bit mad. We've all been there. It's never pretty.

She went to Gay Pride, ate her body weight in pills, snorted poppers till her lungs bled, and danced in the blazing sun at a free party in a field. She had an amazing time with her wonderful friends and she didn't once think of him. She was getting over it.

"I'm so impressed with the way you split up with him," said the best friend of her last long-term boyfriend earnestly, as he put an arm about her shoulder. She hadn't seen him since the break-up two years ago. It was he who had bought her the strap-on as a joke on her ex, as he knew she would try to use it on his best mate. He had never let her though. "You could have really fucked him over, and he would have deserved it, but instead you sorted him out and left him in a really good place. I will always be impressed by the way you handled that."

She wasn't being treated the way she had treated others and it wasn't on. On Monday she finally sent him an email. It said the following:

246

I have come to the conclusion that it is time to move on in my life. It has been one hell of an adventure and I had an amazing time for a while there, but the ride ran out and I have been very unimpressed with the way you have treated me this last month. I've decided it is time to get on with my life, before things turn nasty, and so I'm going to do this without you in it. Please don't contact me anymore. There are no hard feelings. I'm just moving on.

Best of luck with everything.

Esmeralda

"Why, oh fucking why, does the tannoy on the train have to be so loud that it invades every fucking molecule in your body? Why does it have to fucking tell me that there is CCTV in operation on this train? Do I give a fuck that there is a ticket guy called Nigel serving us today?" Esmeralda was in a very bad mood. "I fucking hate trains," she huffed.

"It's not right if I'm feeling more confident than you in a social situation. I want to kick that bloke's fucking head in." Esmeralda knew that her brother was right. If he was outdoing her on the confidence front, then the balance of the universe was all out. "It will be great to have you back!" Everyone was very excited to hear that she was moving to London.

For the third time that month, one of her best male friends tried it on with her. This recent attempt was from a friend who was currently in a full-blown relationship. She was thoroughly enjoying playing the moral high ground. It was driving them all wild with desire.

Unfortunately it was also piling up the evidence on what a bunch of weasels the male race are too. He failed to leave her alone. By Monday he phoned her. She waited for it to go to answerphone. *I need to speak to you about something. This is life-changing stuff...* he said. So she rang him up. It wasn't life-changing stuff. Well, it may have turned out be at some point in the far away future and only for his life, not hers. Once again he was only thinking about himself. How original.

"You can't ring me any more. Do you understand why I'm asking you to leave me alone?" She had to spell it out to him. He didn't see what the problem was. Thankfully the emails she had written in the last week, no matter how obsessive at the time, assisted her immensely in making it all plain and simple for him. When she got off of the phone she had to laugh. She laughed down the phone to her Mother "It's funny how all he wants to talk about is himself. I went around to see him today to pick up the bits and bobs I had asked for and he wanted to know what I had been up to, which he sat quietly and listened to dutifully. Then as soon as I had finished he spent the rest of the time excitedly telling me all about his life, telling me his plans, and showing me all his photos. It was a bit like babysitting." "I think most men are like that," replied her Mother. "They always seem to think that what they're doing is so much more important."

Time does heal everything. It's wonderful like that. At first you really, really, really don't want to give it up. But after a while things just stop mattering. It's one of the very few certainties in this godforsaken world. Like death.

See it as an inoculation, rather. Briefly painful, but providing immunity for however long it takes. Given the occasional booster, another face, and another reminder of the pain. It can last you half a lifetime. - Alan Bennett, *The History Boys.*

"It's true that he has a lot that I don't have. He is very well-educated and well read. He knows lots of interesting things. But I also have a lot going on that he doesn't have, emotional maturity and inner contentment, for a start. The

248

difference is, I can go and learn all the stuff he knows. I can gain it any time I like. Seeing as he was always going on and on about himself, I've had all his areas of interest drummed into me like it was the times tables, so I won't forget them. But he will never learn the stuff that I know. Not just my areas of expertise, because he never showed the slightest bit of interest in them and so hardly discovered what any of them were, but he will never have the emotional and spiritual intelligence that I have. Not that I don't wish him all the best of luck with finding whatever it is that he is looking for and want nothing but the best for him but, you know, I just don't think he'll ever figure any of it out. He is an emotional and spiritual idiot."

A colon is a promise:

Life is nothing but chances and choices.

"You can't escape your problems by packing up and leaving. You'll just put them in your suitcase and take them with you," Esmeralda mused.

You'll laugh at it long and hard one day.

A day had gone by in which she hadn't thought of him once. Lucky her. The offers were coming in but no one was tickling her fancy. She couldn't be doing with anything but the best anymore. It wasn't that she didn't like the men who liked her, it was just that her life was on the move and she wasn't sure how things were going to pan out. At the moment she wanted to concentrate on getting everything sorted and then see what the lay of the land looked like.

For as all true loves know: Love is perfect kindness. - Joseph Campbell.

He hadn't been kind. Part of Esmeralda was in hell. Her heart was so broken. She had not done with crying yet. It wasn't so much him that she missed. There was no him, really. There hadn't been enough time for him to ever form properly into a real human being. She hadn't ever relaxed enough to fart around him. He hadn't ever comfortably stared deep into her eyes. He had not grown into the very fibres of her being, like an extra limb. No, it wasn't long enough for it to matter that she wasn't with him. The reason her heart was burning as hot as molten lead was because she had been robbed. Her heart had been opening like a brave flower and then some spiteful little schoolboy had plucked off its head before it had fully bloomed to display its magnificent prize-winning splendour. And that really pissed her off. The bud had deserved to grow. She had tended the soil, watered the roots lovingly each day, and had done everything that one is meant to do to prepare oneself for the big bang. And that bastard had burst the bubble just as the dream was taking flight.

She hated him more than she hated any of her ex-boyfriends. Even if some of them had right royally fucked things up - cheating on her, rowing about nothing for months on end - at least they had given love a chance. Whereas he, on the other hand, had abandoned her and left her all dressed up for love but with nowhere to go. And she was still refusing to admit defeat. She wasn't ready to go home yet, take off her glad rags and wash off her make-up. Instead she slouched in the darkness on the empty stairs of her heart and wept bitter acrid tears into the scattered remains of her emotions. "I can't wait till I've forgotten all about him."

It was a balmy evening and the bushes were heavy with blackberries. A year had passed by again. Soon Esmeralda would be twenty-nine years old. Her "Saturn Returns". When she had had her birth-chart read, it said that next year would be a very big year for Esmeralda and somehow she knew this to be true. She could feel it in her waters. This last year had been a big year for the young lady already. She had moved into a room of her own, had been embroiled in many exciting love affairs, had fallen in love and then had her heart broken. She had discovered S&M, renting cottages and twitching. She had discovered sobriety and had become a woman. And had begun looking beyond the up-coming period of her life where she would realise her dreams for the next stage - starting a family.

She liked the word "balmy". But not as much as she liked balmy evenings.

"Inspiration: the thought comes when we breathe in."

"To learn something intelligently means just that: In Tell I Gently."

"You're a bad girl and I love it."

"Not as much as I love being bad."

The inflatable mattress was an absolute luxury. It was the closest they'd ever been to actually doing it in a bed. Normally it had been under carts and in hay barns. It was nice to have normal sex again, even though it had been very vigorous and she wasn't interested in anything more from the gentleman. It had been just what she had needed.

"Having sex with Esmeralda is an endurance test."

"How does it feel to be called an endurance test?"

"It's not the first time," smiled Esmeralda smugly.

The duck looked like a piece of origami made out of a crisp white napkin. It was in love with a chicken, which looked as if it were wearing a large pair of bloomers.

Be you Pope, Priest or Prince with crown,
King, Kaiser or Knights keen,
If you run then your reasons shall be found,
For this be the day of reckoning. - The Last Judgement.

"Seriously, you're the best," said Esmeralda's sixteen-year-old best mate. Everyone was being so lovely and supportive at the moment. She made use of the top, skirt and shoes he had bought her.

"After last night you are officially a paedophile."

"Why is that?"

"Your gimp is fifteen!"

"Really? Wow, he looks much older."

"I know. But he's not."

"This is wrong on so many levels!"

The sign read "Sub Wanted." "Really?" asked Esmeralda, "It just so happens I'm down a Dom."

"I've found a new Master. He's into Japanese rope bondage."

Bath is so beautiful. Taking the waters in Bath was a delightful experience. Despite the fact that the waters had chlorine in, which therefore defeated the whole point of taking the waters that had spent thousands of years filtering through precious minerals and ancient rocks. It didn't get rid of her athlete's foot, which it did in Europe where the waters came straight out of the earth, chlorine-free, with that meat pie stink of sulphur.

Esmeralda was officially a mess. Her confidence had been knocked. And for the first time in a long time she was genuinely scared of life. "I'm scared." There was an anarchy symbol scribbled into one of the tables. "I'll sit here," she said.

"I'd be a lesbian too, if I didn't have this insatiable fetish for cock."

"I wish I didn't like cock."

She hated people thinking that she had always been a non-smoker. The smoke poured around him in exactly the same way that bricks don't. It was the ritual that she liked.

"God knows the resting place of every little sparrow."

She saw him through the window of a pub with his new lady friend. It nearly made her throw up. She hoped that this new lady wasn't kinky. That would throw a spanner in his works. She clearly was, though.

Have I been assigned to your photo folder yet, along with all your other unsuccessful, short-term girlfriends? Have you told her how recently we broke up? Has she seen your cupboard of rubber? And the relics from all your failed love affairs? Have you made her suck your cock yet? Has she swallowed down your spunk? Or are you still pretending that you like simply putting your cock in her cunt? And have you told her about the ghost of your ex? The one who still stalks the empty corridors of your insipid heart?

Esmeralda had never been so heartbroken before in her life. All her other relationships had run their course. This one was absolute torture. *What doesn't kill you... hurts like fuck.*

The gold light poured out of her solar plexus like the beam of a headlight. She had moved through the first stage of mourning and had entered the second stage of anger, re-gathering a sense of identity and self worth out of the fury. *How very dare he!* An angel had come to her aid the day before. A lovely older gay man standing outside a pub had caught Esmeralda lost in comical thoughts as she had soaked up some much-needed rays of sunshine. She realised her face had been quite animated and laughed when she noticed he had been watching her. And as her cheeks turned red he called to her across the street, "You're looking fabulous! Someone ought to tell you that." It had actually made her well up.

Her insatiable appetite for cock had returned and it felt great.

"How are you doing?" asked her friend.

"I'm growing more hateful and bitter every day." She said.

"Excellent. Why's that?"

"Oh, just 'cause I hate men. Except you of course. I think you're great. But the rest are all stupid fucking bastards."

It was fair to say at this precise second in time she categorically hated him. Hate and love join together in a circle. On one side they meet where love goes wrong and passes through into hate before love for that person can be found again on the other side. But it always can be re-found if one keeps moving forward. And equally it can be lost again as time goes on.

That's why unconditional love is a dangerous concept. Love can't just be a given. You can't sit on your laurels. Love is a continued effort. As are other life choices, such as living with integrity and living by your own moral compass whilst maintaining an open tolerance to everyone else's perspectives. You have to choose to live by these choices every time you make a decision to do something. At any point, any one of us can choose to do what the fuck we like and screw the consequences. And we all do, regularly. Love is an effort and one that is worth making simply because it makes the world a better place for you and everyone else in it. But you've got to put the work in. It doesn't come unconditionally. And it shouldn't do either. But it should always be given generously and with good faith.

She would stop hating him at some point and the time would come when he meant nothing to her. Like the moment before the wave draws back into the sea; she will rediscover a love for him based on a nostalgia for all that he contributed to her life, painful or otherwise. And it had been a contribution. Women grow by men.

All dictators die.

"She's no lady. But she's all woman, pointed out her chum."

Cocks were coming at her again from all sides but none of them were good enough.

"So what happened with him then?"

"Well what you saw was most certainly not what you got. And what you got you were not allowed to actually have."

"What do you mean? That there was no give?"

"No, I mean there was nothing to give."

Esmeralda found herself picking her way through a field of cocks all lying flat and flaccid like blades of grass in an overgrown lawn. As her delicate bare feet brushed against each expectant member, the field curled its way up her leg, clinging on like a schoolchild on its first day, leaving in her wake a path of erect penises, peering towards her with their unwinking eyes.

There were films and stories that haunted the back of Esmeralda's mind's eye. A film with a prostitute in a grey Victorian dress lowering herself onto the grate of a prison, so that the inmates could feel her up underneath her long skirts, and a beautiful blonde lady having her shift ripped from her so that a man could whip her and brand her.

The first news story where Esmeralda was awoken to the fact that the media sensationalised everything, and had also taken to including all the gory details, had been the story of Rosemary West and her girls in the cellar. It gave the adolescent Esmeralda nightmares during the whole course of the trial and she found that she had to switch the news off whenever it came on so as to be spared the ordeal of their explicit revelations. And all these years later Esmeralda still felt that it had been inappropriate. It's mental how we dull down Grimm's fairytales to pathetic Disney nonsense because we feel that they're too dark for the sensitivities of our children, and yet we are happy to pump each living room full of the most horrific stories day in, day out, in the name of freedom of information. The greatest crimes of the modern age...

The Right to Sue?

Mass Media?

Political Spin Doctors?

FUCK OFF! FUCK OFF! FUCK OFF! FUCK OFF! FUCK OFF! FUCK OFF!

It doesn't matter who you vote for. The government will always get in.

Part of us knows we're more than they see; part of us fears we're less than we hope. - Julia Cameron, *The Artist's Way.*

This time next year, Rodney, we'll both be millionaires. - Del Boy, *Only Fools and Horses.*

And then the *Eureka!* moment struck. After a week of talking to inspiring artists whom she respected and admired, Esmeralda suddenly realised that she hadn't once mentioned that she had just finished drama school or that she was looking for an agent or that she was simply shitting herself with worry that she might never amount to anything. Instead the week was spent in a whirlpool of passionate conversations about art, politics and life. She fell in love with everyone and everyone fell in love with her. And suddenly Esmeralda peeled back the wallpaper on her life and again revealed the rising damp that was really the problem.

All her recent fears and pain had been because she had lost touch with her artistic integrity, which was the central pivot of her soul. By losing touch with this, her whole centring had gone awry and on rediscovering it, her perspective on everything changed. She didn't want to be in

Eastenders, she didn't want to scramble for adverts or corporate work, she only wanted an agent if they represented her needs and she most certainly didn't want a man in her life who thought that she wasn't good enough for him.

It suddenly became clear to her that there was no power in trying to convince herself that she was better than him and he was wrong. There was no right or wrong. In his world she wasn't good enough for him. Fine. But in her world there were plenty of men who as far as she was concerned were better-looking, smarter, funnier and cheekier than him, who thought she was the absolute bee's knees. This realisation meant that not having him in her life was no longer a painful yet necessary treatment for her broken heart, but had become a powerful choice and one that made Esmeralda feel great.

At last, the poor little poppet.

A whole week went by when he didn't once pop into her mind.

The young man turned up at her flat at 8pm prompt, just as she had told him to. Esmeralda was dressed in smart, quality woollen trousers, a crisp white shirt, black PVC braces, and a blue slanting Luftwaffe flying hat. She hadn't bothered with make-up because she couldn't be bothered. If there was one thing she had learnt of late, it was not to ever bend in any way for a man. If he didn't like her the way she was then he could sling his hook. Her bum was spotty and she hadn't shaved her legs, but her confidence was back in full swing. After providing him with a successfully cooked meal and wowing him with her witty intellectual conversation, they quite literally ripped each other's clothes off and he hammered her hard and fast against the back of the sofa with his great big balls slapping against her clit, just the way she liked it. A whole night of fornication proceeded, incorporating the toys and costumes she had appropriated over the last six months and they slipped in and out of roles, in between more funny and invigorating conversations.

The evening was an absolute triumph. He went on his way after they'd had their fill and Esmeralda curled up in her own bed with her own smell and a great big grin across her lips. She was back.

"You'll never guess who I bumped into last night?" Esmeralda greeted her best friend over the phone.

"Who?" she enquired.

"The Unworthy One" replied Esmeralda.

"Oh no…" fretted her friend.

"Don't worry. Couldn't have been more perfect. It was at the theatre and I had been training all day with the woman who was performing. I knew everyone there and I was having a full-on passionate conversation with someone when he came over and, in the words of my friend who was with me, I was 'civil, but non-committal'. Luckily the doors for the show opened as he came over so I went straight upstairs, leaving him hanging at the bottom of them. If his new girlfriend had been watching she would have seen him being snubbed and if she didn't know who I was already, then her interest would have undoubtedly been aroused. After the show I was whisked away to a quiet corner with the incredible woman we had been watching perform and who had given the most sublime performance, so I had completely forgotten about him. When I switched my phone on there was this odd message from a number I didn't recognise so I texted back *Who is this?* before realising it was probably him."

"Because you had deleted his number?"

"Of course."

"Brilliant!"

"I know," smirked Esmeralda. "It couldn't have gone better if I'd planned it. Thank you universe." It's all about the minor victories. Life was back on track and each moment filled with new excitements. And she had nearly finished her book. And that was very exciting. In fact there was very little else left to say.

What have we learnt dear reader? Are there any gold nuggets of truth between these pages or are they the pointless and obscene witterings of an uncouth wench? Is this yet another example of the butchering of the English language? A piece of work responsible for bringing about the degradation of all that we hold dear?

Nothing really matters. And that really doesn't matter either. Don't judge, just do…

She stood before the blank easel of her life. A *tabula rasa*. Beneath the whitewashed canvas was the painting of the life that had happened to her: the rubbish father, the judgemental God, the crap schooling and the upbringing within a small town mentality. Now all that mess of a picture was gone, covered in a thick coat of crisp clear whitewash. Now Esmeralda tried to figure out what she would choose to paint on her new canvas now that she was creating her own life:

A multi-eyed God

A glittering and inspiring career

An exciting, gorgeous, talented and committed man

A passionate and extraordinary marriage

A family of two vivacious children

A beautiful communal house in the countryside

A canal boat for when jobs came up in London

A well-kitted campervan

A gypsy cart that transforms into a stage
A working process dripping in integrity
A bird of prey
A dog that doesn't need a lead
A bunch of cats
A fit healthy body
A well-travelled passport
An old age near the sea...

As her brush skipped across the canvas a smile danced across her lips. What a wonderful world this would be. Why not?

Esmeralda looked up at her author. "I'm done here," she smiled. The paint swirled around the water brewing a storm of colours.

Esmeralda caught the train. The old man opposite her looked like a Basset Hound. He had big droopy red eyes and dripping jowls. He looked like he had been a good man. He had a gentle disposition. "Are we nearly there yet?"

"I'm not really an autobiographical character," explained Esmeralda to the man on the train. "You see, my author and I are clearly similar creatures, but we live in totally separate universes. In her universe, my author has had the linear experience of plodding through every single minute of every single day on the planet we call Earth, for the last twenty-eight years. She bears all the wear and tear, insights and exasperations that such an experience exacts upon a person. It gives her more depth, more facets, but there is also a lot of unnecessary crap. Whereas I reside in the realm of fiction, where time can do whatever it wants. It doughnuts, flashes back, stands still or plods along. I have aged a year in these pages, whilst chopping and changing to flashbacks and memories that I didn't even know existed until they were written down. At the beginning, I was not born, I simply 'woke up'. I have been in existence for a year so far, but now that the book is finished, I will be forever twenty-eight. As my author grows old, withers away and dies, I will continue to be this distilled antenna of a twenty-eight-year-old woman at the beginning of the millennium. I will continue existing until the last copy of these letters are lost to the mists of time and the last mother tells her daughter about a book she once read that was all about a precocious young lady, struggling her way through the stormy world at the start of the twenty-first century. Some of me was loosely based on real sources and some of me was simply plucked from the air, but all of me sprang from the time and space in which I was created. The author lives in the universe of 'If and When'. Whereas I, my fine fellow, will forever reside in the universe of the 'Here and Now'. I'm her simulacrum. I mean, her favourite book is *My Family and other Animals* and personally I think that book is really rather dull."

The author felt insulted. She thought the aforementioned book was an absolute masterpiece. "And I can't stand the smell of her body odour. She smells like cat wee," continued Esmeralda. The author wondered if she could engineer some kind of sticky end for this insolent young lady. But she decided not to. After all, the author had created Esmeralda and so her rebellion was only to be expected. In fact the author would have been very disappointed if Esmeralda hadn't rebelled against her. No one wants a boring child, now do they?

"How dare you describe me as a child!" shouted Esmeralda. "I'm your fucking equal! I may have only been in existence for a year, but I'm the same bloody age as you!"

"Don't over-use the exclamation mark, Esmeralda. It's tacky." The author smiled as she clicked shut the laptop on

Esmeralda's unruly cursing, pleased with a job well done. The book was finished.

Esmeralda and the author left the café and made their separate ways home, through the warm golden glow of the sunshine and into the mists of time.

ACKNOWLEDGEMENTS

Thank you to Mish Maudsley for the wonderful cover design. Thank you to Rachael Beaumont for her generous guidance. Thank you to Steve Rudd for believing in me. Thank you to the people who read the manuscript and gave me the confidence to carry on. Thank you to Buffy for making me jump. Thank you to Freddy for always helping out. Thank you to my ladies for holding me up. Thank you to all my friends and family for all the fun and love and support and for putting up with me, especially my mum. And last but not least, thank you to my patient husband, who is not allowed to read this book, but supports me wholeheartedly. Love you all.